Butterfly

Butterfly

Paul Loewen

•

St. Martin's Press

New York

Design by Kay Lee

Library of Congress Cataloging-in-Publication Data

Loëwen, Paul.
   Butterfly.

   I. Title.
PR9250.9.L64B88   1988   823   87-28695
ISBN 0-312-01395-7

First Edition

10 9 8 7 6 5 4 3 2 1

For Marie

Acknowledgments

I wish to express my gratitude to all those who in one way or another have helped me over the years in preparing this edition. In particular, I want to thank Paul Liepa of St. Martin's Press for his advice and encouragement; my interpreter and guide Noriko Kanda, whose unflagging good spirits kept me going on long searches that too often seemed hopeless; Mrs. Susan Harrington Choate for her gracious contribution of three letters written to her grand-uncle William Harrington; Ikkyū Roshi for his cordial reception and permission to publish our conversation; Jennifer Haley for invaluable help in the transcription of my interview with Mrs. Davenport and other arduous tasks; Columbia University Press for permission to quote from Burton Watson's translation of *The Complete Works of Chuang Tzu*; my friend Norman Kurz, without whose suggestions and aid this edition could never have seen the light of day; my wife Marie Keller Loewen, who read the manuscript and generously put up with the long hours it stole from our life; and finally my stepdaughter Julia Keller, who enlightened and entertained me on every related subject from orthography to Krafft-Ebing to Zen.

Editor's Preface

The unusual nature of the text that is being offered here to the public makes it incumbent on me to say a few words about its origins and my own relationship to the manuscripts upon which it is based.

In the spring of 1944, I was home in Heidelberg on furlough. The war was going badly for Germany, and there was little to be hopeful about, either by way of victory or defeat. In that dark time, the eight new Gramophone records I managed to procure seemed a windfall. It so happened that my mother, whom I had invited to listen with me, stepped out to fetch more coffee just as I put on the young Elisabeth Schwarzkopf singing the aria "Un bel dì" from *Madame Butterfly*. When she returned a minute later, she seemed distraught and asked me to stop the record. She did not like it. I protested that the singing was good; besides, it would be over in a minute or two. Ignoring my arguments, she insisted. I was not used to such capriciousness from my levelheaded mother and tried to make a joke of it; to my amazement, she responded by slapping my face. I cannot recall Mother hitting me even when I was small; and she herself was, if anything, more shocked by her act than I. Her aggressiveness vanished instantly, and she broke down in sobs. But for this little incident, my mother would never have revealed her origins—so she has assured me more than once—and I would not have known of the manuscripts that were to dog me for three decades.

When Mother calmed down, she was ashamed and felt obliged to explain. Did I know who Butterfly was, she asked. Thinking that she was unfamiliar with the opera—which surprised me, because she had a vast musical culture—I began to recount the plot in a garbled manner. "No, no," she stopped me. "I mean the real Butterfly, the one in life." I stared at her; I did not even know that there had been such a person. How should I know who it was?

"A friend of yours, perhaps?" I jested, my mother being half Japanese.

Mother did not smile. "No, no friend," she said gravely. "She was my mother."

I stared at her with incredulity. Was this her idea of a joke? But my mother was not in the habit of joking this way and the expression on her face excluded the possibility. For a moment I was afraid that she had become deranged over my father's prolonged absence—he was in fact never to return from the eastern front.

"I know it must sound farfetched," she said gently, "but it is the truth."

"Are you trying to tell me that Oma Sachiko is Madam Butterfly?" My alarm was rapidly rising.

"No, my real mother—not Sachiko. Butterfly."

Half humoring her as one might a victim of hallucination, I attempted to ease the conversation to a more realistic plane. But once launched, my mother would not be stopped. Her story came out as it had to now, in halting, almost choked phrases that gained momentum and eloquence as they swept before them her recalcitrance and my disbelief. In the end I accepted her account, though it seemed stranger than any fiction I knew.

Sachiko, who until then had been the Japanese grandmother whom I had never seen, was the original Suzuki of Puccini's opera. As might be expected, the opera departs widely from the facts, though in this case history makes grand opera seem very tame and sober. My mother could tell me only what she had learned from Sachiko before emigrating to Germany. The real Butterfly did live in Nagasaki, she did marry an American who abandoned her, and she did commit suicide; she also left behind

· *Butterfly* ·

a child, though not a boy. That child was my mother, Itako. Itako was brought up by Butterfly's maid Sachiko, who identified with her mistress to the extent of denigrating Itako's father—whom we shall call Pinkerton, since the world knows him as such—just as if she herself had been the one abandoned. Itako, who looked foreign and yet had no foreign parent to look to, suffered considerably from her anomaly and at an early age turned to her Occidental heritage. Her talent for music led her to study piano at Tokyo University.

In 1920, Itako met a German doctor who had been invited to Japan as consultant for a new clinic in Tokyo. When he returned to Germany, she accompanied him as his wife, thereby fulfilling her mother's aborted destiny. She was able to continue her studies in Berlin under Eugen d'Albert. In 1924, I was born, and eventually the family settled in Heidelberg, my father's home-town.

After the war I studied to become a civil engineer and in 1952 had the opportunity to go to Japan as part of an exchange program organized by the U.N. Although Mother had decided to bury her Japanese past—she never considered returning to Japan even for a visit—she relented somewhat and charged me to visit some "cousins"; Sachiko herself had died during the war. Since I knew I would be going to Nagasaki, she suggested I might look for traces of my grandfather—"Pinkerton"—whose last known address (ca. 1914) was in that city. By this time she had mellowed and permitted herself to be curious about him.

In Nagasaki I was able to visit Madam Butterfly's house, but people were nonplused by my inquiries about Pinkerton, who they assured me could not have come back. The address I had was in the low hills to the west of the city, which had not been touched by the atomic explosion. My ever helpful interpreter, Miss Noriko Kanda, suggested we look about. Nobody had heard of Pinkerton, but some knew of a foreigner called Taizan, which was the kind of name given to Buddhist acolytes. This Taizan was an eccentric old fellow, a sort of philanthropic recluse who had been around for as long as anybody could remember. Unlike other foreigners, he had not been interned during the war, but no one seemed to have seen him since. On the scent now, Miss Kanda and I spent the next day asking around and were finally directed to Midori, a woman who had been Taizan's housekeeper. She unfortunately was not able to tell us very much about Taizan—she had gone two or three times a week to his little house to clean, wash, and do a little cooking—though she clearly held him in great affection. After I had explained that Pinkerton—we were not yet sure that he and Taizan were the same person—was my grandfather, Midori went and brought me a large bundle of papers. They were manuscripts that Taizan had asked her to burn just before he died, but she had not had the heart and kept them without really knowing why. Perhaps I was the one they had been waiting for. She had once shown them to an American soldier who could make neither head nor tail of them. I understood why when I opened the packet. There were close to a thousand pages, covered mostly with a fairly illegible scrawl and chaotically thrown together. However, to my intense excitement, I immediately spotted the word *Butterfly*. There could be no doubt: Taizan was Pinkerton, and these were his writings.

I stayed up half the night deciphering those untidy pages. What I read shocked me profoundly. Some of it was scabrous and perverse beyond anything I could have imagined; in spite of my deep loathing for Nazi rhetoric, I could not help thinking of the term they used for anything they disliked: *zersetzend*—"degenerate," "pernicious." I felt ashamed, both for the man capable of living and writing such perversities and for myself who descended from him and read of them. Indeed, I had doubts about the veracity of the account. At the time, I could not believe that

· *Butterfly* ·

anyone could behave like the Pinkerton of the manuscripts. Had it been a novel, I would have condemned the author for lack of verisimilitude; as it was, I strongly suspected Pinkerton of mixing sick fantasies with some rather gruesome facts.

I did not mention the manuscripts to my mother or to anyone else. I was young then and in love with a girl with whom I intended to build the ideal marriage; for the illicit, not to mention the perverse, I had little interest or tolerance. And it must be remembered that I was living in a very different epoch as regards sexual morality. *Lady Chatterly's Lover*, for instance, was, if I remember correctly, still suppressed in America at that time.

Yet I did not forget Pinkerton's manuscript, though I would have liked to. My repulsion notwithstanding, I had read through all the pages (it took more than one night), and they had made an impression.

More than three decades have gone by since. The world has changed. Today pornography of whatever description can be bought at every street corner, and there are facilities catering to any perversion. Our sense of what is obscene has been considerably modified; we have learned to be shocked at things more serious than kinky sex. And I myself have changed as well. My ideal marriage failed, and I have had to confront things in myself that at twenty-seven I would not admit existed. Thus when I took another look at the Nagasaki manuscripts a few years ago, they seemed less provocative and more interesting than they had in 1952; for all their faults, I found some parts moving, even beautiful. And Pinkerton himself no longer appeared so incredible; if his tale remained fantastic, it seemed in the main no longer impossible to believe.

The decision to edit the manuscripts, however, was again connected with my mother. At the very end of her life, she became suddenly preoccupied with the father she had tried all her life to banish from her thoughts. When I visited her in the summer of 1976, two months before her death, she made me repeat again everything I had learned about him in Nagasaki. "All my life," she said one day, "my mother has been a shining light for me; I associated everything that was good and beautiful with her, and I often felt her guiding me. My father, on the contrary, was obscure and threatening; he was the darkness that swallowed the light. I hated him, and I feared him like an evil ghost. But now I am no longer afraid. Now I can think of him, of what he became later in his life, and wonder what really happened between him and my mother. She must have meant more to him than just a woman he played with and abandoned, if he later returned to Nagasaki to live. There is a story there, and I wish I knew it."

Her words made me uneasy. If there had existed a legible version of Pinkerton's manuscript, would I have had the courage to put it into her hands? The idea of editing and publishing the manuscripts, in any case, surely had its beginnings in a belated desire to satisfy my mother's wish. Butterfly and Pinkerton will remain in people's memory, Puccini has seen to that. It is time, however, that their true story be told, and not for curiosity's sake alone. Pinkerton felt he had something to say when he wrote his autobiographical account; there is ample evidence that he returned to it more than once, and that one version at least was written with a view toward publication, although the project was apparently abandoned. Perhaps the task was an impossible one, for I do not believe that we—prospective readers of whom I was the first—were ready then to hear what he had to say. Not in the 1920s, nor in the 1950s. Today it may be different; for myself, at least, it is. In the intervening years, there has been a sexual revolution, and more recently, a revival of interest in the spiritual side of life. If Pinkerton's experiences are explainable in terms of sexual pathology, his written confession takes on more meaning

· *Butterfly* ·

in the spiritual context. I say this not in apology for the lurid contents of the manuscript or its occasionally garish style, but simply in the belief that the time is ripe for its dissemination. Ultimately, it is for the reader, not the editor, to evaluate and to judge.

Since 1976, I have made a sustained effort to gather documents and information that would supplement the Nagasaki manuscripts. In this I consider myself extraordinarily fortunate. It seems little short of a miracle to have found a number of private letters pertaining to one or another of the people who were associated with Pinkerton. Most useful of all is the essential information provided by the late Mrs. Milly Davenport, whose first husband was a grandson of George C. Sharpless, the American vice-consul at Nagasaki in Pinkerton's time. She also provided portions of Sharpless's diary, which unfortunately did not survive intact. Relevant passages, together with her testimony, have been incorporated almost integrally in the text, along with other documents and testimony that have come into my hands. My acquaintance with Mrs. Davenport came about unexpectedly. After my mother's death, I found the name Sharpless in my mother's address book. I sent a notice of her death, and received a note of sympathy from Mrs. Davenport that eventually led to a meeting.

Finally, a word concerning the text. The manuscripts were written over a period of many years. The first version probably dates from ca. 1914, when Pinkerton settled in Nagasaki. Parts were rewritten or added at different times after that. Finally— probably between 1934 and 1937—there was an attempt to put together a version for publication; this comprises the most legible and coherent pages of the manuscripts, but leaves out a very substantial portion of what the earlier pages contain. As Pinkerton became older, his vision inevitably changed, and he exhibited an increasing tendency to select and to censor. In the beginning, one feels, he wrote with abandon and indeed a certain relish in exposing himself. By contrast, he was more self-conscious in preparing the later version and apparently wanted only to tell what was necessary to convey its "meaning"; some of the more lurid details were accordingly suppressed, as well as large sections concerning his relations with Butterfly. However, this radical revision seems not to have satisfied him, and there are signs of flagging interest toward the end. The final version was half-heartedly finished up and laid aside; publication plans were evidently abandoned. It might also be noted that minor discrepancies occur in the different versions.

Memory itself being subject to spontaneous and often unconscious transformation even among those with unassailable motivations, it is hard to judge the reliability of any particular portion of the manuscript. I have tried to present the available material in as complete a fashion as possible. Pinkerton's "final version" is reproduced in its entirety and designated as "the Nagasaki ms.," somewhat arbitrarily, since any section of the entire text can with as much right be called that. Passages from the earlier pages have been interpolated where they seem most meaningful; these I have rewritten in the third person, partly to emphasize their omission from the author's final version, partly to give them coherence, for some are no more than notes or jottings. In the interest of readability and ease of comprehension, I have distributed the supplementary documents and testimonies on the same principle. Except when permission has expressly been given to use a family name, I have changed them, using where I could those by which the historical personages are known through Puccini's opera.

—*Paul Loewen*
La Tranche-sur-Mer
August 30, 1987

· *Butterfly* ·

Part One

Halb zog sie ihn, halb sank er hin . . .
(She half pulled him, he half sank in . . . .)

—GOETHE

1

From Nagasaki, it took two days to sail
down the western coast of Kyushu and around Cape
Sata, its southern tip. During this time, Butterfly never left
me; at all times something of her enveloped me like a magnetic
emanation and held me in a mildly euphoric state. As the ship
coasted, so did my spirit insensibly float on, drunken and joined
still to hers in a rapture of welded loins.

The third day we broke away from the shores of Japan; by the
morning of the fourth, we were out on the open ocean, heading
east at a clip as if already harking to the call of the continent
beyond. Then Butterfly's presence began to fade. Where it had
wrapped firmly as a cocoon around my soul, it now became but a
strand of silk drawn ever more tenuously across the widening
depths. I desperately tried to hold on to her, but the queasiness of
a separation I had been dreading for months was already upon me
like the first upsurge of anticipated seasickness. My mind
clouded; thoughts beginning and ending nowhere tangled in
nameless anguish; and those toward whom I was cruising—my
father, my mother, my sister Lisa, and Kate, above all Kate—rose
unbidden in my mind's eye, their importunate images rudely
eclipsing the Butterfly in my heart.

At noon the sky became strange; without being altogether
overcast, it hung low like a huge worn canopy sagging under
accumulations of moisture and dirt. By midafternoon, great gusts
filled the heavens and swept the sea, swelling and heaving and
lashing the clouds. Many were ripped to shreds, others blown this
way and that; billows and tatters hurtled together and as quickly
came apart.

High still above the western horizon, the midsummer sun, refusing to cede, blazed a spectacular iridescence into the volatile clouds. The sky became a kaleidoscope of swirling colors; the tones were strange, their intensity preternatural. It was uncanny, almost frightening. Crew members told me later that they had never seen anything like it in all their years at sea.

But there was to be more. From the starboard quarterdeck where I stood, I saw, at a point directly under the sun, a powerful vortex suddenly form. An unimaginable force seemed to be sucking in everything in sight, including—such was my impression—our ship. Within minutes, the sun had vanished behind a massive concentration of clouds dark and dense as a mountainous clump of black earth; to either side, shifting arrays of unearthly hues were being pulled together. Yet amidst the violent movement, a pattern became discernible.

"Butterfly!" I cried under my breath. Spread overhead like a stupendous goddess's mantle was the figure of a butterfly whose wings spanned half the sky.

An indescribable blend of anguish and esctasy wrung my heart while my eyes stared disbelievingly on. Already the sun was boring from behind into the dark body; at the center a needle of light had penetrated and was making a fissure. At first no more than a jagged silver line, it deepened as a supernal force pried apart that black substance too compact to be cloud; deepened and widened and stretched until the cleft opened into a gaping oval, a luminous monstrance of liquid gold set within that terrific mound suspended in midair. The mammoth butterfly hovered closer, as if about to sweep down upon us. And the gold, quivering with energy, grew brighter and brighter; near the center it glowed to incandescence, to a sizzling white that intensified, intensified still until at last the sun in blinding glory burst through the butterfly's body.

The effulgence struck me full in the face. Inwardly reeling, I

· *Butterfly* ·

crumbled to my knees; it was as if I had, in the split second before my eyes gave way, seen the face of God.

When I recovered my senses, I was almost surprised to find I had not been plucked off the deck. Instead, the giant butterfly had receded, its presence seemed less immediate, less overwhelming; its form was looser, and the opening in its body had grown considerably. The great solid chunk had transformed itself into a dusky tumid ring, almond-shaped like a Byzantine mandorla; through it the sun shone in a golden haze, sovereign and serene. The air felt freer, the winds had calmed. I picked myself up and stood leaning against the side of the ship, shaken and entranced.

For a moment I thought with a pang that the butterfly was taking its leave: it was diminishing, its wings were slowly losing their contours and would soon dissolve imperceptibly into the approaching sunset. But I was wrong. It lingered on, drifting slowly and desultorily into the distance like a fantastic kite, yet continuing as if magnetized to frame the setting sun. And stretching toward me from the sublime apparition on the horizon was a path of light that beckoned and pointed like a shimmering phallus. As if in response to its pull, a longing as I had never known rose to swell my breast and loins; I felt my soul being irresistibly drawn to the waiting butterfly. Oh, Butterfly, if only I had let my life spill forth then! And I would have, the very next instant, for you already possessed my senses, and my soul was about to jettison its body and fly to you, and there was no hesitation, Butterfly, only the glimmer of a joy greater than any I would ever know. But already the voice had sounded—the devil's own, I've often thought—inviting me to dine at the captain's table.

2

Her hands were small and soft and as white as pear blossoms. With the wide sleeves of the festive kimono trailing, they glided about like creatures of living grace. No other part of her was exposed—even the face was entirely covered by a masklike layer of powder and paint. Sometimes when they strayed close to his face, Pinkerton perceived a faint but distinctive fragrance. Surely the sleeves had been perfumed, but Pinkerton, intoxicated, scented in it the enticing nubility hidden deep within their folds.

When Goro explained in his jocose, ingratiating manner that the dance represented the transformation of a chrysalis into a butterfly, Pinkerton had to restrain an impulse to shush him into silence. The dancer's gestures rendered all explanation superfluous. Pinkerton marveled at their clarity and suggestiveness. How eloquent those hands were, how wonderfully alive! They lured his senses like the first ritual offerings of a precious fruit. Restrained by the measured steps and the delicate rhythms of plucked strings, her sensuality seeped ineffably through. He seemed to see her passionate soul beckoning in the curving of a finger, in the sweep of a hand; yet the eyes, when he sought them out, were wholly without expression: two dark drops coolly glistening in a powdery mask.

As the performance went on, even Goro became too entranced to offer insipid comments. Using a pair of huge folding fans brightly painted to resemble butterfly wings, the dancer made her audience partake of the miraculous transformation. She captured to perfection the butterfly's awakening, its emergence from the cocoon, the first instant of hesitation and the tentative flutter of wings before it soars into open space and sunlit air. Long afterward, whenever Pinkerton told of the performance, the magic of this moment would flicker in his face and flit across like an electric spark to his interlocutor.

Pinkerton, in lavishing praise on Butterfly—she had come to be identified with the dance for which she was famous and was now known under no other name—made it clear that he wished to spend the night in her company. So he was surprised and annoyed when another woman came to him in his room. Perhaps they thought him too drunk to notice. But he was not one to be treated so lightly. Where was Butterfly? he asked, repeating the name several times like an invocation. The woman, embarrassed, tried to explain, but she spoke little English, so he could not understand. Ruffled, she left the room and returned a little later with Goro, who immediately began to bluster about the virtues of his companion. Pinkerton insisted on Butterfly. Money was no consideration, he impatiently pointed out; but apparently it was not a question of money. What was it then? Goro answered with evasions, but Pinkerton, becoming more and more heated, would not desist until the man had explained that Butterfly belonged to a class of geisha who could only be obtained through a formal arrangement. Pinkerton impulsively declared himself ready to make such an arrangement on the spot. This brought a smile of amused disdain to Goro's lips. A serious matter like that could not be settled so precipitously. The conditions had to be discussed; there were gifts and settlements to be made, formalities to be observed. It would be an elaborate transaction. Pinkerton, exasperated and suddenly tired, dismissed Goro and the girl and spent a fretful night alone.

The following morning, however, he sent again for Goro. What would an arrangement entail? That depends, the little Japanese answered cautiously, but, after some prodding: a house for the girl together with means for its upkeep, a sum settled on *mama-san*, plus gifts of various kinds—say thirty thousand yen, all included. The figure was rather alarming, but possibly because of that, or because he felt the Japanese snickering behind his placid mien, Pinkerton did not flinch but charged Goro to do what was necessary to conclude an agreement on his behalf.

After the man had scrambled off, Pinkerton asked himself whether he was not foolhardy to enter into an arrangement that seemed inconveniently binding and cost a small fortune. His father would not be pleased; but then, his father had promised to foot all expenses if he agreed to spend a year in Japan, away from Kate and abjuring all communication with her. Surely his father had reckoned with a mistress; in fact, now that he thought about it, there had been positive encouragement in that quarter—after all, if he was to forget Kate . . . though not a hundred mistresses could make up for Kate, he thought in a belated surge of passion. Well, he had no intention of renouncing Kate; he would do as his parents demanded, he would sit out his year in Japan, and then he would go home and marry Kate—with or without their blessing, but in any case uninterfered, which was enough. In the meantime, secure in this intention, he would enjoy himself; why shouldn't he, since Kate herself had entered into the spirit of his father's game? "Suppose," she had discomfited him by saying, "we really do live apart for a year, without writing. It might be a useful test for us. After a year of freedom, if our feelings are still the same, nothing's lost; and if we feel differently, then your father will have been right." The logic, though it stung him, was impeccable, he had had to admit. But if that was the way she wanted it, he would make the most of the freedom she was foisting on him.

"Well?" he questioned impatiently when Goro came bouncing in late the next afternoon. His longing for the dancer had grown obsessively during the last thirty hours. The prospect of such a novel engagement excited him and lent urgency to his desire; desire in turn compelled his mind to dwell on her person and in

· *Butterfly* ·

particular her hands. Her face, oddly, eluded him: when he tried to picture it, he saw not hers but that of the woman sent in her stead. To that would-be substitute he had paid no attention, yet her features—he had not noticed at the time how pleasant they were—now intruded again and again into his revery, so that he began to regret having refused her favors. In the end he could not have said which one he wanted more, so mingled had the two become in his simmering lust.

"Forget Butterfly," Goro exhorted with an exaggerated bluffness. "I find girl for you, ten times beautiful."

Pinkerton, wound up to an excruciating pitch of desire, was hardly prepared to renounce its object upon this offhanded recommendation.

"No use," Goro finally stated after meeting Pinkerton's adjurations with a number of evasions. "Butterfly belong to Miyamura. Miyamura big merchant, very rich."

Pinkerton's eyes blazed, but his manner was calm. "How much would it take to get her?" he asked coldly.

"Sah, you don't understand, she is mistress of merchant Miya—"

With a violence that made Goro draw back in alarm, Pinkerton brought both palms crashing down upon the table. It was a gesture he had seen his father perform on more than one occasion, invariably with effect; though he had always thought it unnecessarily brutal and melodramatic, he now performed it spontaneously with appropriate panache. "I don't care!" he shouted. "I don't give a damn about your fucking Miyamayas! I want that girl, and all I want to know is what it'll take to get her. You just go and tell them that."

Goro looked at Pinkerton as if he were a madman. But immediately he took hold of himself; his face became impenetrable and his person took on a military gravity. "*Hai, wakalimashita,*" he barked and made a stiff bow.

Alone, Pinkerton found himself trembling. He had brandy brought and between glasses feverishly paced the room. Goro returned an hour later, though it seemed longer to Pinkerton. He had spoken with the old lady and explained Pinkerton's wish; the old lady had understood, but it was a delicate situation because of Miyamura's wealth and position. All things considered, the only way Butterfly could be ceded to another would be through a formal marriage. Goro's forthright manner of talking indicated that no compromise was possible.

Marriage! This was the one eventuality Pinkerton had not considered, nor could he envision it now. Distractedly dismissing Goro, he flung himself face down upon the bed. Wild thoughts raced through his head. Could he make a deal with Miyamura? Buy or force him out? Or should he abduct the girl? And take her where? To America? His fantasies subsided; he saw he had no choice but to put Butterfly forever out of his mind, and bravely he set about it. Every effort, however, only conjured up still more vividly the beautiful hands of which he had been dreaming. No, it was impossible that his body should forever be denied the caresses that his imagination had so lovingly tailored; impossible that his eyes should never behold the mysteries yet to be unwrapped but his already in anticipation. And where would his desire, swaying so high and heavy on its stalk, go if she should not be there to catch it when it burst?

Inadvertently he had reached down into his breeches, but as he touched the painfully constricted parts, a thought jolted him. He flung himself around and sat up on the edge of the bed. Why shouldn't he marry her? What could it mean anyway, since he was leaving in a year? Whether he left behind a wedded wife or a kept mistress, where was the difference? The marriage, unconsecrated, would not even be recognized. It was a show put on for Miyamura's sake, no more. This reflection lit up Pinkerton's spirits like sunlight streaming into a heavily curtained room. He rang and ordered Goro to be fetched at once.

· *Butterfly* ·

* * *

The wedding was fixed for the end of May. Pinkerton had conceived of a small private affair; the old lady, in charge of the arrangements, had other ideas, and against these Pinkerton protested so futilely that he began to suspect Goro of not transmitting his views. The wedding, in the Japanese style, ended up being quite an expensive and elaborate production; the entire consular staff was invited, as well as all the old lady's entourage and familiars, including the merchant Miyamura and his cronies. The rationale was that Miyamura must not lose face, for that might incite him to take action against the marriage. To Pinkerton, however, it seemed clear the old lady was using the publicity to ensure that her protegée would be treated equitably by her new spouse. There was plenty to do, what with purchasing and fixing up a house, furnishing it, hiring a staff, preparing gifts, so that even Pinkerton, who through special consideration was assigned very light duties at the consulate, had trouble fitting everything in. During the fortnight before the wedding, Goro spent several afternoons coaching him in his role of bridegroom. Instruction notwithstanding, he felt clumsy and ridiculous performing the newly learnt gestures in an outlandish Japanese costume, but at least he would be able to go through the ceremony without overtly embarrassing anyone.

What would his compatriots think? He resisted the temptation to speak to them about it. They of course would understand, but however indulgent they might be, any explanation could only confirm him as a rake and a cad. As the wedding day drew near, excitement and desire gave way to a nervous disquietude. Wasn't he really behaving badly, he on occasion wondered? However much he assured himself it was only a sham formality to outmaneuver a troublesome rival, he could not quite shake off a vague feeling of shame. But then, he invariably retorted, she was only a high-class whore.

The night before the wedding, Pinkerton dreamt of Kate. He

could not recall the dream, but it left him with a vivid and troubling sense of her presence. The instant he shut his eyes, her image reappeared; he saw her as she had been at their parting. On that occasion she had been as reserved as he had been passionate. She did not disavow his impetuous affirmations of their love; she was only unusually quiet, and a strange, distant smile played about her lips, a smile full of melancholy and unspoken meanings. Finally, in a frenzy, he had seized her gloved hands and pressed his lips to the sheer black silk. Underneath, the flesh was cool and curiously inert, which made her hands seem inexorable in their sleek perfection. But his kisses had eventually brought them to life, and they had stroked his cheeks and his hair. At the moment of separation, they had suddenly pulled him to her with such force that for an instant—no more—his lips were crushed to hers. Before he had had time to respond, she was gone. The reassurances he sought so desperately were not to come.

Recaptured in his mind, her smile took on a hint of mockery. Innerly he protested: he was not really marrying the girl; surely she did not think he would marry anyone else. But the sardonic expression remained, he was powerless to change it or shut it out. Her presence, if anything, became more vivid; he felt he had only to reach out to touch her, and yet he could not do that either.

Beside himself, he rang violently and shouted his order to inform Goro that the wedding was off. This radical action calmed him, and he sat in a stupor, emptied of feeling and thought. But when Goro bustled in half an hour later wreathed in smiles and ostensibly ignorant of Pinkerton's change of mind—even though his man later affirmed that the message had been clearly conveyed—his bubbling good humor drowned his patron's protests and swept them so vigorously out of the way that Pinkerton himself lost their gist and let them drift from his mind. In the end Pinkerton felt positively sheepish for having irrationally wanted to cancel what they had taken such pains to secure. So all went as planned after all.

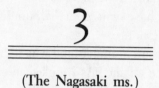

3

(The Nagasaki ms.)

My mother and Lisa, both formally attired in black, looked so serious that for a moment I feared the worst. I was genuinely moved to see them and rushed to embrace my mother; she kissed me, but the rigidity of her body and the shadow of a frown reminded me that demonstrations of emotion—even after a year's absence—were not well-regarded in our family. My sister's welcome was warmer, but she had barely got her arms around my neck when we were admonished that my father was waiting.

The man I found sunk in the pillows and bedclothes seemed at first sight to bear little resemblance to the father I had known. The flamboyant silver mane had become sparse and lusterless; the muscular face had shrunk. His extreme emaciation and pallor presented a picture of frailty that wrung my heart. I was reminded of a broken branch on which a few dry leaves still dangled, tenuous and forlorn. Though he saw me enter, he did not—apparently out of weakness—so much as twitch while I traversed the room. How he had degenerated! At close range his condition appeared even more pitiable. For a moment we looked at each other in silence. The enmity I bore him evaporated. Too choked with emotion to speak, I took one of his hands in mine and tried with all my will to communicate something of the warmth and natural affection that had hitherto been missing in our relations.

My inquiry about his health met with neither reply nor acknowledgment. His eyes turned from me and stared vacantly into space, and the crooked line between his desiccated lips twisted into a thin and mirthless smile. In a voice that, faintness notwithstanding, crackled with I know not what malignant spirit, he asked, "Well, have you come around?" A familiar rasp punctuated his question.

It took me an instant to understand what he was talking about. Then I felt my face aflame. As I looked into my father's flinty eyes, a knifelike hatred cut through the good feelings I was harbouring: nothing had changed. I saw the same malicious lips; the same steely, supercilious regard; the same ambiguous chuckle with its volatile mixture of menace and mockery. And that insufferable expression of cold superiority. A terrible rage stirred in me, rose and reared and towered beyond reason, beyond sanity. My neck quivered, my head swelled; a mad, demonic impulse possessed me to throttle that helpless bag of bones. I was almost surprised that I did not do so; instead, I heard myself answer loudly, my voice hard with spite, "Yes sir, I have!" A malicious pleasure crept over me as I proceeded to announce my marriage to Butterfly. My words, like barbs on a whip, were chosen to draw blood—they were explicit about Butterfly's condition and status—and I savored their effect like so many crimson droplets on a tortured skin.

"You are joking, I presume." My father's face was blotched and he nearly choked on these few words, though he made a supreme effort to control himself.

"Oh, I would hardly joke about such a matter," I replied in accents that parodied my father's habitual pompousness of speech. "Possibly you feel surprised that I made no mention of this in my letters. It's because I wanted personally to bear the good tidings—I trust you remember how pointedly you expressed yourself: the greatest gratification I could ever hope to give you

· *Butterfly* ·

would be to take a legitimate wife, any I damn pleased excepting Miss Hamilton, and to beget a decent heir. Well, this gratification is yours now, I'm happy to say, because by the time I see my legitimate wife again, she will have given birth to your grandchild, whose complexion I hope for your sake you will find decent enough for your heir."

At that something burnt out in his face. The words, when they came, teetered upon his trembling lips and dropped tonelessly: "Get out." For emphasis he gave a little wave of his right hand, the faintest of gestures but no doubt the best he could manage. "Go, go." His eyes were like smouldering glass. It was the last time I saw him alive.

4

The photograph was inspected with the disdainful curiosity and aversion of women being shown a specimen of insect. No one had spoken; there had not been the usual little cries and phrases of admiration. Pinkerton understood perfectly how the stiff figure in the picture with its blank, inexpressive face appeared to them. His mother, when the photograph was passed back to her, tossed it negligently onto the coffee table, as if loath to touch it any longer than necessary.

They—Mother, uncles and aunts, family friends, cousins, Monsignor—said:

"Isn't it enough that you've killed your father?"

"You cannot, simply cannot live here with a Japanese wife."

"Think of *us*, if you don't care about yourself. How'll it look for us?"

"You have a duty to the family, young man. Now that your

father's passed away—God bless his soul—you have to step into his shoes, you know."

"I can't believe that you've really married her, and I don't believe *you* can either."

"Don't you think about who we are sometimes? Five generations ago, your ancestor fought in the Revolution, and since then every generation of Pinkerton—I repeat, every generation—has risen to a position of eminence. Don't you feel that in your blood?"

"A heathen woman . . ."

"You're a Pinkerton, you know, like it or not. You're not a gipsy who's here one day and gone the next without anybody noticing. You got a family to consider, and a tradition to uphold."

"Jesus, Henry, don't America mean anything to you? Don't God mean anything to you?"

"Your mother needs you, boy. Don't forget that."

"You'll never make your way in society with a Japanese wife, I can guarantee you that."

"We'll bring up the child."

"If it's not consecrated by the Church, it's not a marriage. In the eyes of God and the civilized world, you are not married to that woman."

"Bring the child over here and have him baptized, if you must. Personally, I wouldn't recommend keeping around a half-breed bastard, but if you must do so, at least let him be a Christian one."

"Don't think I blame you, Henry. I don't. You're a young man, and young men have their little escapades. I know, I was one myself not so long ago and, by golly, I don't know as I'd have acted different. But now your dad's gone and somebody's got to take charge. Now that's serious business, and you're gonna need

· *Butterfly* ·

all the assets you can get hold of, so it's time to put away childish things, as we say in the Scriptures."

Lisa said:

"And what about Kate?"

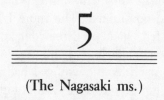

5

(The Nagasaki ms.)

My father's death put everything in a different light, or so it would seem. I was now my own man, and a rich one. Yet fundamentally nothing had changed; my main concern was still to return with all possible speed to Japan, and in that I continued to be frustrated.

Our family had substantial and diversified holdings spread throughout the country; uninformed as I was of my father's affairs, I found myself faced with the formidable task of managing a vast estate whose details were entirely unfamiliar. My initial anticipation of an early departure—my first thought when my father died was that I could now be with Butterfly during the final months of her pregnancy—stretched and finally dissolved in a morass of paperwork. I began to realize that I would be lucky to get there for the lying-in, and gradually that I would miss even that.

At the same time it became more evident with each passing day that I could no longer live away from Butterfly. It was as if I had left something behind in Japan whose existence I had ignored but without which I was severed from reality. Listless and indifferent to the world around me, I would sometimes catch myself touching parts of the body to reassure myself of their solidity, so curiously disembodied did I feel. Not that Butterfly occupied my mind to the exclusion of all else; for all that I loved her, she in no way impassioned me as Kate had a year before. But at times I would be overcome by a feeling of want that, unlike passion, went beyond sentimental or physical yearning—it was more like missing some part of my own core.

During this period of impatient waiting, I became conscious of the enormity I had committed. The more I missed Butterfly's presence, the less I felt I had ever deserved it; and the more others condemned my present attachment and urged me to break it off, the less I forgave myself for the wrongs I had already done her. Had I not married her on a caprice, without giving a thought to her feelings or to the position I was placing her in, or even to the consequences for myself? Reviewing what had passed between us, I now discovered offense in a thousand details. My callousness and cynicism mortified me. Even my love for her began to seem suspect. Had my unwillingness to part from her been more than, say, a momentary reluctance to quit a warm bed? Did I miss her so much only because she had made my life so comfortable? True, I had become devoted to her and no longer thought of abandoning her. But would I spend the rest of my life in Japan or take her back to America? That question had been held in abeyance and never confronted.

Perhaps we are not given to reflect upon matters that cannot hurt us. Perhaps our moral sensibility is no more than a generalized sensitivity to pain which, like an insurance policy for the furniture within our walls, covers only that through which we can sustain sensible damages. So long as Butterfly remained a plaything, however favored, I imagined I treated her well and was well-pleased; but once I took stock of what she had become for me, I felt uneasy for having treated her as less. And the deeper my remorse, the worse I endured our separation, for only her physical presence could palliate—by suspending, not canceling—the moral sting. Alas, what we seek so avidly in a woman's body is often not pleasure but oblivion from the knowledge of turpitude knotted indissolubly in our heart.

· *Butterfly* ·

6

Early in September I announced my decision to sail for Japan on the *S.S. Putnam*, scheduled to leave San Francisco on the eighth of November. My mother, after giving me a withering look, continued to cut her meat; Lisa drew in her breath and averted her face. Neither commented. The silence was uncomfortable, but I felt relieved that they seemed to acquiesce.

Three weeks later, to my considerable surprise, Lisa informed me that Kate would be coming to stay for a while. "You needn't look so consternated," she said with a little pout. "She's not coming to settle accounts with you. It's me she's coming to see. Now that Dad's gone, there's no reason why she should stay away—except maybe for your presence."

I made a vague protesting gesture that led Lisa to declare, "Oh, don't think she's afraid to see you! She just didn't want you to feel embarrassed, but I told her you had the skin of an elephant and wouldn't mind in the least. Wasn't I right to do that?" My disapproval no doubt showed on my face, because a sly little smile animated her lips. "She's an angel; she doesn't hate you for being a cad. She doesn't even seem to hold it against you. How she does it I'll never understand." The smile was gone, and her throat had tightened. "Hen, if it were me, I think I'd scratch out your eyes." I nearly flinched; a savage rasp in her voice had made the threat feel like a beast ready to spring. She glared at me for an instant, then turned away and stalked from the room.

Lisa's words did not reassure me; on the contrary, they aroused my suspicion. Was this not a last-ditch attempt on the part of my mother and Lisa to dissuade me from returning to Butterfly? When I broke off my engagement with Anne, my mother had reacted even more violently than my father; given her subsequent aversion to Kate, Lisa could not have extended an invitation without her consent. And Kate for her part would not have chosen this moment to visit; why should she wish to see a faithless lover who had jilted her for another? Unless, encouraged by Lisa and my mother, she was coming in the hope of reconquest—or revenge.

I was vexed at what seemed an underhanded scheme, and a dark premonition made me wish I were safe on the open sea. At the same time, the prospect of seeing Kate again held a secret sweetness that seeped into my heart; I tasted it furtively, and apprehension rippled through my veins like cold sparkling champagne.

7

(Pinkerton's letter to William Harrington, dated September 10, 1895)

My dear Willy,

A hundred and thirteen pardons—one for each day—for having subjected you to the ignominy of learning about my broken engagement in the society column. My one excuse, weak enough I grant, is that I've been meaning to get down to New York and thought I'd break it to you in person and in detail.

To answer your questions: Yes, I did jilt Anne in a dastardly fashion. And yes, it was for another woman. Charges of ignoble behavior will not be denied; I'll put myself at the court's mercy with only the extenuating plea of a lady's beauty. And who is this lady? Her name will mean nothing to you, and as I do not wish to have to apologize to you a second time for a like reason, I announce to you herewith that we are engaged to be married, which will justify me in referring to her as Kate. She went to Vassar, and it is there that Lisa met her and—God bless her sisterly solicitude!—brought her home for the spring holidays.

Now, imagine a morning like any other and you're going in for breakfast and suddenly you see in front of you, right there in your own breakfast room, a woman more beautiful than any you've ever seen or imagined! Lisa had written about a girl in the Senior class—two years ahead of herself—who was the *ne plus ultra* and whom I simply *had* to meet, but being already engaged to Anne, I did not take this to heart; and certainly I did not expect something so dazzling—excuse the choice of words, I really was dazzled! I hate to think how I must have looked—surely very foolish, because Lisa laughed at my being starstruck and asked if she wasn't even going to get a kiss to welcome her home. I felt every bit like a schoolboy.

I'm afraid I can't quite tell you what happened during breakfast, Willy—only that we took our time and that by the time we left the table, the sonorities of her rich, mellifluous voice had entranced my soul and I knew that I wanted never to leave the side of its owner. It was as if I had stepped across the threshold of the breakfast room into another dimension. My life before that moment was left far behind; everything in it seemed distant and without substance. Anne, whom I had thought charming the night before, now appeared a callow debutante whose every word and gesture betrayed a depthless, conventional spirit. My love for her evaporated—that is, what I had taken to be love; indeed, I understood no longer how I could have imagined myself in love. The fluff and frills of her coming and going, the coy little games she played with me, even her prettiness and physical charms, suddenly seemed insipid, even irritating. I knew then that I could never marry her.

Lisa was an absolute dear during the ten days they were

home. She practically arranged our first tête-à-tête and did everything to bring us together—not that we needed encouragement! After that visit, I was running down to Vassar every second week. Kate, who has a small income and no close kin, took up lodgings in Boston after her graduation, so we've been seeing a great deal of one another (though never enough for me). Willy, I cannot tell you how happy I've been; I hope with all my heart that you'll someday find out for yourself what true happiness is.

Our relations, by the way, remain as chaste as new snow, not for lack of desire, mind you, but rather out of its abundance—a kind of mystical reverence that makes the approach to the shrine a stately if steady procession. Don't laugh, Willy! One day you'll know what it's like. The very strength of our desire quenches its urgency, because in the core of our being we know that our love will be with us as long as we are together—and what can part us, Willy? Nothing! By the way, I speak of the carnal aspect only to forestall the indiscreet questions and insinuations that I know would come if I didn't.

Joking aside, when will you be coming up? We all miss you, and I can't wait to have you meet Kate, and to hear about your latest adventures. In the meantime, Lisa joins me in sending our most affectionate regards,

HENRY

(From Pinkerton's letter to Harrington dated September 23, 1895)

. . . . You demanded a description; well, think of Helen appearing on the ramparts before the old men of Troy, or of Phryne wowing the Athenian jurymen. But if you must stick to being your prosy old Willynous self, then think of

· *Butterfly* ·

Vivian Pearson, but in a transfigured version, or better, think of that stunning dark-haired girl at Madame Pons's —Liddy? or Lydia?—the one with the extraordinary wild eyes who married a Russian count, to the despair of two gallant sophomores I remember who would have vied with each other in ruining themselves over her! I don't mean to say Kate really resembles either of them, but you get an idea of the type. . . .

(From a letter written by George Collins to William Harrington dated October 19, 1895)

. . . You might be interested to know that I ran into Henry the other day in the Fine Arts Museum accompanied by Anne Courtland's successor. Like everyone else, I had been surprised by the news of the rupture—as far as I was concerned, Henry and Anne had formed a couple since they were still practically children, and a perfectly assorted one at that. I remember how they used to go off cooing together when we were still in short pants, and with their parents' blessings *par dessus le marché.*

Henry and his new paramour were both very amiable and we ended up spending the afternoon together. Well, after that I understood. Anne is a lovely girl and a Courtland, but she simply cannot hold a candle to her rival, whom I shan't presume to describe; like any great *oeuvre d'art,* Miss Hamilton has to be seen. I can only say that she is a woman such as one would put on the Ark were there a second Deluge; or on the throne if our country had a queen. I am not a pursuer of the *éternel féminin* like you or Henry, but I do believe myself to be at least as sensitive as *vous autres fins connaisseurs* to those qualities not so immediately seized upon by your roving eye; and there I declare *sans hésitation* that I have rarely if ever beheld a woman of Miss Hamilton's stamp. In the loftiness and depth of her mind, in fineness of sensibility, in nobility and poise and that *je ne sais quoi* of feminine grace, she is the equal of a Beatrice. The Pinkertons should be on their knees thanking God for sending such a woman to their son, who *entre nous* hardly deserves this munificence. Instead, they raise a hue and cry because now the Courtlands are offended and their dynastic ambitions are foiled. As if the Pinkertons needed to expand their dominions! But they probably think of themselves as Aragon and covet Castile. . . .

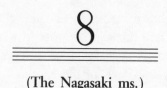

8

(The Nagasaki ms.)

Kate was standing with her back toward the door when I entered. I had resolved to be composed, but my heart beat wildly when I saw the rich, heavy coils of dark hair poised inimitably over that proud neck whose contours I knew so well. Hearing me, she turned.

The sight of her stopped me in my tracks; for a moment I stood stock-still, as one might in suddenly beholding a masterpiece. No, I had not forgotten how beautiful she was. Who could forget the miracle of harmony that was her face, or the skin that breathed with endless sunshine and spring, or those eyes, dark and vertiginous like the deepest well? But remembering was one thing, meeting in the flesh quite another.

Yet even as I stood suspended in admiration, I took stock of the inner distance that separated us now. I felt acutely how we were detached from one another even as I was merged with Butterfly. At that very instant Butterfly was so strongly present to me that I could all but feel her looking through my eyes, as I sometimes did through hers. Never had I been so clear about my position with regard to the two women. Released all at once from the apprehension that had been troubling me a second before, I strode confident and smiling toward Kate. My only uncertainty was whether to kiss her in greeting, for I wished to spare her any awkwardness.

Of this there was no danger. Kate, unambiguously offering me her hand, was open, even warm, and apparently without embarrassment or rancor. She congratulated me like an old friend on my marriage and did not shy from talking about Japan; but she invited no confidences and left no opening for intimacy. The ease in her demeanor made my suspicions seem absurd and mean-minded; I, who had feared unwelcome intentions on her part, was now almost piqued to find her manifestly lacking any beyond that of reviving her friendship with Lisa.

In the days to come, Kate neither sought nor avoided my company, but I seldom saw her alone. She was a model of social amiability, no less and no more. Her behavior could not have been more perfectly tailored to my wishes, for what I had most desired for our reunion was peace of mind, hers and mine. Yet if I felt grateful, it was not for long. Soon it began to rankle—not seriously or excessively, but there it was nonetheless—that I should receive so little of her attention while seeing so much of her person. I took to wondering about what she felt in my presence, about what and whether she thought of me, about what she did with memories of moments I still treasured. Surely it was not possible for her to forget how happy we had been together, or remembering, to be unaffected. I, well, I had Butterfly; but she? Had she truly put me out of her heart, or was she only maintaining an outward dignity? I spied in vain for some telltale sign of unavowed interest and retired each evening a little more convinced of her indifference.

9

Already close as children, Lisa and Henry had been drawn ever deeper by their mother's aloofness into what that distant lady irately called their "conspiracy." When Henry went to Japan, their intimacy had continued—or so Lisa thought—in the form of an assiduous and detailed correspondence. It was thus a rude shock for Lisa to learn of her brother's marriage—something of which he had never breathed a word. When her mother announced the news in her best tragic manner—her dying husband had informed her—Lisa at first broke out in laughter; *she* knew it could not be. Yet it was, and in the weeks that followed she felt she no longer knew anything at all, only that a constant pain had lodged itself in her chest. For if she did not comprehend how her beloved brother could have betrayed her lovely friend, deep down she forgave him as she forgave all his foibles; but that he should have failed to confide in her—that shook her to the core and hurt her more than the darkest infamy. Such a breach of complicity was the one thing she could not find it in her heart to forgive.

How could he have married that woman in the photograph, so like a Japanese doll? Again and again she asked herself as she perused the placid sepia image or searched her brother's face across the dining table; the question awaited her every morning when she awakened, and she pondered it in bed, all the while wishing he would come in and stretch himself beside her the way he used to and tell her the answer. Yet when, after weeks of silent sulking, she finally put it to him, she realized even as the words formed on her lips that he had no answer. "No, don't try to reply," she went on quickly without giving him time for evasions.

· *Butterfly* ·

"Just tell me one thing, it's all I want to know: how do you feel now, I mean about Kate? Have you forgotten her, or what?"

He did not answer. She, reading the pain that came into his eyes, pursued. "Do you still love her then?"

This time she waited. A minute or two passed before he could get the words out. Yes, he still loved Kate, he always would.

"Then marry her!" Lisa burst out passionately. "Marry her— nothing is preventing you now that Dad's gone. You wanted to so badly then. Well, she's yours now, take her!"

He looked at her, half perplexed and more in sadness than indignation. "Lisa, I'm married now, don't you understand? I have a wife, and soon I'll have a child. Please, Lisa, you must accept that, you and mother and everyone else."

"Hen, oh Hen," she pleaded with a desperate fervor. "Didn't Monsignor himself say that the marriage is void? The Church doesn't recognize it; it's as if it didn't exist. You're not bound by it, not at all! And I'm sure Kate would take the child—if she doesn't, I will."

10

(The Nagasaki ms.)

Kate's presence in the house was like a gust of fresh air that vivified its inhabitants but occasionally sent them shivering. Her conversation, which even my mother began visibly to enjoy, was the more piquant for being interlarded with provocative opinions, just as her impassioned fingers at the piano brought out dissonances and basses that jolted but captivated the ear. One incident alone was jarring. It occurred early during the visit and left me profoundly and rightly troubled, even though at the time I had only the vaguest intuition of its significance.

Kate had come to us accompanied by a striking girl of nineteen or twenty. With its angular lines and overripe lips, her face, though arresting, fell short of beauty. But she had the lithe, powerful body of a magnificent feline (I learned later that she had been trained as a circus acrobat). I instantly whiffed an odor of sensuality that must either attract powerfully or repel. Her proud carriage and an indefinable something in her face suggested some other status than a maid's; certainly I had never had a servant greet me with a stare of such brazen curiosity.

I was not the only one to wonder about this exotic girl who conversed with Kate in a mixture of French and German. The second evening we sat together, my mother asked Kate where she had found her unusual servant.

"Oh, Marika isn't a servant, really," Kate casually replied. "She's my slave. I bought her last year in Hungary from the owner of a circus that was being disbanded." We did not know what to make of this. Kate, sensing our incredulity, had her maid summoned. "Marika," she called out as soon as the girl appeared at the door, "*ich erzähle gerade den Herrschaften* . . . I was just telling our hosts that you are my slave, but they won't believe me. Come here and show them." The girl blushed—with shame or pleasure it was impossible to tell—and her naturally crimson lips curled ever so slightly in an enigmatic smile. Lowering her eyes, she went to the right side of Kate's armchair and dropped ceremoniously to her knees. In the stillness one could almost hear her fluttering heart, almost feel the suspirant syllables swell and rise from its voluptuous chambers and sibilate under her breath: "*Maîtresse!*" She bent her mouth devoutly to Kate's hand immobile upon the armrest in a kiss which, tender at first, intensified until her lips seemed soldered with passion to her mistress's skin. "Enough," Kate said, but the command went unheeded. Finally she had to draw back her hand and shove the girl's head away like an importunate dog's. "*Geh!*" The girl

· *Butterfly* ·

swayed a little on her knees and let out something between a sigh and a sob; then she darted from the room.

My mother tittered uncomfortably. Lisa, her face decomposed, cast about like a mystified theater-goer who did not know whether to walk out or applaud. "Isn't slavery against the law?" she ended by asking in a small voice.

"Does it look as if I'm keeping Marika locked and chained?" Kate laughed. "She's perfectly free to leave whenever she wants. In the eyes of the law, I merely delivered her from certain contractual obligations. She's the one who wishes to stay on and 'play' at being my slave, if it makes you happier to think of it as playing."

Playing what twisted game? I had half a mind to ask. But I could not find my voice, so lost was I in the strange new vista that had opened. More than once in the past, I had been surprised and delighted to come upon some hitherto unseen facet of Kate's cornucopian personality, but this time it left me uneasy and estranged. Her words and the scene I had witnessed shocked me, for they would not square with what I imagined to have intimately known. Whatever comprised her game with Marika, I darkly sensed, lay not only outside the charted precincts of our love but beyond any possible annexation. I scented something sinister, something terrifying and feral, and suddenly wondered what she was whom I had once so trustingly held in my arms.

"Is it very amusing to play at being a slave?" Lisa asked a little shrilly.

Kate did not immediately reply.

"Amusing, no, I shouldn't think so. Though some do have a taste for it. For them it's more than amusing; it is most serious."

She suddenly looked at me. I met her eyes, and for the first time since our separation, I found myself plunging once again into their fathomless depths. Partly to resist the magic, I fumbled for something to say.

"But the taste is surely not a natural one!" My little laugh sounded silly and false to my own ears.

"Are all your tastes natural ones, Henry?" There was banter in her voice, but her eyes drank me in. "If so, you don't know what you're missing. An unnatural one might widen your horizons. Try it sometime."

"I suppose playing mistress is also an acquired taste?" I retorted.

Kate smiled a faint, mysterious smile. "Acquiring a taste is not hard," she said with a strange look. "Nor is it very rare." With that her eyes left my face and she abruptly changed the subject.

11

(Editor's note: this early page, though not part of the Nagasaki ms., has been left in its orignal form because of its personal tone.)

It had become a habit of mine to take Butterfly mentally through the day's events, explaining one thing and reflecting on another as I was wont to do aloud in her presence; and I tried in turn to imagine her responses and comments. The spurious sense of Butterfly's participation in my life helped bridge the distance between us. These imaginary exchanges were as spontaneous and free as our intercourse had in time become. The scene I had witnessed, however, left an aftertaste of ignominy which I preferred to spare her, and for the first time I felt inhibited.

Did the sale of Marika so disturb me, I wondered, I who had bought Butterfly without compunction? Or was I merely unhappy to be reminded? But surely I was not alone to indulge in this sordid commerce. Did not men the world over traffic in beautiful women? What pretty woman did not sell herself, if not for cash, then for shares in power and status and property? Or was it the acknowledgment rather than the fact that shocked?

And if my action was ignoble, had Butterfly not redeemed it by bestowing love for the pleasure purchased? If such love could come of it—and her love, as I already suspected then, was the best thing I would know or see—could the act be wholly bad? Who can say what ultimately is good and what bad? Is the good or bad in the act itself, or rather in the way we live out its consequences? As the soul winds along its labyrinthian path, what mortal eye can see beyond the bends?

12

Pinkerton, having paid a handsome price, expected pleasures to match. In this he was disappointed. Butterfly was lovely, she was well-versed in the ways of love, she was eager to please, but she could not give Pinkerton the pleasure he had come to anticipate through his fantasies. Her clever, sensitive hands performed wonders upon his body, pressing here to relax and there to tonify, but he did not find in them the magical instruments of sensuality that had obsessed him in his longing. It was not a question of proficiency, for her nimble fingers could do anything, but one of attitude. Pinkerton found her constantly at odds with his desires. Where he wanted his senses driven to new, uncharted intensities, she would coddle and lull them to quietude if not to sleep; where he would be titillated and seduced, she was full of wifely solicitude and ministerings. After a week of vain attempts to coax her into becoming the seductress of his dreams, he gave up and let his longings flock back to Kate or stray to other women he had known. Not without nostalgia, he recalled the heady visits to

Madame Pons and her stunning bevy of demi-goddesses that always filled him with a secret awe; yes, the girls there had been more exciting, he reflected, thinking peevishly of Butterfly. He had bargained for an exotic courtesan, he had gotten a foreign wife.

What he missed in her was wantonness. It was clear that she had been trained to please, clear too that she very much wished to. She catered to every desire he manifested, but she contributed none; in his frustration he took her in all the ways he knew, and in each instance she was amenable, even eager. But she herself remained unmoved. His sighs and spasms washed over her like waves and tides over the smooth white boulders along the shore. Infinitely patient and docile, untiringly cooperative and painstaking, she had the qualities, Pinkerton sardonically noted, of a "perfect" whore: whereas a good one pricked one's lust with her own and shared in the pleasure or at least in its display—and here Butterfly fell sorrily short.

But as a wife she was unimpeachable. She molded herself to his habits and personality, to his likes and dislikes, and did all to make his life agreeable. Not content with what her eyes observed, she applied herself to improving her English: by year's end she spoke almost fluently, though her vocabulary was limited and her constructions often uncertain. After their first week together Pinkerton, dreading boredom, would have moved back to his bachelor's quarters had Butterfly not appeared so hurt; but his fears were unfounded. Once she had made the necessary adjustment, Butterfly became an excellent companion. She had a way of infusing her remarkable artistic sensibility into the smallest things, so that the most ordinary day would quicken with little touches of poetry and color and come aglow with gentle pleasure. There were to be no sensual extravaganzas, however much he might desire them, but their life together was permeated by a quiet, steady sense of well-being—a refreshing

· *Butterfly* ·

breeze never absent and never too much there—and that in the long run was a far richer gain.

At first Pinkerton did not notice; he only found himself engaged always in some pleasant activity or another that seemed to be of no particular consequence. Although seldom aware of doing anything interesting enough to report at length—during his first weeks in Japan he had written pages and pages to Lisa— he was never discontented or bored. His appreciation grew by imperceptible degrees, but it grew. One day, waking at dawn and feeling Butterfly's warmth beside him and his own hard urgency, he drew himself up over her. It would not have been the first time he roused her from sleep with his caresses or entered her as she still dozed, but this time he refrained and let his eyes alone grope in the semi-darkness over her sleeping form. Outside the birds had begun to chirp. For a long time he watched over her; as the half-light filtering through the translucent paper screens turned whiter, a feeling of tenderness stirred and spread through him until his entire being tingled with delight; he had never felt so happy.

He knew then that he loved her.

13

(The Nagasaki ms.)

Marika's performance was distressingly theatrical, yet it fascinated me and I could not help reviewing it again and again. Floating in my revery, the images took on a subtly different coloring and seemed less repellently bizarre; presently I discovered a peculiar appeal in the girl and her extravagant surrender.

I was more than ever intrigued, but Kate did not speak of Marika, and something restrained me from bringing up the subject. Marika herself was seldom visible, and what glimpses I had were fleeting. Once or twice I caught the sound of her laughter mingling with Kate's, which further sharpened my curiosity.

Kate, however, presented the greater enigma. It was as if a passage of moonlight had revealed a strange nocturnal visage unsuspected and at odds with the one seen in the light of day. Fired by dark intimations, I studied Kate for signs of I know not what baleful doppelgänger. But I detected nothing; my attention only reconfirmed her qualities, so that each time I came away more dazzled by her loveliness. Imperceptibly my thoughts drifted to my long relinquished claims and memory after memory came flooding back.

Suddenly all that I had imagined buried for good was there again before me. Oh, to lay my head upon that lap, to surrender to those eyes—that such sweetness could be so close to hand and yet denied! A world so rich and bright, forever forfeited, because of an irresponsible caprice! To be sure, I had been amply recompensed for its loss, but what about Kate, who had an equal claim?

Remorse made me crave doubly for Kate's attention. I could no longer enter her presence without hoping for some sign of forgiveness or continued affection—a touch of the hand, a word, a look. But such was not forthcoming. Unable to speak openly of what lay so heavily upon my mind, I beseeched her with looks and oblique words, all in vain. Nor was my desire for a tête-à-tête acknowledged. Lavish with amenities and smiles, Kate refused to see or hear. Her friendliness was a curtain drawn between her heart and mine; I tugged at it but could not, or dared not, tear it away.

One day, stranded in the drawing room after Kate had adroitly parried a bid for attention, I sank heavily into an armchair, the same from which I had witnessed Marika's odd exhibition of

· *Butterfly* ·

fealty. Overcome by frustration, I felt a sharp envy for the girl. If only I too could clarify and redefine my turbid relationship with Kate through some such extravagance. Indeed, was not Marika's gesture an apt expression for my own turmoil of remorse, guilt, admiration and passion? Idly I began to recreate the scene, but with myself in Marika's stead. I conjured up Kate where she had sat that evening, imperious and distant; never had she seemed more beautiful. I envisioned myself crossing the room, approaching, standing before her, and squirmed as imagination bent my knees. Her splendor towering over me, her eyes bearing down . . . I trembled, yet the anguish was ineffably sweet. I felt a pang of terror and shame; it was as if something monstrous and sublime had stirred in the caverns of my soul.

This moment of weakness did not last. I soon berated myself for my absurd imaginings and even laughed aloud; but from that day forth I was to regard Marika's strange homage with different eyes.

14

Henry and Lisa invented a game called Procrustes in which they took turns playing the bandit and the victim he stretches or truncates to fit his infamous bed. Each role had its attractions. Procrustes could lord it over the other in a fierce and fiendish manner, while the victim might indulge in the most amusing grimaces and screams. All of which provoked endless peals of laughter and childish excitement.

One day Lisa as Procrustes decreed that the captive be tied down and flattened with a roller; she had seen workmen use one to press a macadam road. The rope she found being a long one, Henry presently found himself completely immobilized; this provoked a certain anxiety in him, and whether because of that or because Lisa was particularly absorbed in her role that day, she seemed truly menacing. Meanwhile, spurred by her success with the rope, Lisa decided to gag him as well on the pretext that Procrustes had an earache that day and could not revel in his victim's cries. The idea did not appeal to Henry, but his protests only made her keener. All he could do was to shout and agitate his head, but this resistance was taken, perhaps a bit disingenuously, to be part of the game; in any event, it proved as effectual as any offered in Procrustes's own day. Lisa, who knotted a handkerchief no less adroitly than a cord, then proceeded to roll an empty beer keg over her captive. Caught up in her own giggles, she paid no attention to Henry's distress, and when she did take notice, that too was interpreted as due contribution to the game.

Fear and anger gripped Henry when he found himself helplessly trussed and gagged, and it took a great effort to refrain from crying—less because of any real pain than out of frustration and outrage—as the barrel passed over him uncomfortably and in his opinion for far too long. Yet there also came a strange feeling of voluptuousness, which grew more pronounced when Lisa in cruel triumph palpated the victim with her foot to count the "broken" bones. Towering over him, she seemed bigger and no longer a child. Her face was barely recognizable; it had become that of a strange and beautiful woman.

Freed at last by their nanny—Lisa having proved more adept at tying than undoing—Henry gave vent to his displeasure; then Lisa was very sweet and contrite, but when she tried to kiss him, he shrank in consternation and made a show of temper to hide the queer new feelings he could neither express nor comprehend.

Later in life, Pinkerton was struck more than once by the beauty of a woman's face viewed from below, even when that face

· *Butterfly* ·

normally held little appeal for him. He became aroused on these occasions and wished for the woman to "continue," though he did not know precisely how. Nor could his desire be told, for however she might proceed, it had to be on her initiative, not his. The longed-for "continuation" never once took place; the woman would kiss him or in some other way deflect rather than give substance to what remained a tantalizing foretaste of desire.

On this point Butterfly fared no better than others. In the early days of their marriage, it often excited him to see her masklike face hovering and swaying over him. For a brief moment, she would seem indeed to embody the erotic mysteries he so eagerly pursued. Light enough for him to lift with aplomb, she would stay on top for long periods, delighting him with her stamina and supple grace. But unaware of his mute, hidden desire, she like the others failed to draw it out, though unlike them, she had the art to make him forget it was ever there.

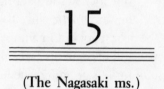

15

(The Nagasaki ms.)

One day I went down to breakfast a little earlier than usual and found Marika alone in her preparations. There was little for her to do in our well-staffed house, and as she had a room adjoining Kate's in a wing I seldom visited, I rarely saw her except in the morning, when she prepared freshly ground coffee on an alcohol burner, and little enough even then, for she was very discreet and—after looking me over so boldly the first day—hardly ever glanced in my direction. This suited me despite my curiosity, for I felt strongly her allure and clearly it would not do to flirt with Kate's maid.

On this morning, however, she smiled prettily when I entered, but left it to me to utter a greeting. I amused myself with the thought that slaves were perhaps not subject to the same rules of politeness as servants. Smiling back, I asked her in halting French where she was from and how long she had been in the country. She answered in English, in a mixed accent whose charm was enhanced by her low, purring voice.

Did she like America?

"Some things I like," she replied in her decided manner. "I like the trees. The leaves are beautiful." I waited, but nothing more came. She started to measure out the coffee beans.

Anything else?

She thought for a moment. "Peanut butter," she said and lapsed back into silence.

And what didn't she like?

"Coffee," came the instant reply. "No taste, no bouquet." She sat down on a chair next to the sideboard with the coffee mill between her thighs. "And men," she continued as she looked across into my eyes. "They are *frustres*, like the trees. They don't know how to . . ." The rest got lost in a noisy burst of energetic cranking, but her eyes, still fixed on my face, glinted suggestively. After a minute or so of furious grinding, she left off and gave her hand a little shake.

"Hard work," I sympathized.

"*Ah oui!*" she agreed, breathing deeply. "You want to grind for me?"

I had seated myself at the table a little distance away and now expected her to pass me the grinder, but she leaned back on the chair with arms dangling and did not move. When I rose and went to her, she looked up at me with laughter in her eyes. "You are nice," she said softly. As I reached down for the grinder, she caught my hand and pressed it to the crank; with both hands over mine, she guided it slowly into motion.

I was bent over her uncomfortably, but there was little I could

· *Butterfly* ·

do to change my position short of crouching down or disengaging my arm. Her face was lifted toward mine; our eyes met and held for what seemed an eternity while the aroma of fresh-ground coffee wafted up from under our awkwardly moving hands. At last the crank turned without further resistance, but our hands continued absently for a few empty turns before slowing to a halt. In that instant our lips touched. When they parted, her eyes were wide with excitement; taking my hand from the handle, she plunged it deep where her legs met.

Somewhere a door opened and jolted me to my senses. It took a moment to withdraw my hand from the grip of her thighs. Approaching footsteps propelled me back into my seat. While I tried to calm my pounding heart and assume a natural expression, Marika proceeded with perfect composure to light the alcohol stove, after casting me a half-amused, half-contemptuous look. I remembered that I had not rung for service; just as I reached for the chord, Kate appeared at the door.

16

Discomposed by the incident with Marika, Pinkerton wandered listlessly from the library and eventually strayed into his bathroom, constructed like most things in the house on a grandiose scale. Without thinking, he locked the door and started to undo his trousers. A sweet, stale feeling of familiarity drew him up short; his gestures and surroundings transported him back to an earlier period when, aroused from wrestling with Lisa, he would shut himself in to relieve the tension in his loins, purposeless as yet but already imperious. Later, this solitary pleasure had been largely relegated to the morning or evening hours; since his return from Japan, he had rarely sought it and then only in bed.

With a feeling of vexation, he left off and decided to draw a bath instead. He was glad his father had had the latest plumbing put in, which permitted bathing at all times, for in Japan he had gotten used to soaking daily in a hot *furo*. The warm water made him feel better, but the image of Marika was not long in reappearing and once more his desire rose up. He gave it a few half-hearted strokes, and when that made it only more exigent, he indulged it in a torpor, pulling the skin back from the head and pushing it over again, off and on and off. Shutting his eyes, he imagined himself back in the breakfast room: once again he is bent over Marika; this time he removes the coffee mill and slides the hem of her skirt up toward her waist, while she, sensually odorous, impatient, fumbles at his crotch; and he, fingers in the dense tuft, exploring, desire brandished, ushered in; her jouncing rasping desire, her moans rising, urging him on. . . And Kate, suddenly . . . Her piercing eyes, suddenly there, bearing down, boring into him, penetrating his gasping loins to the teeming semen rallied to charge. Her beautiful eyes. Watching.

He let his head tilt limply to the side as his lust dispersed in the quiescent water and floated off in languid milky wisps.

At the moment of bursting forth, with the abruptness of pictures changing in a magic lantern, Butterfly had suddenly been there to engulf him, mind and member and all, as she was each time when his loins opened, whether in company or alone: present herself or absent, it was always to her womb that his desire strove and in her flesh that it ebbed.

Sinking back in the warm water as into her arms, he could almost feel them folding him to her breast. Thus comforted, he lay thinking of Butterfly.

· *Butterfly* ·

17

That summer they copulated spectacularly, almost in the manner of a performance, as if to prove how well they could in spite of what each lacked from the other. Pinkerton marveled anew at Butterfly's skill, marveled too at her lack of inhibition. Nothing shocked or repelled her; she did everything with a heedless innocence. Was the lubricity he desired impossible, he wondered, because she was innocent of sinful ideas, or because she was untainted by ideas of sin?

After the first frenzied week their amatory activity had fallen off, and for a time it had taken on a moribund cast; but a revival had come with the warmer weather that reduced everyday clothing to a light cotton *yukata* worn against the skin. The flimsy ankle-length robe revealed all too readily any anatomical modification, and it took only a slight effort to get past the single sash that fastened it; with the coming of summer heat, even the *yukata* was often dispensed with. Yet his eyes, if not his other senses, found her more appealing clothed, more elegant; her body, soft and smooth and lithesome, was pleasurable to the touch, but to one brought up on Grecian ideals, its proportions seemed less than perfect, and the rather short and stocky bowlegs in particular went against the esthetic grain. Her features, on the other hand, he supposed to be beautiful, and they did often appear so; but he could also see them at times as ugly, for her face was above all foreign—implacably, invincibly foreign—a fascinating mask even when cleared of powder and paint.

As the summer wore on, his body became more able to relax, his mind to relinquish its overwrought erotic obsessions. Her face, imprinting itself day after day upon his retina, began to appear as lovely as it had once—was it just a few weeks ago?—

seemed alien. Had love changed his vision? Or was love only the awareness of vision's subtle changes? He took endless pleasure at her sight and delighted in gazing until she, more pleased than embarrassed, sent him on his way; to touch her then seemed a bounty too great to conceive. Everything about her took on a fascination for him—her clothing, her combs, her powder; he delighted in them like a child. In time their love-making lost its acrobatic flavor; its rhythms broadened, its modulations became more subtle. More and more he allowed himself to sink into her softness, to abandon himself to the gentleness of her ministrations. Where he had dipped into her body with the ambitions of an angler casting for fish, he now went in like a diver enamored of the sea and underwater life. And Butterfly, now as always, showed herself to be wonderfully pliant to his newly awakened love; she would receive him and hold him and listen to his passionate murmurs without seeking to understand, and rock softly to his more urgent rhythms, and press him to her when he injected into her the distillate of his love, and cradle his spent body with words of soothing endearment.

Exactly when it happened he no longer knew—it was sometime during the fall, because he remembered groping past folds of kimono—nor could he have said at what moment he noticed. Her eyes were shut tighter than usual, her breathing was more intense; contrary to her usual comportment, she held him off by begging, "Not yet . . . not yet . . ." Surprised, he made an effort to comply, but already he felt the gush and it was more than he could restrain; just then, however, she dived slightly with her body and a deft finger at his perineum stopped the flow. "Don't move, please don't move!" she softly cried as her legs clamped tightly around his hips and held him immobile. Only her buttocks jiggled ever so slightly. All at once she let out a little gasp and tightened her embrace, then gasped again, clutching him desperately to her and heaving; and from her gorge

· *Butterfly* ·

came a guttural sob that mounted with repetition into a high, floating wail: "*Yurushite* . . . Forgive me . . ." Her body shook uncontrollably and suddenly was drenched in sweat, her face was awash with tears. He felt the wetness on his neck and chest as he lay enfolded on top of her, overcome with tenderness and awe; while her venter continued to pulsate from the erupted passion, nipping him with its vigorous throbs and sending thrill after thrill up his spine.

(The Nagasaki ms.)

I made a point of leaving the two girls to their daytime activities, but I saw enough of Kate at meals and after dinner to fall each day a little more under the charm of her intelligence and beauty. One evening they persuaded me to join them in their music making instead of being the passive listener; I had not sung for over a year, but as we went from song to song, my courage rose and we wound up the soiree with Schumann's *Dichterliebe*. I was touched as never before by this cycle of unhappy love, and each song brought me closer to identifying myself and my accompanist with the lover and his beloved. The girls too seemed deeply affected; the last chord of the beautiful reminiscing postlude died into a long silence upon which we were all reluctant to intrude. As it was already late, we quickly said good night. Once Kate had left the room, Lisa took my hand and, twining her fingers in mine as in former days, remarked pensively, almost as much to herself as to me, "You're fine together . . . the two of you suit one another so well."

I would have been the last to disagree. We did suit one another extraordinarily well, to me that was painfully evident. Our interests, our tastes, our education, all fitted together like the teeth on a pair of cogwheels. Had my parents been blind not to see that? What a potential was in the couple we might have formed, I thought as I now took the full measure of what was lost forever. And I, had I not let it slip through my fingers, heedlessly, like so much sand on the beach? I could have wept as for a stillborn child, or one which I myself had caused to abort.

Thus was my recrudescent admiration for Kate dipped in despair like a kite in tar. I longed to speak of it to her, to beg if need be on my knees for forgiveness, for absolution, and indeed—oh, the unparalleled egotism of a masculine heart—for consolation; but she never left a crack through which to slip into the precincts of intimacy or even their purlieus.

Such sentiments did not ease my perplexity with regard to Marika. I was unhappy at having allowed myself to go so far with her, and I had resolved to go no further; on the other hand, Marika had aroused me powerfully, and memories of that morning would not cease to prey on my imagination. Her intriguing relationship with Kate, moreover, redoubled my interest.

Profiting from a series of balmy Indian summer days, the girls and I took to breakfasting outdoors on the terrace. It was so pleasant there that I would remain and spend the morning working in a shaded corner. The first two mornings passed without incident. On the third, having dozed in a chaise longue, I awoke to the sense of someone's eyes upon me. When I looked, I saw Marika sitting on a chair at my feet. Instead of the usual outfit worn by housemaids, she had on a white pleated dress open at the neck and permitting a good guess at the contours underneath; her feet were bare. She had the watery look of an Ondine fresh from the waves, and without knowing why, I blushed. Unthinkingly, I asked what she was doing there.

"I look," she replied archly without softening her impudent

· *Butterfly* ·

regard; she did not smile, but a hint of derision played about the corners of her mouth. "I look at the pretty *monsieur* sleep, and I think it is nice to sleep with him. But he don't come to me. I wait a week and he don't come. So what do I do, eh?" Her voice was low and husky and melodious. "Well, I think to myself, and I put my hand under the skirt, like this." So saying, she tucked up the dress and her right hand disappeared under its folds; I could see it moving up her thighs. She continued in a lilting, mesmerizing monologue. "And I touch the pussy and I think, it is a nice pussy. I think it is even nicer if the pretty *monsieur* kiss it with his pretty mouth. Then I think I feel his mouth there under my skirt. Yes, it is there, it is looking for pussy. I feel the lips, soft red lips, and the tongue—oh, it is moving! Good, he is kissing pussy, not like American—a nice deep French kiss with the tongue inside, yes. Big tongue to little tongue, lip to lip. *Poétique*, no? So now I feel with my fingers and I feel it is wet, very, very wet." She stopped and suddenly winked at me with a saucy smile. No doubt my amazement was writ large over my face, for she broke out laughing; under the dress her hand continued to move.

Her laughter provoked a flush of anger in me. "Stop it, Marika!" I admonished sternly in what I intended to be an authoritative tone of voice. "That's enough of this nonsense! Your little show isn't as amusing as you think." But my throat was tight and a tremor ruined the effect.

"No?" Marika put on a look of mock surprise. With that extraordinary way she had of focusing her eyes like a searchlight, she fixed them on the bulge in my trousers. "Ask your little brother—I think he is very amused."

At that very moment, as if to signal its assent, the little beast gave a visible throb which to my dismay I was unable to suppress. Marika squealed with delight. I could not deny what was so palpable, but still I would not enter into her game. "Please, Marika," I demurred, this time almost pleadingly. "You're very

· 45 ·

attractive, I admit that, you're irresistible even, but you must understand that I cannot be your lover. Not because I don't want you, but because your mistress—"

She rose without listening and in two strides was before me; her hand came up unhurriedly to my face. She let it hover, the bedewed and glistening fingers almost touching my lips. The penetrating odor of her womanhood rushed to my head like a shot of pure alcohol, tumbling in an instant the last bastion of restraint. My lips parted to kiss her proffered fingers, then, maddened by the potent aroma, closed over them with abandon. As I sucked them, she drew my head to her and cradled it invitingly between her thighs; presently she took her hand from my mouth and rubbed it caressingly against my face, first the back side, then the palm, so that her pungency was smeared all over my cheeks.

19

(Fragment of a letter from Kate(?) to Cécile X., translated from the French by the editor. The beginning is given here, the end in Chapter 56; a middle section is missing. The pages were among Pinkerton's papers; from their crumpled condition, they would seem to be part of a draft that had been discarded and later recovered. Dated May 6, 1910, they were written well over a decade after the events related in the first part of the Nagasaki ms.)

My dear Cécile,

You are right about my putting you off with false promises of a written explanation—I wasn't at all sure a young person should acquire such knowledge, nor was I persuaded that a godmother should teach it; I suspect that your mother, liberal as she is, would not approve. But your letter was so eloquent in its pleas and so libertine in its arguments that I am beginning to wonder whether I *can* teach you anything! In all events, know that I am succumbing to its charm rather than following my judgment.

Your apparent competence makes it superfluous for me to say anything about the art of attracting a man; the subject at hand is, as you say, how to "keep him under your rump." In either case it is a matter of playing on his mind through his senses; the emphasis alone is different. In the former you are inciting him to dream, so the means is more visual and vocal, whereas in the latter you are imposing your body upon his dreams, hence the engagement of the more material faculties.

The first rule in domination is this: lead him by the nose. Remember that of the five senses, the olfactory is the most powerful. An odor is part of something external that enters your body and becomes a part of you; this is why the effect is both immediate and haunting, more powerful than that produced through the other senses and at the same time longer lasting. It inebriates where other agents merely delect.

Although certain odors are inherently pleasant or noxious, more often our response is determined not by the odor's purely sensuous appeal but rather by the meaning we give it. A dog will sniff casually at its droppings, but in us strong odors arouse disgust or ecstasy, depending upon the associations we make. Thus an odor essentially reinforces what attraction or repulsion—active or latent—is already there. What is a good or bad odor? One that comes from something which you would or would not willingly make a part of yourself.

Therefore first make sure that he is attracted; men almost always are to a young girl, whether or not they know it, especially if she's as pretty as you, but it still pays to be attentive. Once the ring has pierced his nose, a few little tugs will bring his face down to where you wish it.

I'll list the parts where odors are concentrated to give you a quick overview:

gentle:	*hair*	
	skin	
strong:	*armpit*	*sweat*
	feet	
powerful:	*sex*	*effusions*
		secretions
		blood
		urine
	anus	*concentrate of oils, etc.*
		feces

Each of these can and should be used, except possibly the last, which out of hygienic considerations and personal preference I avoid manipulating, even though it can be used to strong effect. I am told that a certain lady at the ancient Japanese court once sent a faithfully confectioned simulacrum of her excreta to an admirer. But I'll talk more about tactile and visual aspects later. In any case, you see that you are limited only by your own imagination.

What is of paramount importance is that you be absolutely certain yourself that *all* your odors have the power to excite and to subjugate. Do not doubt! That is the whole secret. The more you take it as a matter of course, the better. The worst is to be self-conscious or embarrassed or ironic with regard to what you do: you won't be able to hide it. So first convince yourself. Unless you can, don't

· *Butterfly* ·

start anything; once you start, don't hesitate. Never forget that to him you smell divine—on every occasion, at all times—and never let him forget it. If you have not washed, have him clean you like a cat; if you have been in your boots all day, make him kiss your feet before washing them. Henri IV would not let his mistresses wash before his visits; but he was a king and dared to say what he liked. The ordinary man does not, he has to be coerced into enjoying what he dares not admit. Within his strutting breast beats the heart of a slave that wants to abdicate responsibility for the desires he is ashamed to own. Whence his need for whores and for casting stones at them.

Intuition and discretion are of course essential, here as anywhere else. You have to judge your man. In some cases he is all too eager to plunge. In others you have to lead him gently step-by-step or he will rebel; his sense of incongruity will rouse him to derision, he will hide behind an ironic detachment, and your game will be lost. Laugh at him all you like, but never let him laugh at you—never even imagine it possible.

Always stay a step ahead of him. If he kisses your hands, make him kiss your feet; if he sniffs in front, offer him the back. You must direct his attention to that which he has not yet dared to approach, to push his nose in where he is hesitant; by doing so, *you* create the erotic context, *you* give erotic meaning to your odors, and their power becomes yours to wield (whereas if he supplies the erotic context, he controls it as well). And once this erotically charged odor goes to his head—in most cases immediately—he is lost, he will never rise from beneath your . . .

20

Even after a year with Butterfly, Pinkerton could still not be quite certain if the fragrance that enveloped her person and permeated her clothing was entirely natural or came in part from a perfume she used. When he asked, she would only smile. Ethereal rather than exciting—her body was very discreet with odors, he had early noticed—the distinctive and subtle aroma reminded him a little of sandalwood or fine incense. On winter evenings when they lay crushed under a mountain of heavy covers, Butterfly would tell him stories from old Japanese romances, and in one there had been a prince who exuded an exquisite perfume. "Just like you!" Pinkerton had exclaimed in spontaneous delight and, snuggling close, had covered her with kisses. Then he had stopped listening, his mind had wandered; with his face pressing into her shoulder, he had tried to imagine what a butterfly would smell like to a sensitive enough nose—exactly like his wife, no doubt! This conceit had made him bubble over with amusement and an absurd sense of pride. Ordinarily, however, he took her fragrance for granted, like so many other things. It was only when he left her that he began to miss it. In a moment of loneliness it occurred to him that he could have taken along a *yukata* or some other piece of clothing impregnated with her scent. Had he known how long he would be away, he might have asked her to send one; more than once he wished he had, but each time it seemed too late to write and ask.

21

Marika was to come to my room that night. Scarcely able to contain my desire, I had pressed her to accompany me immediately, but she said she had to attend Kate, who would be returning shortly from riding with Lisa. I could not argue against that and waited out the rest of the day in a state of extreme agitation.

Once alone, I was no longer so sure I wanted her to come, and this uncertainty added to my unrest; at moments I positively wished that she would not, for it would be awful beyond conceiving if Kate were to find out. Furthermore, I sensed that my lust for Marika was somehow tearing me from Butterfly. It was only three weeks until my departure: soon I would be back with her, my wife, far away from all that was troubling me: Kate, Marika, family, business. More and more I was realizing that my stay in Japan would be a long one. What I should do there was a moot question, but the last five months had persuaded me that Butterfly and I could not live together in America. And if ever there had been doubts about our marriage, they were gone. My whole being, I felt, was joined to hers in a lasting and unfathomable way, and my flesh cleaved to her with a tenacity that I noticed above all when I visited other women, for without exception I found myself loving Butterfly through their bodies, so that after a few times I ceased going to them. As for Kate, my feelings were strong and complex, but they made no inroads into my life with Butterfly. My love for Kate—and I could not deny loving her still—was founded upon my appreciation of a potential, whereas with Butterfly the potential, lesser perhaps in scope, had already become reality, a reality to which I now belonged.

Never had these thoughts been so clear in my head; yet the wayward excitement remained. Marika's wanton perfume stuck to my skin; again and again, like a milkmaid, like a snake charmer, it drew out my desire and made it rear. Drunk as I was on her sensuality, I at first did not want to wash it away and for one brief instant had even considered skipping lunch so as not to have to. In the end I reluctantly yielded to reason, yet my careful ablutions did not expulse her from my nose, which continued to be so boldly haunted that I looked about fearfully lest someone else should notice the smell. For all that I craved Marika's favors, however, I was certain that in the end it would be no different with her as with the others. This conviction made me feel detached and rather aloof even as I was consumed with desire.

But my detachment deserted me as the evening advanced. By eleven I had bathed and made myself ready; I tried to read, for I did not expect her quite so early. At midnight I gave up any pretense of being occupied: she should be there, she would be any minute, and I was waiting. On the stroke of one I opened the door and left it ajar so that she could be guided by the light. Then it was two, and three, and four, and still she did not come. I stretched out on the bed, but I could not sleep. The slightest sound made me want to jump up, but each time I resisted and lay as if asleep so that I could nonchalantly ask the time when she woke me and then exclaim, "Goodness, I've been sleeping for hours!" Minutes would go by and at last I would rise to confirm what was only too clear: that the noise had been something else, and that she had not come.

I dozed off with the intention of going down early for breakfast to demand an explanation. When the alarm rang at seven, however, I did not feel up to a confrontation and procrastinated until it was too late to catch Marika alone; then there seemed to be little point in going down at all. It was very late when I finally rose; I could think of nothing better than to lounge around on the terrace in the hope—vain, I need hardly add—that Marika might appear. After dinner I retired immediately on the pretense of a headache. Again I secretly hoped—since Kate seldom went up before ten or ten-thirty—for a visit from Marika, although this was unrealistic, for how should she know that I had gone to my room? At midnight I found myself once again holding an involuntary vigil.

The following morning, bursting with recriminations, I made sure that I was the first in the breakfast room. I had my breakfast brought to me; despite a conscious effort to eat slowly, I was finished in no time. I wished I had taken along something to read. At last footsteps sounded. I drew a deep breath and made myself ready. To my disappointment, it was Kate who entered. When Marika came a few minutes later, she as usual took no notice of my existence. After failing several times to catch her eye, I seethed in bitter silence. But as I was stepping out after the girls, Marika motioned for me to return.

Why was I not at breakfast yesterday? She had come down early to wait for me. The night before Kate had been indisposed and had kept her; last night, too. Perhaps this evening she would be able to slip away. But she had to be very careful, because Kate would sometimes ring for her in sleepless moments. "She will kill me if she know I go out to fuck you," she whispered in melodramatic earnest.

She had put her hand on my breast and rubbed it gently up and down while we talked, so that I could not refrain from taking her in my arms and kissing her. She returned my kiss with ardor but soon pulled away. Her mistress would be waiting, she had to go. Her eyes, as I looked into them, glowed with promises, while her hand closed firmly where my passion was most assertive. "Keep it for me," she breathed, her eyes still locked with mine.

"Don't let it out." As if to seal the injunction with a gage, she drew my face forcefully to hers; a jet of liquid as from a spring spurted into my mouth. She turned quickly and was out the door by the time I had swallowed the poison liquor that would make my blood furiously itch.

22

Neither of them could sleep. They had lain together for a good part of the afternoon, then they had bathed, dined, and loved inexhaustibly into the night. Spent and famished, they had gotten up for tea and *norimaki*; Butterfly had proposed *sake* and brochettes, but Pinkerton had developed a taste for rice rolled in seaweed—lately he had veered sharply in his tastes—and wanted to have it once more before departing. It was close to five, Sachiko would be coming in with their breakfast in an hour, for Pinkerton was to be at the ship by seven-thirty. The time left to them seemed very precious, yet they did not know what to do with it—everything had been said, everything had been done twice over. Restored by the tea and food, they lay in a pleasant torpor, their lips and organs hurting from the long embraces.

Outside the rain had subsided; somewhere water was dripping in heavy, languid drops. "It has stopped raining," Pinkerton said. As if that were a signal to do something, he began idly to untie Butterfly's sash. She let out a little gasp when his cheek touched her skin, for he had grown a light stubble since the evening before. Raising his head, he quickly kissed the profaned spot. "Should I go and shave?" She giggled and pulled his head down again to her. "No, I like it. I like to feel you . . . how do you say, *chiku chiku suru.*"

"Scratch?"

"Yes, I like to feel you scratch me." She pressed his cheek to her skin and rubbed it gently against herself. "I like to feel you."

Little by little he moved down along her body's rolling slopes until he reached the small crater on the rounded hillock rising where there had been none before; he thought with wonder of the creature underneath joined to her just as she had once been joined to someone now lying under a mound of earth. Looking from above at the smooth surface, he could not understand how he could have penetrated it to deposit his drop of life; yet it was in there, it was growing, it had even begun to move.

"Is it a boy or a girl?" he asked as if she knew or could choose.

"Do you want boy or girl?" They had discussed it more than once before, but the topic seemed inexhaustible. Answers varied according to their mood.

"A girl, like you."

"Sure?"

"Sure!"

"This time no more change?"

"No, no more changes."

"It will be a girl."

Her earnestness amused him, yet he himself half believed that she really had the power to determine the embryo's sex. Sliding down the curve of her belly, he rubbed his cheek against the small hairs bristly from the fluids that had soaked them and dried. With gentle fingers he pried apart the lips; pursing his own, he sent a breeze over the moist tissues. A sigh of pleasure echoed it; her hips swiveled in his direction, and her right leg lifted and encircled his neck so that their lips could join. He held her open with his two hands and peered into her secret depths even though there was not light to see. From within came an odor of semen that slightly repelled him, but he approached his mouth nonetheless and pressed it softly into the wetness of her flesh. The kiss was long and quiet and tender; he licked her once, affectionately. Drawing away but still keeping her folds parted with his hands, he lovingly blew upon them with light, long breaths.

"Will your girl miss me very much?"

"Yes, very much."

"And what will she do without her boy?"

"She will miss him. Perhaps she will cry a little, but she will wait."

"It'll be hard for her."

"Yes, my girl is very spoilt. But she is good girl, she will learn to be patient." Her thighs tightened about his neck, her hands reached down and again drew him toward her. "She is brave, but she will suffer, so you must . . . comfort her a little now. After, she can play again with her boy, yes?"

Later Butterfly said to him, "Be gentle with your boy . . . he will be lonesome. Let him play with girls. My girl has your baby to keep her company, but your boy will be alone. I and my girl, we like him to be happy."

It was light by then and he could see her face; like her voice, it was quiet and touchingly serious. He felt his eyes misting and did not know what to say.

"Promise me?"

Pinkerton almost could not find his voice. "Yes," he said chokingly. "I promise."

23

(The Nagasaki ms.)

Almost another week passed while Marika kept me on tenterhooks. During this time I was constantly expecting her to turn up, but every day there was some reason why she could not. I did see more of her after one of the maids that served at table took ill and, upon Kate's insistence, Marika was put in her place. This was a double-edged blessing, for while it was gratifying just to look upon the object of my desire, it also heightened my frustration, the more so as Marika used every opportunity to stoke my passion with incendiary words and deeds. After four or five days I was so ravaged that I could endure no more. A scheduled trip to New York which I had looked forward to with mixed feelings now came as a welcome relief.

24

With the lightness of a dancer, Marika swept in and was standing in front of him before he had quite had time to look. "I have something for you," she said softly. Behind her Pinkerton could hear footsteps and voices approaching, but they did not seem to bother Marika. Trussing up her skirt, she put her right hand under it and crouched down a little; when she straightened up, there was a large prune glistening between her thumb and middle finger. She held it gracefully to his face like a magician displaying a conjured object and then slipped it into his mouth. "I put it in for you when I go to sleep," she whispered. Over her shoulder Pinkerton saw Lisa and Kate appear in the doorway. He could only hope that he was not quite as scarlet as he felt himself to be; fortunately his breakfast had already been served, otherwise it would have seemed odd indeed for him to greet them with a full mouth.

This was the first of several love offerings impregnated with her juices. Each time his heart skipped a beat as if heavenly snow had dropped upon it. Beside dried fruits, he once got honey that she spread messily with her fingers on a piece of toast, and another time half of a hard roll.

Now that Marika served at meals, she seldom let one go by

without some form of provocation. They dined at a table long enough to accommodate eighteen people; when there were no other guests, Mrs. Pinkerton and her son took the ends, while Kate and Lisa sat facing one another in the middle. The distances between them were not conducive to conversation, but Mrs. Pinkerton insisted on keeping up the family tradition; in any event, she did not approve of excessive talking during meals. This arrangement, however, made it possible for Marika to carry out the most outrageous acts under the very eyes of the three women. Unusual pieces of food appeared on Pinkerton's plate, surreptitious caresses sought out their mark, and lewd phrases were whispered, all under their noses and without their noticing. Marika went about it with a composure and brazenness that took away Pinkerton's breath. His digestion suffered, for he was always tense from being aroused, and half the time he sat numb with fear lest the others should witness Marika's latest caprice. Yet with the fear came voluptuous feelings such as he had dreamt of but not known. For nothing—not fornication in the pews, nor masturbation in the confessional—could compare with sitting at table with his mouth full of the serving girl's secretions.

25

(The Nagasaki ms.)

When I announced that I would be going down to New York, Kate asked when I was leaving and then suggested a little celebration the following evening, since she would no longer be present on my return: she had rented a house at the seaside and would be moving there in the next few days. I was quite taken aback and could not hide it; in my dismay I protested rather too vehemently, while Lisa, who evidently knew more about Kate's

· *Butterfly* ·

plans, merely expressed her regret. "Kate will come again to see us once she's settled, Henry," admonished my mother to cut short my entreaties. "Won't you, my dear?" Kate looked at me playfully and remarked that she did not know her presence meant so much to me.

A private talk with Kate had been increasingly on my mind. Even though my wish had so far been frustrated, I had assumed that before my departure for Japan I would be granted an occasion to see her alone if I asked. Now, however, it was my unconsummated passion for Marika that seemed more pressing. Not that Marika meant more to me; on the contrary, I had become painfully aware of how strong my feelings were for Kate, and there were times when I came close to imagining that my desire for Marika was in some strange way a deflection of my love for Kate. Still, it was for Marika that I burnt.

The news of their impending departure increased tenfold my desire, and my disappointment was proportionally worse when Marika again kept me waiting that night. The thought that my passion might never be satisfied drove me wild. Should I postpone my trip to gain a few days? It might look odd, and it would be inconvenient; but anything was preferable to being cheated out of the one thing that could release me from my agony.

To my relief, the weather was lovely the following morning, and Kate and Lisa went riding after breakfast as I had hoped. The moment they left, I rushed to Marika's room. I entered without knocking and found her sorting laundry. If she was surprised, she did not show it. *"Tiens, Monsieur Henri,"* she half greeted as one might the milkman. Her tone of voice irritated me, and I reproached her bitterly for not warning me of her imminent departure and for not making better use of the little time we had.

"You did not know?" she asked as innocently as you please.

"No, I did not!" I almost shouted for vexation. "Besides, I'm going to New York tomorrow and won't be back until the end of next week. By then you'll be God knows where!"

Marika took my face between her hands and showered me with kisses and consolations. She was sorry she did not come to me last night. The reason was that her monthly indisposition had started, and it was bad luck to let a man enter when one was polluted. If she had known I was leaving, she would have come anyway, just to be with me. In any case, I had no cause to get so excited; I could come visit her at their new house, she would write to me and let me know when. She even intimated that she would enjoy more liberty then, since her room would not be next to Kate's as it was in our house; there I could stay all night and all day should I so desire.

While she calmed me, she drew me to the bed where our bodies could more freely mingle. Gradually our words took on a different coloring, our hands became bolder, our lips more avid. When at last I removed her corset and looked upon the perfection of her breasts and inhaled the strong musky scent of her nudity and rubbed my face against the unctuous smoothness of her skin, the gnarled frustration melted in me and ten days of pent-up desire broke forth in an avalanche that robbed me of my breath. Pressing myself to that naked flesh toward which all the atoms of my body had so long and so vainly been striving, I felt faint from ravishment.

But I was not allowed into the sanctuary. Time and again she would pull away from my insistent yearning, or else push it aside with the very hand whose caresses spurred it on. Driven beyond endurance, I entreated, I begged. "Next time," she murmured. "Can you not wait?" But why should she mind her condition when I did not, I protested. She shook the head that was buried in my neck. No, she couldn't. I moaned in despair. She raised her head and looked piercingly into my eyes. "Shall I, with my mouth?" It was not what I wanted, but my desire had become so

· *Butterfly* ·

painful that I nodded in resignation. At that moment a shadow of disillusionment tinged with shame passed over me, and my body subsided into a taut passivity.

The vigor of her lips made me gasp; over and over, they brought me to the edge only to hold me back, each time closer still, each time stretching my senses to yet a higher pitch. Her hands, strong and relentless, tore into me; two deft fingers set afire my bowels and made them writhe. My body became an instrument that her virtuosity drove into spasms of wild, unfamiliar pleasure. I lost all control, all sense of where my physical existence ended and began; I heard myself heaving and crying out in strange animal cries; and then it was as if my insides were gushing out in a sea of tears and sweat and effusions.

I jackknifed to reach Marika, but she slipped from my embrace and darted into the adjoining bathroom. I heard her spit out the contents of her mouth in one great glob; I heard her rinsing, spewing, washing. A heavy stupor weighed down my limbs, an indistinct sense of lassitude and futility. For the first time Butterfly had not been there to receive me; the living presence that I had once carried within me was gone. I had soared to a sensual intensity I had not known to be possible, and there had been nothing to catch me when I dropped. I felt alone and lost in an impenetrable emptiness. Although it was late and I knew that I must hasten away, I remained indifferent and inert.

Marika, who had handed me a towel, eyed me with impatience and proceeded to dress. "They say a man is sad when you spit out his *foutre*," she remarked with a touch of irony. "He is *rejeté*, he think. Is this true, *Monsieur Henri*? Do you feel *rejeté*?" I forced a smile and a denial, but her taunt had punctured something in me and now the sadness spilled out, spreading and suffusing. For a long time afterward, gall flowed in my veins.

In retaliation I commented on her remarkable expertise and asked where she had learnt her skills. "I do it, how do you say, pump?—*pomper le dard*—when I was ten year old," she replied unruffled. "I should know how, no? But I pump you too much, I think. You will maybe not have enough when I want it." She had finished dressing and looked at me with a malicious smile. "Here is something to help you recover," she said as she picked up a pair of small drawers from the soiled laundry and held them out to me; as I hesitantly reached for them, she stuck them at my nose. A whiff made me color with unavowable pleasure and shame. Casting down my eyes, I let her keep the garment pressed to my face; through the sheer fabric I kissed her hand. *"Petit cochon,"* she purred, her voice a Circean caress.

As I prepared to tuck the unpresentable object into my pocket, she suddenly exclaimed, "Oh, it is one of hers!" Embarrassed by the awkward error, I wavered; her eyes, drinking in my predicament, danced with I know not what deviltry. "No matter," she quipped. *"Monsieur* will find that the *effet* is the same . . . or maybe even better." With that, she laughed pertly and pushed me toward the door.

26

Even the bathwater, run very hot in the Japanese manner, stung more than usual; it made Pinkerton draw back in surprised irritation, as if bitten by a normally affectionate pet. He had fled to the bath vaguely hoping to find something of Butterfly; but today the water seemed to be charged with a mute resentment. Her name pronounced in invocation brought no answer into his heart. For the second time that morning, he felt rejected by Butterfly.

With his eyes closed, Pinkerton recalled the miniscule bathroom in Nagasaki, half of which was taken up by the sunken waist-deep *furo* with its ledge for sitting in the water. When they took their bath in the late afternoon, mellow sunlight would filter in through the little bamboo grove and surround them with spots of gold. The mottled pattern changed from day to day as the seasons turned in a loose, modest rhythm; immersed together, he and Butterfly seemed to float along with that ineluctable cosmic progression. The temperature of the water discouraged touching, though once in a while they would snuggle together or nestle in a still, tenoned embrace; most often they were joined only by the water, but in an intimacy unique and seldom surpassed. In the heat, the boundaries of their bodies seemed to dissolve, and a vital current of energy would flow around them and through them, untrammeled by bodily confines. More than once, Pinkerton felt himself merged with the water, and his identity melted and diffused through everything that surrounded him: Butterfly, the water, the begonias and bamboo, the sunlight and sky—all were as one whole, inviolate, intact, immutable. In such moments he was not conscious of anything in particular, but afterward when he thought back on them, he would be overtaken by a religious fervor that he had known as a child and not since, for after his adolescent revolt against the Church he had eschewed anything that smacked of piety. There were no words to describe his feelings, so he did not attempt to tell them; he would have liked to, though more out of exuberance than any real need, for he obscurely felt that Butterfly, always present on such occasions, must share his experience in some way he would have been hard put to specify.

The quality of sunlight, the hues of bamboo, the smell of steamy water and wet wood, the peace, the communion—all this Pinkerton now summoned up with great vividness, yet it all seemed far away; it had taken on the distant quality of childhood memories, of things that despite indelible traces are irretrievably of the past.

27

During luncheon, I could hardly look at Kate, though my eyes were more than ever drawn to her. Face to face with her whom I had after a fashion violated, I had a difficult time maintaining my composure, the more so as my soul was entranced by a strange and turbid voluptuousness.

Immediately upon regaining my room, I had locked the undergarment in a cabinet. I handled it gingerly, like a stolen article that the illicit possessor trembles to unveil. The sight of it filled me with consternation, almost with awe, for the memory of its odor and of its texture against my mouth made me thrill with an emotion very different from what I had felt when I had imagined it Marika's, and this prurience filled me with shame and dismay. I had, even if unwittingly, stolen something whose very essence lay in its being given, for intimacy melts in the face of force or stealth like boiled snow.

What would that noble lovely woman, whom I had once courted so ardently and yet so chastely, whose lips I had kissed as reverently as a chalice and whose hand I could never touch without agitation, what would she think if she could have seen her irreproachable if faithless lover but two hours ago? In all the months when I had enjoyed a clear claim to her love, my mind had never erred so near its portals as my nose that morning. But that one whiff had been enough to arouse the animal desires that I had long kept down; unleashed, they now rushed in a pack for that forbidden spot, so that a flood of images assailed me even as I contemplated the beautiful, pure features of her face—lurid, lewd images of other features hidden under her skirt. My

· *Butterfly* ·

obsession was such that, had I been able, I should no doubt have transformed myself into a dog and crawled on all fours to bury my nose in her lap.

Mercifully, Marika was not there to add to my confusion, for the maidservant she'd replaced had resumed her functions the day before. Even so, my balance was precarious and several times I felt myself skidding out of control. For the first time, I experienced a drunkenness that came from within and learnt how it felt to be "unhinged." As we got up from table, I was relieved as well as genuinely surprised that my inner turmoil had gone unnoticed. But my heart nearly stopped when Lisa took me aside on the way out and asked whether anything had changed in the way I looked at things.

"I mean," she elucidated, no doubt misinterpreting my pallor, "I could ask Kate to stay longer—if you want me to."

"Why should she?" I asked a little sharply, terrified as I was by the thought that Lisa might somehow have perceived the emotions that had been so close to overwhelming. "She's not interested in me."

"But that's not true!" Lisa protested. "I know, because I've been sounding her out. Of course, in her position she can't leave herself open to ridicule, but if you're willing to take a step toward her, a really sincere step, I know she won't refuse to listen."

At that moment, the prospect of being reunited with Kate poured into my feverish mind like a cataract of all that was most desirable on earth, and I was dazed by the realization that it might indeed still be possible. But it was the flitting, eruptive images of the flesh that made the temptation so immediate and incisive, that made my head spin in contemplation of the insuperable emotional distance to her secret entrances; it was the thought of putting my head between her thighs that took away my reason and my breath.

Partly to steady myself, I took a sardonic tone. "You mean if I go and tell her that I'm ready to repudiate my wife if she'd marry me instead?"

Lisa gave me a long look. "It's your life, Hen," she said quietly. "All I can tell you is that, as of now, you still stand a chance, and if you want me to speak to her for you, I shall. It's up to you to decide what you want."

Temptation made me feel faint, and I must have looked distraught, for Lisa put a consoling hand on my cheek; she seemed about to say something but in the end only shook her head while the shadow of a smile crossed her face.

I went up to my room in a tizzy and flung myself on the bed, literally swept off my feet by the new erumpent desires I instinctively knew to be more dangerous than the lust for Marika. However it might have been in choosing between Butterfly and Kate, there was no question but that I had loved Kate, and perhaps with the greater passion. That passion, never dead, had lain inert like a powerful acid that needed to be brought in contact with the flesh to manifest its terrible potency.

But if I felt its power, I had not yet yielded to it. I thought of Butterfly, of the child she was carrying, of our life in Japan, so peaceful and content. Could a man ask for more? My passion for Kate was a *furor*, divine or demonic I knew not which, a veritable malady that would surely consume me if I let it; whereas Butterfly's cool and gentle hand would just as surely succor and restore, if I could only reach it. To depart instantly, to return to Butterfly and not see Kate again—that was the most sensible, the only viable, solution. Happily, I was scheduled to leave for New York the next morning, so it was only a matter of getting through the evening without succumbing. That did not seem so impossibly Herculean a task. By the time I returned, both Kate and Marika would be gone. And a week after that, I myself would be on my way to Japan. Such were the reassuring thoughts with

· *Butterfly* ·

which I reasoned myself into a calmer state; in the end I was smiling at my own exaggerations, though deep down I felt, darkly, like a man in a lion's den imagining how he would wake up safe in bed.

Without any particular intention, perhaps without thinking at all, I went to the locked cabinet and took out the baneful garment. Bringing it into the clear daylight, I proceeded to examine it with a cold eye. The satin was soft and smooth, and it was finely cut and sewn, almost immodestly, as if destined for a man's eye. A slight yellowing and a small stain marked where the material had lain most intimately; I looked at it unmoved, if anything with a certain distaste, and I might have followed a modest impulse to turn away were it not for remembering the emotion I had felt when Marika presented it to me as her own. Would I not at that very instant be throwing myself on it if I thought it still to be Marika's. But what if Marika had been mistaken in her identification? Or mendacious? Or—and here my breath caught—what if Kate had tendered it to me with her own hands; how would I feel about it then? The idea made my heart contract. If she had, if she would! Fully conscious of being ridiculous, I slowly raised the garment and breathed in once more, deeply, deliberately, the impregnations of the woman I loved and could not possess. A feeling, inexpressibly sweet and acrid like the odor that captivated my senses, rose in me until, uncontainably, it seeped forth from my eyes; I kept the garment pressed tightly to my face as tears, mingling with her emanations, penetrated through the fabric and moistened my fingers.

28

On his return from New York, Pinkerton found a thick official envelope from the U.S. consulate at Nagasaki. Sharpless, the vice-consul whom Pinkerton had charged to take care of financial and other practical matters in his absence, reported that all was well and that he had continued faithfully to execute his instructions; he awaited any others Pinkerton might have, and his return if he had none. A letter from Butterfly was enclosed; it was written on beautiful Japanese paper and lightly perfumed. In her touchingly childish and yet not unpleasing hand, Butterfly announced the birth of their daughter. The girl had been named Elizabeth, as he wished, after his sister; for her Japanese name, Butterfly had chosen Etsuko, a common girl's name meaning "happy child" or "child (daughter) of happiness," because she had been conceived in such happiness. She had been born in the hour of the dragon; her horoscope indicated musical gifts and a life abroad.

Embedded among the sundry details and sentiments were two little poems of the sort Butterfly, following an ancient literary tradition, composed to adorn her letters. These she wrote in Japanese with a brush. In her translation, the first one read:

> *Fire from January to October, soughing autumn winds;*
> *I watch for the woodcutter returning from the hills.*

And the other:

> *Happiness in my garden, the fragrance of chrysanthemums;*
> *Yet would I join the boys and girls at play.*

Pinkerton was not untouched by these delicate expressions of her longing, but they did not brighten his day as their predecessors

· *Butterfly* ·

had. Instead, they oppressed him; rather than bringing him closer to her, they only made him feel more acutely the tremendous distance that now seemed to lie between them. He tried to steer his desire back to her, tried to rouse himself with images of her beauty, with memories of their joys, but to no avail; it was as if the electric current had been cut: however much he might connect and reconnect the wires, he would not be galvanized. Peevishly he laid aside her letter and did not read it again. Yet he persisted in the belief that once he got back to Japan, all would be as before.

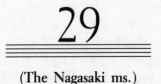

29

(The Nagasaki ms.)

Was it because it was our last evening together that Kate seemed twice as enchanting? Never had I seen her so goddess-like in beauty, so sovereign in intelligence, so endearing in manner; she enthralled me and at the same time put me at ease despite my inner tumult. I became more enamored with each passing hour. Perhaps the champagne we drank had gone to my head; more likely it was Kate herself. I could have thrown myself at her feet then and there, in front of my mother and Lisa, to implore her forgiveness and her hand. This impulse was so contrary to my will that I did not give it rein; my eyes, however, could not be deterred from their unabashed adoration.

It was midnight when we separated. My mother had retired earlier, and Lisa left us in the hallway to say our good-byes. Seizing the hand Kate offered in parting, I glued my lips to it; to my relief, she did not withdraw but let me keep it. My heart was full to overflowing, but my tongue was mute. What indeed could I say, if it was not to blurt out all as I longed to and yet could not? I covered her hand with burning kisses as if to impress upon it the passion I could not declare. All at once, I thought of Marika kneeling in her bizarre devotion, and through the length of me passed a yearning, endlessly long and sharp like a thread of cold blue steel. Dizzy from a temptation I scarce dared contemplate, I felt my heart fall like a stone dropped into an abyss.

"My poor Henry," Kate said softly. For the first time since we had seen each other again, a hint of emotion appeared in her eyes: sympathy perhaps, possibly love, and most certainly, pity. Her hand, disengaging from mine, touched my neck; she approached, and I felt the fleeting brush of her lips against my forehead. I bent forward to lay my head upon her shoulder, if only for an instant, but already she had drawn back and was turning to leave. Stifled by anguish, I watched her go. The cry that rose stuck in my throat, for I knew that if she were to come back, I would be forever lost to myself and to Butterfly.

I had persuaded myself that my trip to New York would deliver me from the temptation Kate increasingly presented. I could not have been more deceived. Before leaving I had in a fit of determination consigned Marika's pernicious gift to the fire, but this in no way expelled it from my mind. Soon I regretted my virtuous action; at home the hope of Marika coming had kept me from sleeping with my cheeks upon it as I should have liked, but in my hotel room, freed of that consideration, I longed for it with rage. Needless to say, the woman who had worn it was also constantly on my mind. Often I caught myself wondering how I could visit her in Creighton without being indiscreet. Determined as I was to break away from her, such thoughts made me angry, yet the daydreams continued, and once caught in them, no greater sweetness seemed possible than to gaze again upon her face. For all that I ridiculed it, the thought came to me that I should willingly give my life for another look at her.

Marika, too, was in no way forgotten. The flurry of business appointments, personal calls and sumptuous dinners failed to distract me, nor did the women introduced by a friend in New York do anything to allay my unquenched desire. The night before my departure, I had against all expectation been awakened by Marika slipping into my bed. She had come, she explained, since I was leaving in the morning, just to keep me company; hadn't she said she would? Although my passion remained unconsumated, the caresses we exchanged and the pleasure of holding her fucksome, odorous body in my arms was such that I shed tears of joy and gratitude and perhaps of relief over the fact that she had finally come to me. Before she left, she made me swear to visit her in her new home—as if I could, after half enjoying her, have stayed away.

A note in French came the day after I got home:

Chéri,

It is lovely by the sea, but the water is cold. Come and make me warm. The mistress goes riding every morning at nine. Don't be late. Come soon—my womb cries out for your inundations.

M.

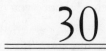

30

The house seemed deserted with Kate gone. Both Pinkerton and Lisa were impatient to talk about their recent guest, but neither wanted to be the one to broach the subject. When Pinkerton finally asked after their friend, Lisa described the house outside Creighton and told of her trip down with Kate to help her get settled. She had spent two nights there. "By the way, I am to tell you that if you'd care to join her for tea, you're cordially invited."

Ignoring Lisa's expectant look, Pinkerton asked, "Why was she in such a hurry to go there?" His voice betrayed his irritation over Kate's departure.

"You mean, why couldn't she have stayed until you left?" Lisa returned a little sharply. "For all the attention you showed her, I can't think why in the world she should. In any case, she had arranged to rent the house on the twentieth."

Pinkerton, at a loss for a rejoinder, made a vague gesture of dissatisfaction and silently looked off into space.

"You will go, I hope?" Lisa pursued.

Deep down he knew he would, but he was loath to admit it. "Maybe," he said with a studied indifference to cover the heartbeat that had quickened when Lisa mentioned the invitation. "If I can find the time."

At this Lisa rebelled. "Henry, what has gotten into you?" she cried. "Who are you trying to fool? I have eyes, I saw how you were looking at her. If you're not in love, then I renounce all hope of anyone ever falling in love with me!" As he did not immediately respond, she went on, her passion rising. "Why do you pretend to me, Hen? We . . . you used to tell me everything. Why do you hide from me now? Anyway, you can't—I know you too well. I know you're troubled, and I understand, believe me, I do, but . . ." She stepped close to him and put her hands upon his chest. "If you'd just follow your true feelings, just listen to what your heart tells you. You think I don't know what you feel like in there, but I do. You love her, Hen, you can't hide it. Your heart is so full of her that I can feel it with my hands. You loved her the minute you saw her, and now you love her even more, much more . . . you love her so much you . . ." Lisa was close to tears. Her emotion, however, made him calmer, and he put his arms around her.

"You're the one I love,' he said, stroking her and kissing her on the forehead.

· *Butterfly* ·

"You're silly," she remonstrated, but she smiled with pleasure and let her head rest against his neck. "Silly Hen, you're just an old silly." Then her voice became serious again. "Go see her, Hen. Go tomorrow."

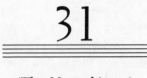

31

(The Nagasaki ms.)

Creighton was an hour and a half's ride away. To economize on time—for I still had more business than I could attend to in the week remaining to me—I decided to see Marika in the morning and Kate in the afternoon, even though the thought did not make me feel entirely comfortable. Setting out at daybreak, I arrived in the little resort town shortly after eight, but to avoid the risk of being seen by Kate, I waited until almost nine-thirty to approach the house. Marika greeted me with a quiet, enigmatic smile. She did not kiss me but, taking me by the hand, led me straight to her room under the roof.

The stairs leading to the attic were narrow and steep. I was guided up by her callipygian sway, obscenely lovely and so close that by leaning forward I could have buried my face in the pert jouncing cheeks. Breathless more from arousal than exertion, I put my arms around her as soon as we reached the top. My hands cupped her breasts as I kissed the nape of her neck, and my desire pushed out at her as if wanting to pierce the layers of material in the way. Half scuffling, half embracing, we got through the door and to the bed.

Her large hazel eyes seemed pensive, almost melancholic, and I was disappointed not to find in them the lubricity that had tuned me once to such a pitch of desire. Her lips, too, lacked fire.

My passion, however, needed no stoking; heedless and feverish, I woed her with ravening kisses. In my hunger for a union so cruelly postponed, I fumbled to raise her skirt. To this she made no opposition, less still to the caresses I lavished on her uncovered parts; but it was not long before she turned her mouth away. "Down there," she said in a clear unemotional voice, and to confirm her wishes gave me a gentle but unequivocal push. I let my head roll down between her breasts and further until the Mount of Venus jostled my cheek. As I groped to clear away the skirt bunched high around her thighs, she suddenly twisted over on her stomach and tucked in her knees. The skirt, swept up toward the waist, exposed her thighs and buttocks; there was no mistaking what I was being offered. The initial shock, as so often, became a deep thrill, and charmed by her sighs of pleasure, I discovered the flavor of love in the tangy, slightly bitter taste on my tongue. I soon began to tire, but she urged on my flagging efforts. Just when I thought I could no longer hold out, she rolled over. Across the length of her body our eyes met. Hers were dark and misty. Unable to wait further, I tore at my trousers.

"Please close the window," she dismayed me by saying in a dispassionate tone. "I am cold." Impatient with the new interruption, I looked up and saw that a dormer was open on the far side of the large room; the attic was in fact a little chilly for us to be undressed. Reluctantly and with considerable awkward-ness—for I did not know whether to discard my trousers or pull them up—I stood up and dashed to the window. By the time I returned to the bed, Marika was lying naked. Her powerful legs opened like a pair of scissors and wound around my waist. In one beautifully fluid motion and without a break in contact, she rolled me over and rose triumphantly astride my loins. With her thick brown mane loose about her splendid shoulders, she resembled an Amazon mounted proudly on a broken stallion. Overwhelmed with admiration, I cried out to her under my breath.

· *Butterfly* ·

Her rhythm was deliberate and languorous as she rode me like an equestrienne at an amble. Rocking upon the enchanted stalk, her rapturous cheeks churned unrelentingly until a great tenderness washed up in me like an ocean tide, and in its depths life's seed rose straining toward the feminine fount. Like the insect that in mating yields up his life, I was at that moment so completely absorbed that I would have abandoned life itself to our union. Surging toward consummation, I cried out her name and my love for her. She, sensing the imminence of my inebriate offering, breathed her assent but quickly amended, "No, not yet! Wait . . . wait." Our eyes locked. She slipped a finger into my mouth, as if to placate my urgency.

Then, as in a dream, the voice came, calling Marika's name. It glided by my ears without at first touching me, for the world and its realities had fallen away like so many dry petals around my generative core. "Oh, my God," Marika sobbed, "oh, my God." For a moment, she continued her gyrations as if hoping the intruder would go away. But the voice came closer, boots clattered up the stairs. We froze, our fingers tightly entwined, swaying in a suspension of ecstasy.

The door flew open. I saw Kate framed in the doorway, and still I did not quite grasp the reality of her presence. She was dressed in a black equestrian outfit, her right hand clasping a riding crop. Marika, erect on top of me, had her back to the door and out of shame or fear did not turn. I too would have looked away, but my eyes were irresistibly drawn to the livid face frozen in its petrifying beauty.

For just a second—it could not have been more, though time seemed to have stopped—I was all but sucked up by those dark burning eyes. And I saw in them, as in a magic crystal, the entire length of my love and the depth of my betrayal. I saw myself falling endlessly amid a dazzling flurry, as if a celestial diamond had shattered to dust. At that same instant, even as I looked into her eyes, my lust broke. I could not doubt that Kate saw. What I felt was beyond remorse, beyond despair. I remember wishing that my life would flow out with my desire, and that she would plunge her riding crop through my heart.

A terrible hardness that I had never seen came into Kate's eyes, but instead of venting her rage on me, she turned on Marika. "Shameless hussy!" she let out in a voice trembling with fury. The next instant she fell upon the girl. Immobilized by the latter's weight, I looked on in helpless consternation as the black-gloved hand rose and descended in one swift, deadly movement; I heard the crack of the whip on Marika's naked back, heard her scream; I saw her face crumple in pain and felt the violent recoil of her body hurtling from my embrace.

Indignation broke through my shame; I completely forgot—to my later astonishment—my own state. "Stop that!" I shouted. Already the whip was rising for a second blow. I lurched and threw myself between the menacing arm and its victim. "What do you think you're doing!" I demanded, outraged.

Kate glared at me. "Get out of my way," she hissed. Oblivious of my nakedness and all else, I moved forward without flinching to take the riding crop away from her. To my shock and disbelief, it darted out swift as a serpent and lashed me directly in the face. A searing pain blinded me; tears came to my eyes, I gritted my teeth to keep from crying.

My shock gave way to an unprecedented fury; never in my life had I encountered such wanton violence. All my love for Kate had flown without a trace; I saw only a dangerous animal ready to mutilate or kill. Without thinking I charged at her.

The riding crop caught me full in the chest, with such force that my body whirled and crashed to the floor. The pain nearly made me faint; I could hardly breathe—a rib had cracked, but I would know that only later. From what seemed a great distance away, I heard Marika screaming something in German and Kate retorting that she should worry not about my skin but her own.

· *Butterfly* ·

Marika whimpered in terror. I was almost too weak to move; my head reeled and I felt nauseous. Summoning all my strength, I propped myself up. "Don't," I gasped. "Don't hit her again . . . please."

"How touching." Kate turned and looked down at me with contempt. "She pleads for him; he pleads for her. A pretty pair of lovebirds!" Something in her voice, in her eyes—I knew not what cold scorn, malice, mockery—sickened me and made my gorge rise. I would have sprung at her again, but in my condition it was hopeless; it I had only suspected in the beginning how adroit she was with the whip and how brutal . . .

But my rage lasted only a few seconds; already it was ebbing. I felt more than anything stunned, and unreal as in a dream. For all my pain and outrage, I could not quite believe that the murderous fury before me was the woman I had loved and imagined I knew. Nor did it seem in character for the agile and spirited Marika to cower so helplessly and without resistance. I recalled her shocked face contorted with pain, and once more felt an overflowing tenderness.

"If you must beat someone," I muttered through clenched teeth, "beat me. Do with me what you like, but leave her alone. It's not her fault."

For a moment Kate looked as if she might take me at my word. But she checked her fury.

"Very well," she said coldly. "Take her and go. All I ask is that you leave my house, both of you." She said this in a matter-of-fact tone and turned to leave without another look at Marika or me.

"*Maîtresse!*" Quick as a flash, Marika darted over and dropped at Kate's feet. The grace and splendor of her moving body took away my breath and made me momentarily forget my pain and my emotion. "Don't make me go away, Mistress. Anything but that!" As always, Marika spoke to Kate in German.

Kate looked down at her with distant curiosity. She spoke softly, half to herself. "You disobey me, you behave in a bestial fashion with that one there, and you still want to stay?" Using the tip of the riding crop to raise Marika's chin, she scrutinized the uplifted face as if for telltale signs; with pokes and taps, she turned the girl's head this way and that. "Do you realize what your punishment will have to be?"

Marika whimpered.

"I hate even to think of it," Kate mused as if undecided, all the while letting the whip promenade lightly over the girl's face and shoulders. "All that lovely skin . . . it would be a pity, wouldn't it?"

Marika continued to whimper softly without answering, but she was trembling now.

"No, it's time you left," Kate concluded. "You should consider yourself fortunate to escape. And with such a devoted paramour, too." Kate negligently threw down the whip and made as if to leave.

"No!" Marika cried, shuffling forward on her knees. "Punish me!" she begged. "Beat me, do with me what you like, kill me even, but don't send me away—anything, but not that!" She looked up at Kate with pleading eyes. Then, blushing, she lowered her head once more and said almost in a whisper, "The slave thanks the Mistress . . . for her gracious correction." She bent forward and picked up the whip; holding it with both hands, she brought it to her lips as if it were some holy relic, then presented it ceremoniously to Kate. When the latter did not take it immediately, she prompted softly, "Your slave begs for her punishment."

Kate sighed, but I thought with more pleasure than resignation; she darted a glance at me before accepting the offering. Very deliberately, she touched the girl's left nipple with the small leather flap at the whip's terminal end. I heard Marika whimper

· *Butterfly* ·

and saw a strange expression steal over her face. Her eyes were shut, her brows contracted as from intense concentration; her face glowed with a strange expression I knew not of fear or rapture. As the soft leather tip slowly grazed over her skin, her expression grew in intensity and her breathing became labored. A command from Kate brought her head and shoulders down to the floor; at the same time she raised her hips so that her posterior and sexual parts were obscenely exposed. When the whip's probing tip descended down the cleft of the buttocks, her whimpering took on an edge of hysteria and I felt that at any moment she would break out into sobs.

After what seemed a long time, Kate's arm suddenly flew up and in quick succession delivered two lashes. They were casual and apparently effortless, and certainly Kate did not put her strength behind them; nonetheless I could clearly see a dark red streak where one of the blows had landed, and this was matched by another on the side hidden from my view.

"Get up," Kate ordered. "That's all for now. But be careful, because the next time . . ."

"There will be no next time," Marika sobbed. Rising on her knees, she solemnly kissed the instrument of her torture once more before taking it from her mistress's hand. Her face was streaked with tears, as she murmured her gratitude and her protestations of obedience.

The scene had thrown me into the most complete disarray. I no longer knew what to think. What was this perverted game into which I had been drawn? What was Marika, what was Kate, and what was my love for the one and the other? Surely this depraved and savage virago could not be the same woman whom I would have chosen in all the world as the model of cultivated femininity? The two were as night and day—but then, what is night but a half-turn of the earth on its axis? What garden will not have its terrors in the dark of night? As for Kate's shadow side, I remembered that I had suspected it, that indeed I had glimpsed it once.

But deeper than the shock of discovery was the horror of recognition. For the obscurities of my soul were drawn to the nocturnal side of Kate's personality like shadows to a black sun. My revulsion had given way to fascination; a longing slithered forth like some primeval monster emerging from the bowels of the earth to show its Medusa-like face. What had formerly seemed a private crack, an inner fissure, was now revealed to be a chasm that ran through the world at large and opened at my feet. Already teetering on the edge, I felt its irresistible pull and saw myself falling like the damned in medieval paintings that plunge without end into a fiery Hell. Yet my terror was shot through with a reckless joy; I was transported by the presentiment of another life—terrible, no doubt, but possessing dimensions wondrous and unknown.

32

There had been a time when Pinkerton was given to fervent prayer. Every evening he would kneel at the side of his bed and spend a quarter of an hour asking for God's blessing and forgiveness—for precisely what was unclear, as he was at an age when reason had not yet claimed supremacy over other impulses.

His father seldom beat him; his mother never. In fact, he could hardly remember her touching him in any way. But her displeasure would be in her face, in her voice, in her every movement. And the punishment she meted out was always the same: to kneel in a corner for a designated length of time and pray for forgiveness, which God alone, she declared, was qualified to grant. It was hard on the knees, and sometimes excruciating for the bladder, but at the same time he would experience an intense emotion not unlike pleasure. Although he occasionally rebelled by thinking contrary thoughts, he mostly tried hard to pray sincerely, for he did truly believe that his soul's salvation depended upon it. Unbeknownst to him, however, he often indulged in a mixture of passionate repentence and voluptuous wallowing in his faults.

His mother, who never assailed him physically or screamed, inspired in him an unaccountable fear. She had a way of treading soundlessly and towering over him before he was aware of her approach, and though he learned to be quite vigilant, he could never be certain that she was not watching. The most terrible part of being punished was this unconfirmed feeling of being observed; each time, for the entire duration, he would feel her eyes upon his back, watching his every movement, reading his every thought. On occasion, when he could bear it no longer, he would turn to look, and more often than not his curiosity would collide with her flinty censorious eyes. Sometimes, though, she would not be there at all. And that for some reason was almost worse.

At fifteen he took to considering himself a freethinker and suppressed his bedtime prayers. But that did not change his punishment. When it ceased he could not have said; one day he noted with a certain wonder that he had not been formally punished for a long time. Did that mean he was now grown-up, he mused, or had his mother also ceased to believe? The feeling that her ubiquitous eyes were boring into his back, however, never quite faded.

33

Before leaving the room, Kate to my dismay turned and addressed me once again. Her cold insistent gaze made me acutely conscious of my nakedness, and her words cut into me like the point of a thrusting rapier.

"Your behavior, sir, is simply beyond conceiving. Despite your want of faith, I still considered you an equal, a friend, and even extended an invitation to visit—I shudder to think where it might have led. But with your Caliban tastes, you preferred the company of the slave to the mistress. What can I say to you now? You've put yourself beyond the pale of civilized intercourse. Go and don't come back. I'm sorry I hurt you, but you should not have attacked me. I doubt that we'll meet again, but if we do, I shall not know you."

There was nothing I could say to justify or defend myself. Crushed by shame and remorse, I wanted to sink into the floor, to disappear forever; but when Kate started toward the door, the thought that I should never see her again was so unbearable that I called out after her. My voice sounded pathetically weak. Kate paid no attention. Shaken and speechless, I listened to her boots click relentlessly down the wooden stairs.

· *Butterfly* ·

34

In later life Pinkerton was subject to a recurring dream. In the dream his father would be alive again—not as if he had never died, but as if he had returned from a long trip or absence. The circumstances varied but the situation was always the same; hiding his initial surprise, Pinkerton would manifest a joy that often was genuine to an unexpected degree. But immediately thereafter anxiety would begin to gnaw at him, for would not his father criticize the way he had been managing the family affairs? With increasing anguish he would await the confrontation, all the while acting cheerfully in the hope that his errors and transgressions might yet go unnoticed. Then, invariably, came a moment when his father would expound his plans, sometimes in the presence of others, sometimes to him alone. At first Pinkerton would feel relieved that the anticipated criticism seemed not to be forthcoming, but then he would realize with mounting uneasiness that his father's intentions went against all his own and negated dispositions he had already made. As he listened, he would think of arguments, but at the end of the speech, when his father would sweep his eyes over his listeners in his characteristically self-satisfied manner, Pinkerton would be unable to utter a word, for by then his own world would have collapsed like a house of cards and speaking would only draw attention to the unsightly ruins and to his guilt. And this feeling of being reduced to mute, impotent acquiescence—which he knew well from experience—would linger on when he awakened, for the rest of the day and often beyond.

35

With Marika's help I managed to dress and climb into the coach she hired for me, but I was half-dead when I got home. The doctor Lisa frantically sent for diagnosed a broken rib. He examined me with curiosity, but was discreet enough not to ask questions. Hiding behind my condition, I kept determinedly silent.

A high fever confined me to bed for well over a week. During this time the scenes in Marika's room came back to me over and over again; each event, each moment, was relived, ten, twenty, fifty times. Kate's imposing figure haunted me, waking and sleeping, especially her eyes, in which my ignominy was preserved like a beetle frozen in glass. Her eyes were the loveliest things in the universe, and I had irreparably sullied them with my baseness: the thought made me despair, and I would groan aloud in self-loathing. I wanted to die, for I had lost all hope of happiness and felt I could never again hold up my head to those dearest to me. Like a somnambulist who falls and awakens submerged in mire, I saw my skin covered with a shame that was thick and sticky and visible to all. It was unthinkable how I could have brought it upon myself, and yet I understood only too well, for all my remorse and despair did not expunge or reduce by one iota the lust that had fomented such folly and, alas, would drive me to greater madness still.

It was during that fateful, delirious week that my lust underwent its strange mutation. Until then it had been that of any other man—to enjoy through the senses a body I desired, to unite in flesh with a woman I loved. But now any hope, or even dream, of a union with Kate was irrevocably lost, and at the same

· *Butterfly* ·

time my love for her had grown to demented proportions. Caught between the hammer of despair and the anvil of overweening passion, my desires took on a definitively weird cast.

In the beginning my one remaining desire, obscurely recognized, was to die before those eyes that I had defiled, and even better, by her own hand. For somewhere there lurked the hope that in death I might be pardoned and perhaps even loved again. Soon, however, another desire began to worm its way through my despair. Again and again I saw in my mind's eye Marika kneeling naked and lewdly exposed, heard her beg abjectly for punishment, felt the malicious caress of leather over skin, and then the swift rise and descent, the sharp crack . . . and I shivered, for it was as if I myself were reliving the scene but in Marika's place. It haunted me with an obsessive fascination, and prodded at a certain dark spot buried deep in my soul. What formerly I had experienced as at best a vague agitation, a troubled but undefined yearning, now emerged as a true desire. And as my fevered imagination wrapped around it, its shape became increasingly unmistakable: I craved what Marika had so unforgettably shown me, I craved the humiliation of kneeling before Kate, the total surrender of body and will, the words and gestures of submission, even the pain of being whipped. This recognition horrified me, but I was helpless to resist. Judgment and moral sense notwithstanding, I began to wallow in the horrendous events of that fateful afternoon, to relish positively the memory of those two barbarous lashes I still sensibly felt; all too willingly I would have offered myself to more—a hundred, if it took that to appease her anger. The thought of the sickening pain terrified me, and at the same time evoked such feelings of voluptuousness that I felt Heaven and Hell opening on either side to suck me in.

I have heard of men who pay money to be flogged or otherwise mistreated. No doubt I resembled them, yet in those days I would not have seen or admitted a similarity. If the desire for punishment is an inversion of lust, in my case it grew so directly out of my love for Kate and was so indissociable from her person that I could not have conceived of it existing by itself. But if lust could—as it did—pursue a course independent of love, why not in its inverted form as well? This, however, would have seemed unimaginable to me at the time.

For however heated became my phantasies of humiliation, however urgently I craved her punishment and its pain, these did not become ends in themselves. No matter what form my longing took, it always looked to Kate's love. But having become unworthy of aspiring to that love, I in turn could no longer offer love, only submission. My lips, dispossessed of her kisses, stooped to her feet; her caresses forfeited, I yearned for her blows. If love is all that is noble and ennobling, love betrayed demeans and depraves. Thus it was in my abasement, in the mortification of my own flesh and soul, that I nursed a dark tenuous hope for redemption. I was confused then and could not have formulated it so, but consciously or not, such had become my persuasion by the time I left my bed and set off once again for Creighton.

36

During his illness, Pinkerton's mind was unceasingly visited by female figures; they drifted in and out like so many preying ghosts.

Foremost was Kate, who came in two guises. One was the Kate he had known in bygone days. In a flowing white gown, she seemed an angel of light, all softness and grace, who brought with her fragrant breaths of a spring that would never return. The other was the Kate he had last seen; superb in her black riding habit, with devouring eyes, she was like a dark avenging angel—powerful, inexorable, and if anything even more beautiful than the other. Sometimes, for a brief moment, they would both be present, but it was always the latter who remained.

Butterfly also appeared in two forms. One was the discreet, loving wife who, as it were, would slip in under the covers without even being seen and transport him back to Nagasaki. For a brief moment he would feel comforted and safe but after that even worse than before. He dreaded thinking of Butterfly now, and when he did, more often conjured up the other one, as lithe and lovely as a beautiful snake. Desiring her anew as if he had never possessed her, he hated her, and himself, for she was the cause of his misery. He wished he could pluck her from his life and rub out every trace of her existence. He always repented such unjust thoughts, yet it could not be denied that from the depths of his mortification, he would have given much not to remember her at all.

Strangely, perhaps, he had no such bitter feelings toward Marika. With her he now felt a deep bond. At times she seemed almost his twin; for though he trembled still to remember the degrading sensuality she had drawn him into, he no longer saw in her the temptress but the slave humbling herself before the mistress he too adored. She was perhaps the one person he truly wanted to see. To her alone he could speak freely; only in her arms could he hope for a moment's respite. And she was above all a link, perhaps the last, to Kate. He hoped against hope for a visit. But she never came.

When he spoke, it was only with Lisa. But she provided no succor, and her constant presence at his bedside was less than welcome, for he did not want her to see his passion and distress. Somehow his sense of guilt carried over to her, and he was terrified that she might question him. There had been a time when she surely would have, but now she discreetly refrained;

nonetheless she saw more than he wished and was clearly troubled. Sometimes she read, but at other times she would just sit in the darkened room and watch, and that in particular upset him. More than once, waking in the dim light and feeling her eyes upon him, he mistook her for Kate, and though he never gave himself away, each time it left him violently shaken.

Worse, however, was his mother. The sight of her gaunt figure slipping noiselessly in and out of the room took him back to an earlier time of his life when she would enter without warning and on the flimsiest excuse, undoubtedly in the hope of catching him at something forbidden. He had always known her to be cold and irritable, but had there never been a time, he wondered, when she too was young? A time when her eyes were not so hard and dry, her lips less pinched and bitter? He seemed to remember, vaguely, having once had a mother who was different, but the image was buried somewhere and he could never find it. Did it in fact come out of his past? He had the feeling—it was not tangible enough to be a memory—that at some point something had disrupted their relations and banished him from her affections; but this too was probably a dream or a figment of his imagination.

He thought also of other women: women he had forgotten long ago, playmates, servants, casual acquaintances; and Anne, who all in all was quite a lovely girl—would his life not be happier now if he had married her? He did not believe that, of course, yet he felt a lingering regret. How long ago that morning seemed when he first saw Kate! The turns his life had taken since—he had difficulty believing that everything had really happened; at times it all seemed like a dream.

· *Butterfly* ·

37

(The Nagasaki ms.)

For a time I was torn between sailing for Japan as planned and abandoning all to a passion already beyond control. In more lucid moments I was determined not to succumb and anxiously counted the few days I had left before catching my boat in San Francisco. I even had a heated altercation with Lisa, who with the doctor's support refused to let me leave; my condition, I must admit, justified her insistence, and in the end I was secretly relieved at being forced to stay.

My intentions in going to Creighton were vague; I knew only that I had to see Kate again. During my convalescence I had composed speeches and scripts for a projected reunion, but however eloquent these had been in the sickroom, that bright early November morning made them seem tenuous and without substance. As the crisp, fresh air filled and revitalized my lungs, my lurid imaginings began to dissolve like remnants of a fading dream.

Marika, though not surprised to find me at the door, made a slight grimace. We stood looking awkwardly at one another. She did not show me in.

"You come to see me . . . or her?"

"You," I felt compelled to lie.

"I cannot. She do not permit me."

I stared at her, not knowing what to say.

"It is finished. You understand?" She said this impassively and seemed to be waiting for me to turn and leave. When I did not move, she added, as if making a concession, "After what has happened, it is not possible to continue."

Although I had not come to see Marika, I was quite put out by her remoteness. However things might stand, I had expected a little more warmth, not to mention civility.

"All right," I said coolly. "But I should like to speak to your mistress."

"She do not like to speak to you." Apparently Marika did not intend to let me in.

"Look, Marika," I said, trying to keep down my exasperation, "what happened was unfortunate. I'm very sorry for it, and I know that she is upset, but I must see her. Don't you see? It's important."

Marika shrugged. She was still waiting for me to go away.

"Well, you can at least go and tell her."

"No use. She tell me to not let you in."

"Never mind," I said with considerable heat. "Just go and say I'm here!"

"I cannot," Marika replied, as cool as you please.

"Listen," I told her. "If you won't, I'll simply go in and announce myself."

"You cannot."

I was getting angry enough to throttle her. "Do you think you'll stop me?" I asked with scarcely concealed menace.

"Not I will stop you." Again she shrugged and let me glare a moment longer before saying with an air of lassitude: "She is not there." At that she took a small step back, as if inviting me to look for myself. I was on the point of pushing past her but checked myself.

"And you won't talk with me. . . ." I looked into her face; it remained quite blank. She shook her head. For an instant I wanted to argue, to plead, but when she refused to meet my eyes, I turned abruptly and strode away without saying good-bye.

My heart contracted violently when an hour later, from my post across the street, I saw Kate ride up with a man who clearly was not her groom. To my relief, he did not go in but rode away

· *Butterfly* ·

with her mount. I barely had time to rush over and cry out to her before the door could shut.

Frowning, Kate stepped back out onto the porch; she advanced to the edge so that I could not mount the steps without seeming invasive. From below, I looked up a little breathlessly at her; my heart was pounding so that I could hardly speak, and it was she who addressed me first.

"I believe I made it clear that I no longer wish to see you, and Marika has surely said so again today. How many times do you need to be told?"

"I know . . . I know," I stammered; all the phrases I had prepared were gone without a trace. "But I had to speak to you."

"Well?" she demanded impatiently.

I declared that my behavior had indeed been inexcusable, worse than inexcusable, and that I could in no way defend it. But I begged her to forgive me nonetheless—not because I deserved it, but out of mercy, as I could not live without seeing her.

"If it makes you happier, you can consider yourself forgiven," Kate said coldly. "But to see you, I am afraid, is out of the question."

"Then you haven't forgiven me at all!" I blurted. "What can it mean to be forgiven if I am banished from your sight?"

"You want me to continue receiving you, but on what basis? Consider: you were my friend's brother; you made love to me and proposed marriage; you jilted me and married another; you came back and made love to me again though without proposing marriage; at the same time you were seducing my slave, and as if that weren't outrageous enough, you had to steal into my own house and violate her under my very eyes! Which of these colorful personages am I supposed to see in you? A friend? A deserter? An aspiring lover? And whose, if you please—mine or my slave's?"

Merely to hear Kate speak of her slave brought back in a flood all the scenes I had envisioned; but now, in her actual presence, they seemed ridiculously melodramatic. I had with little difficulty imagined prostrating myself before her and imitating Marika's phrases, but to fall on my knees in broad daylight and actually to utter such silly-sounding words were something else again. Embarrassed and overwhelmed by my absurd desires, I stood rooted in confusion. Kate, seeing me unable to reply, curtly bade me good day and turned to go into the house.

At that moment I knew only that if she were to close that door behind her, I should have no hope of ever being admitted again, and that thus banished I could not go on living. Beside myself with desperation, I broke out of my paralysis and, leaping up the steps, caught her hand. Whereupon she turned with a look of such burning indignation that I was utterly confounded. Without being aware of my actions, I fell to my knees and pressed the gloved hand to my lips.

"Get up and let go of me," Kate said icily.

But now I had started and was not to be stopped. "No!" I cried. "Not until you forgive me—really forgive."

"What you want is impossible. I've told you that already."

"It's not true!" Now the words came out by themselves; I listened to them in amazement. "If you can forgive Marika, why can't you forgive me? Beat me if you like, punish me the way you punished her, or however you please. Punish me, Kate, I beg you to, but then forgive me!"

Kate heaved a little sigh of annoyance. "Who are you that I should beat you? I can punish Marika because she is my slave, but you're nothing to me. Please let me by."

"No, not nothing!" I blurted out. "I'll be anything you want . . . a slave if you will. Let me be your slave, if nothing more!"

"Don't be silly," she said wearily. "You're making a fool of yourself."

· *Butterfly* ·

"I don't care! Kate, can't you see that I love you beyond anything I can say? I know how wretchedly I've behaved, I know I can't hope for your love, but don't drive me away like this. Anything, Kate, but don't banish me from your sight!"

Kate only shook her head. She tried to pull her hand away, but I held on tightly.

"This is ridiculous. Let go. You're being extremely tiresome."

Ignoring her, I went on, carried along by a flood of pent-up emotions. "Kate, take me for your slave, yes, your slave! I beg you!" The words made me tingle with shame and at the same time a peculiar gratification; drunk upon their exorbitance, I embraced her knees and let my cheek slide down until it lay against her boot. And between my lips, trembling still from the taste of leather, the word slipped out, half a whisper, half a sigh: "Mistress!" As a prayer uttered after a long aridity calms the heart, the word brought a sudden sense of peace mixed with awe. But I knew that my life had been staked.

"You don't know what you're saying," Kate said as she tried to free her feet from my embrace. My protests she at first refused to heed, but in the end she conceded. "Listen, you have no idea what it is to be a slave. Try it if you must, and we'll see what kind of slave you make. It's just possible that you're born to be one. But go home first and think about what slavery means, and if you're still mad enough to want it, come back at four o'clock tomorrow. Don't come though unless you're sure. You'll have to be ready to obey to the letter and to submit absolutely. And be warned: it won't amuse you! Now let me pass."

38

(Letter from Lisa to Pinkerton dated May 17, 1937, found among Pinkerton's papers. Internal evidence suggests that it postdates the Nagasaki manuscripts.)

Dear Henry,

They say that before you die, you should lay down earthly concerns. But mine still weigh so heavily, and I have little time left. I shall not regret leaving this life, yet my heart is burdened by regret.

I should have written to you long before this. I have thought about doing so ever since I learnt that she was dead. But you know that I am stubborn. It hurt me so much to see what she had done to you. Thinking about it was too painful, so I preferred to have no news. At this moment, I do not know where you are, or even that you are alive, though I assume I should have been told if you were not.

For a long time I felt very bitter toward you, for letting her do what she did. I could not reconcile what you had become to the brother I had known and loved, perhaps too dearly. And perhaps, too, by blaming you, I lightened my own guilt, which otherwise would have been unendurable. My guilt, yes—because I am responsible for all that happened to you. It is to confess this that I am writing, and to ask your forgiveness.

I do not allude to my bringing you together. My conscience is clear on that score, and I still sometimes think that if you had married her when you should have, all would have turned out well. But for what I did later, after your return from Japan, I cannot forgive myself. Oh, if only you hadn't gone! Did you know that Dad had her investigated and found that her family was not quite what she had given it out to be, and that was what set him and Mother against your marriage? I was so furious when I found out. What difference does it make, I shouted at them. Of course they patronizingly informed me that I was too young to understand. The worst part was that they turned out to be right. Only it wasn't a question of age, because today I am an old woman at the very end of her life, and I still don't understand how she could have been like that.

I acted in innocence and with the best of intentions (the road to Hell, as the saying goes . . .); but this you surely never doubted. What you probably do not know—unless she has told you—is that I put her up to it. Well, Mother and I; Mother might even have suggested it by asking about her, though I needed little prompting. I was so sure you were made for one another, and we were all horrified that you had married a Japanese. So I wrote to her and the three of us met and agreed that she should try to get you back. Her only condition was that she be given a free hand, with no questions asked. Her insistence on this point seemed a little curious, but I thought nothing more of it at the time, and even later, when things turned bizarre and I became uneasy, I still had no idea. I simply could never have imagined where it would lead. I still can't.

Was it because I did not want to know? Possibly. She had warned me against inquiries, but there was more to it than that. The more worried I became, the more I tried to turn away. You coming home wounded, however, was almost the last straw. I was tempted to throw up everything then

· 95 ·

and there but persuaded myself that it was in a good cause. Yet my intuition of danger was so strong that several times I was on the verge of going back on my decision.

Do you remember the day you went to see her when you had barely recovered, and came back exhausted? You were as uncommunicative as you always were during that time, but despite my resolution to stay out of it, I had to ask how it went. You only answered that you were to go back the next day, but you had such a strange look. Something gripped my heart at that moment and I nearly cried out to protest your going. Without knowing why, I distinctly felt you shouldn't, and all evening long I argued with myself. I prayed for guidance, for some sign, but got nothing, nothing at all. It made me resentful, and I think from that moment on I began to doubt God. The following day I still did not know whether I should try to stop you.

But when I heard you announce that you had changed your mind and now wanted to catch the next ship for Japan, I was shocked, and horrified anew at the thought of you leaving, for I had mindlessly assumed that missing the first boat meant you would stay. Was it the Devil who incited me to ask about the trip to Creighton and to push you into going back? That moment weighs on me more than everything else together, because before I was innocent but by then I knew somewhere deep inside that I was acting against my better judgment. And that visit decided your fate, didn't it? Because after that you went to her daily and never again spoke about going to Japan.

Looking back now on my life, it all seems like one big mistake—or a grotesque joke. Sometimes I imagine it unraveling so that I can start over again. But would I be sure of doing better? (Though it does seem impossible to do worse.) The house is empty but for the servants and an

· *Butterfly* ·

occasional visitor: one or two old friends, a cousin now and then, the doctor, the lawyer—no children or grandchildren, no beloved ghosts; no priest, no God. I cannot believe a God can exist that would make such a mess of people's lives or allow them to do it.

But somewhere on this earth I have a nephew or niece, and a sister-in-law and a brother. And if I still have one desire left, it would be to see them and tell them of my repentence, and ask for their forgiveness and their blessing. Alas, I have waited too long.

My heart is bitter, but the bitterness is not toward you now. Certainly, I was more directly at fault than you, and I hope that, knowing this, you will forbear from rancor against

> Your unhappy,
> LISA

39

(The Nagasaki ms.)

Exhausted from my excursion, I went to bed after an early supper and slept fitfully through the night. I awakened to a room bright and cheerful from the morning sun.

Lying cosily between the sheets, I thought of the meeting with Kate. Everything about it felt unreal and far away. My words and behavior seemed preposterous: who could have taken me seriously? The remembrance by turns embarrassed and excited me. Would I really consider becoming her slave? One moment I almost laughed aloud at the absurdness, but the next I thought of Kate and of not seeing her, and turned cold. Though ludicrous while not in progress, the game was deadly earnest.

But what was I doing playing such games? I, a grown man with a wife and a newborn child, responsible for a household and a large fortune. It crossed my mind that my daughter's name day was in two weeks and that I had never seen her or even acknowledged her birth. All at once and for the first time, the child took on a real existence for me. I could envision her puckered face and wriggling body, I could hear her laugh and cry.

Memories flooded into my consciousness: Butterfly waking me and cradling my head; the exquisite movements of her hands preparing and serving food; the magical fascination of her rounding form and the conversations about our child inside. It was as if the progression of my days, temporarily torn out of the Nagasaki calendar, had suddenly been restored. Seized by a sense of urgency as immediate as that of an infant crying to be fed, I jumped out of bed.

At that moment my mind was made up: I would depart for Japan on the very next boat. Without taking time for breakfast, I set about calling to arrange a passage and to settle the most essential business matters. I knew I would have to be on my way without delay, the very next day even, for at any moment my resolve might crumble.

I waited until lunch was over to announce my new plans. The two women were thunderstruck. After the initial shock, my mother contented herself with a pinched expression and a sardonic remark, but Lisa became belligerent.

"You're expected in Creighton this afternoon, you had said—are you going?"

My answer in the negative brought a look of bitter reproach. Casting down her eyes, she said in a low but emotional voice, "So you're going to desert her again, without even saying goodbye."

I believe I turned quite pale. "That's a very nasty thing to say,

Lisa," I blustered. "I'll thank you not to make things harder for me than they are."

"Are you afraid to see her again? Is that why you're going to sneak off on her?"

"No, I'm not afraid! Why should I be afraid of her?" I tried for a bravura that I did not for a moment believe.

Lisa looked at me steadily. "You *are* afraid, because you're running away. And because you're a coward, that's why—like Dad aways said!"

"Shut up, Lisa!" I shouted. "I won't be spoken to like that. You should be quite about things you don't understand. Why, if you had any idea . . . If you cared for me at all, you wouldn't be so wrapped up in your schoolgirl fantasies, and you wouldn't try to meddle in what you cannot comprehend."

I regretted my words even as I said them, and I looked on helplessly as tears started to streak down her cheeks. "If I cared for you . . . ?" she sobbed. "Hen, who has ever cared for you if I don't?"

My mother's inept attempt at consolation only made Lisa cry harder, and my words did not calm her either. I was angry and exasperated, and sorry for her as well; resisting the impulse to stomp out, I went around the table to where she sat and, putting an arm over her shouldere, spoke as soothingly as I could. For a time she kept herself aggressively turned from me, but in the end she looked up; her voice was cracked and her eyes were puffed and full of tears.

"Will you go and see her one last time, Hen?"

I looked at her and could not refuse. But as I kissed the tear-stained face she held up to me, my breast was tight with foreboding.

40

He recognized her as soon as he caught sight of her, even though there were two of them and at that distance he could barely make out their features. They said good-bye at the corner; he watched her come down the street alone.

His heart, he thought with a certain wistful amusement, had never beat so wildly for her mother. The resemblance was unmistakable, though a stranger might have been struck more by the differences. Etsuko was a good bit taller, and her face might have been modeled by European hands upon a Japanese prototype. But something in her expression and in the way her fine head sat on the delicate neck made him think irrepressibly of Butterfly. It amazed him that such things could have been passed on by a mother lost in infancy. A mother he had robbed her of.

She abhorred him, Sachiko had said. Well, why shouldn't she? Because of him, she had had neither mother nor father. And had he ever given her anything? Besides, that is, the unwanted foreign touches in her face, another cause of hardship. It had pained him to learn how she suffered from this; yet he was gratified to discern a remote resemblance to Lisa.

It was fairly dark already, and he, half-hidden by a utility pole, turned to the wall as if urinating, so that she passed without a look. During these maneuvers, he lost sight of her for only a moment, but even that seemed unbearable; his eyes continued to strain after her long after she had disappeared into the house.

He was absorbed in wonder. It seemed a miracle that their daughter could have become that girl, who in another few years would be as old as Butterfly had been when they met. And in her own way she would be as lovely—one could see that even now in spite of the drab black-and-white school uniform designed to

· *Butterfly* ·

smother importune charms. Her beauty, not yet a woman's and no longer a child's, was like still-enfolded petals peeping out from an opening bud. It was beauty at its most touching, for it appealed to the imagination rather than the senses, and aroused a desire not to possess but to nurture and to watch.

But he would not see it unfold, he thought with a pang. That was the penalty for having wantonly cut short Butterfly's life and thrown away his own. It saddened him unspeakably to walk away without an embrace or even a word. Yet he was grateful to have seen her; grateful to see that he had not destroyed all. The chain was unbroken, life continued to propagate from seed to seed, and each spring would have its new blossoms. A melancholic thankfulness settled upon him, merging with the damp evening chill: he had wreaked havoc with his idolatry, but he was still in God's world.

41

(The Nagasaki ms.)

I rode to Creighton at a fitful pace, sometimes drawing back in doubt and sometimes feverishly spurring on. It would be absurd and dishonest of me to say that I only went to humor Lisa, though I might indeed not have gone had she insisted less. All along the way I felt myself assailed by conflicting forces greater than myself. "I'll stop at a tavern," I would say to myself; or "I'll turn back." But I kept going. I also tried to fool myself by thinking that nothing obliged me to go in once I got there. When the house came into sight, I even gained a moment's composure by telling myself that I would not.

Chance or fate had it that Marika was outside taking in the wash when I rode up. I wanted to turn around, but she had already seen me. "You are late!" she said by way of greeting. "She wait for you." Without giving me a chance to reply, she started up the steps. I followed indecisively, my heart aflutter.

Kate, sitting in an informal white dress, looked dazzlingly fresh and lovely, and anything but the armored virago I half-expected to find. Her youthful guileless aura transported me back in time to the bride I had once left behind. As my eyes sank into her alluring softness, all that since had come between us seemed like a dream from which I was awakening.

Looking up from her book, she charmed me with a smile. "Ah, I didn't think you were coming."

Put off guard and reassured by the appearance of normalcy, I could almost imagine myself an old friend dropping in for an afternoon visit. "I almost didn't," I said, falling in with her casual tone; in my agitation, I clutched at anything that momentarily provided an orientation. "I decided this morning to leave for Japan—soon, in a day or two."

For a few seconds, Kate's brow darkened with I know not what somber emotion, but then the shadow, like that of a swift-passing cloud, lifted and her face glowed with an angelic sweetness I had never seen nor would see again. At that moment she seemed transfigured beyond beauty.

"I am very glad, Henry," she said simply. Her sincerity was certain, and I felt no attempt whatever on her part to hold or to captivate. I can still see her sitting before me, an incarnate vision of all I had loved and dreamt of, but cast with a perfection beyond my imagining.

"Will you have some tea?" she asked, motioning me to the divan. Her loveliness dazed me; I could not think or speak. As I continued to stand in seeming hesitation, she said, "If you are pressed for time, don't feel obliged to stay. I can imagine all that you have to do." She stood up and came toward me, and for a moment we stood face-to-face.

· *Butterfly* ·

I was aware only of one single overpowering wish, to prolong the moment, to continue gazing at a beauty my eyes would never again behold once I left the room. To be sure, I could still have accepted tea, with a phrase, a gesture, it would have been the easiest thing in the world. But my heart was too full—not with any wayward, fantastical desire but with simple admiration and love. And it was my heart that spoke.

"Kate, I . . . don't want to leave you." The words, unpremeditated and unbidden, jolted me; without warning, my love for her surged up vertiginously, like a giant wave; carried on its crest, I blurted out that I had not come to say good-bye.

Kate sucked in her breath slightly and, frowning, cast her eyes to the floor; then she turned and slowly took a few steps away from me. When she looked up again, she was amazingly transformed. Her eyes, cold and piercing now, glinted strangely.

"Why have you come then?"

I looked at her in bewilderment; her eyes were opaque and implacable. "Why, because . . ." I muttered in confusion. "Well, we had said that I would come today if . . . if . . ."

"Why have you come, Henry?" she asked again, brushing aside my stammerings. Her voice was edged with exasperation, and uncomprehendingly I sensed a tremor of rage in her slim but powerful body, now drawn proudly to its full height. Like petals suddenly desiccated, the softness fell away; even the fringes of her dress seemed to stiffen. A ghostly shadow flickered over her face, giving profile to the splendid features. I was entranced by the mutations of her beauty, heightened at that moment by an uncommon intensity of expression, but the woman I knew and loved had faded into another, strange and darkly enthralling.

It was her eyes that caught me; those fateful eyes, so dark it was hard to determine their color, so deep they seemed a conduit to some mysterious pristine place beyond time and measure—I had known their infinity of shades and meanings, but now I perceived only an intense blue-black void, which so powerfully drew me in that I could not look away.

"Why have you come?" she insisted, harshly this time.

That imperious question, chiming and chiming again, was like a knell summoning back expelled demons to my beleaguered heart. I colored in confusion as the answer to her peremptory question, against reason and will, stirred and rose in a dizzying flush: that I had come to offer myself, yes, as her slave. But a sense of absurdity prevented me from uttering the words, though my throat burned with their strangled cry.

"Go on, say it," Kate prompted, softly now, as if reading into my heart, and when I still hung fire, coaxed in her low melodious voice while her eyes tugged at my wailing soul. "Say it, Henry."

Then I spoke the phrase that was constricting my heart like a coiled serpent; and my eyelids drooped with shame.

"Really?" I heard the frown and did not dare raise my eyes. In the silence I could almost hear something tearing inside her. With sudden, terrible vehemence she cried, "Then kneel!"

The command stunned me, and though my will might have complied, my body, balking at the exotic act, hovered irresolutely. Uncertain, I looked up and was instantly caught again in her mesmerizing gaze. I knew at once that everything hung on this moment, that my entire existence was balanced on a razor's edge. In a flash of heightened awareness, I saw my love in its entirety crystallized into a jewel perched high, high overhead, precariously—more than precariously, for it quivered and was already tipping—over a chasm of such darkness that if it fell, the fall would never end. With all my heart I wanted to reach it, to steady it; my life was nothing in comparison, I should not have hesitated an instant to throw it down if only I could have saved the jewel. But it was so far, too far. Simultaneously, I had become conscious of being still on my feet and able to walk away, and my

· *Butterfly* ·

mind rehearsed with astonishing vividness every movement it would take to turn and reach the door.

But I did not move. Her eyes held me like lacquered pools of quicksand. I knew I must not be caught in them, but it was too late. Yet I struggled, I know not for how long. I only remember the eerie sensation of my will seeping away, as it were, drop by drop, while her eyes' terrible hypnotic beauty invaded and filled my soul until I was but an empty vessel for her greater volition.

Our eyes still locked, we sank downward in a slow and weirdly graceful synchrony, she into her armchair and I to my knees.

42

"Always, Kate, for as long as I live!" Pinkerton protested. "I won't leave you, I can't, not next week, not ever, not even if you drive me away! I'd die first!" In his passion, he shuffled over to where she sat and covered her hand with kisses.

Inertly, her hand accepted the homage; then, suddenly, it slipped away and slapped him with resounding violence. Dazed, he crouched, immobilized by incomprehension and spontaneous rage. The next instant, however, a surreptitious pleasure began to tingle until his cheek, still stinging from the blow, burned with voluptuous shame. He felt a satisfaction deep and mysterious, like an inhalation of opium, for was not her gratuitous abuse the surest acknowledgment of his servitude, the most concrete affirmation of her authority? He lowered his head almost to her feet but without daring to touch them. Mimicking Marika, he crooned in a parched unnatural voice, "Thank you for your gracious correction."

A little grunt of approval mixed with scorn rewarded the effort it had cost him to bring out such a ridiculous-sounding phrase.

"A slave must show respect at all times. He is not to slobber over his mistress or to touch her without permission. Is that understood?"

"Yes."

Her foot came up sharply, the heel catching his lower lip. His head jerked back; a taste of blood filled his mouth. "Yes what?" she snapped. "Mind your manners, slave!"

"Yes . . . Mistress!"

The words had a sweetness on his tongue unlike any he had known. He flushed, but his embarrassment quickly turned into pleasure, and abandoning himself to it he added loud and clear and with savage relish, "Thank you, Mistress, for graciously correcting your humble slave." Already the quaint locution was sitting better on his tongue. As with wallowing in mud, one soon got used to it and more easily let oneself go.

In acknowledgment, Kate held out her foot. Pinkerton kissed it, and when it was not withdrawn, kissed it again with more ardor. Kate let the foot linger against his cheek. Emboldened by her indulgence, he removed the slipper. A faintly vinegary odor of perspiration mounted to his head; drunken with eagerness, his lips closed over her toes.

43

(The Nagasaki ms.)

My indenture was ratified in the following contract:

We the undersigned Henry Benjamin Franklin Pinkerton and Kathleen Hamilton hereby engage ourselves, for a period of four months, to a strict observance of the terms stated below.

· *Butterfly* ·

1· Mr. Pinkerton will present himself at Miss Hamilton's home every day at four o'clock P.M. and will remain for ninety minutes, during which time he will be at Miss Hamilton's entire disposition and will obey her orders without discussion or modification.

2· Failure to carry out instructions will be punished at Miss Hamilton's discretion, without possibility of appeal.

3· Mr. Pinkerton will forswear conjugal ties as well as all engagements of a like nature.

4· Mr. Pinkerton will abstain from engaging in any form of sexual gratification.

5· Mr. Pinkerton will renounce autonomy over all mental, moral, and physical faculties; hence he will at all times be subject, mentally no less than physically, to Miss Hamilton's direction.

6· Unless expressly ordered to do so, Mr. Pinkerton will refrain from touching or asking to touch Miss Hamilton's person. Exception is made of Miss Hamilton's feet and those parts of her leg below the knee; to these he is permitted to render spontaneous homage.

7· Mr. Pinkerton will never in his lifetime divulge the nature of the relationship defined by the present contract, nor will he disclose anything he may learn about Miss Hamilton in his capacity of personal slave.

8· Mr. Pinkerton will neither resent nor seek compensation for any eventual loss or damage to his person or property incurred directly or indirectly by the terms of his indenture.

9· Mr. Pinkerton will of his own accord confess any breach, mental or physical, of Miss Hamilton's instructions; he pledges his honor to maintain absolute veracity in his relations with Miss Hamilton.

10· Miss Hamilton will acknowledge Mr. Pinkerton as her slave and will treat him as inalienable chattel. Beyond this, she is bound by no obligation of any nature toward him. With the sole exceptions of alienation and dismissal, she will enjoy absolute rights over his body and mind, including the rights of mutilation and destruction.

44

"What you tasted of the whip the other day is nothing," Kate warned him, "compared to what may be in store. It would be a grave mistake to imagine that you'll be playing children's games. Once you put your signature to that paper, you'll be bound body and soul. In my eyes you will cease to be a man, and I shan't hesitate to do to you what I wouldn't do to any man or woman. The contract is a temporary one, but the consequences for you will have nothing temporary about them. In fact, there is no guarantee you'll survive to make a retrospective evaluation. Be very clear on this point, Henry. Although I have no plans to take your life, I cannot answer for what happens to a slave—it's in the nature of my role as mistress that I shall have no one to answer to, and a slave's life is worth as much as his mistress's pleasure and not a whit more."

While she spoke, her hands toyed with a small porcelain cup that had been on the teapoy beside her. All of a sudden, she cracked it crisply, like an egg, against the table's edge; the paper-thin porcelain split instantly in two. Kate gazed at the pieces in her hand with detached curiosity.

"It was a fine piece," she mused. "Louis Quinze Sèvres. I've had it for a long time." Her eyes fixed on Pinkerton as she tossed the pieces carelessly onto the table. "So think well on it: unless you truly feel you cannot live away from me—and let me tell you that you'd be a fool to feel so—I advise you to tear up that paper and walk out of this room once and for all."

· *Butterfly* ·

Pinkerton himself would surely have come to that very conclusion, for the document was so outrageous, indeed so absurd, that it was hard to take seriously. But Kate's menaces and her violent, insensate gesture had lent it an intoxicating if sinister reality; her advice, so incongruously sensible, only exacerbated his passion. He shuddered at her words, and threw himself into his folly.

"Take my life!" he cried. "Tomorrow, today, when you will. Away from you, my life will be nothing to me, less than nothing!"

Snatching up the pen, Pinkerton scratched his name at the bottom of both copies and flung himself at her feet. The violent movement hurt his wound so that he nearly cried out, but he was heedless in his exaltation. On his knees, as if initiating the rite that was to become his entire existence, he handed her the document in which he had signed away his life.

Part Two

Wär nicht das Auge sonnenhaft,
Die Sonne könnt es nie erblicken;
Läg nicht in uns des Gottes eigne Kraft,
Wie könnt uns Göttliches entzücken?

(Were not the eye sun-like,
How could it see the sun?
If within us were not God's own power,
How could divine things enchant us?)

—GOETHE

45

[Editor's note: The diary of George C.
Sharpless, vice-consul at Nagasaki during Pinkerton's first two sojourns in that city, unfortunately has not
survived intact (see note p.157). The entries reproduced below
are from the year 1897.]

May 14th.   Pinkerton shipping out in a hurry because his father
has taken ill. Asked me to look after Butterfly in his absence, give
her monthly household money, see to it she has all she needs. I
asked if he really thought he was going to return. He indignantly
countered by asking whether I was considering leaving Japan
without Charlotte? Piqued, I told him straight that, while we took
in stride his setting up house with a Japanese girl, his compatriots
and I did not take it for granted that he considered her his
legitimate wife; nor did he himself a year ago, if he would take
the trouble to remember. He backed down and admitted as
much, but explained that he had since changed in his sentiments
and now considered himself married in good faith. Moreover, he
thought he had made this evident, though apparently not to all.
There I couldn't fault him, for he had expressed his change of
attitude on a number of occasions, only neither I nor Charlotte
nor any other American here took him very seriously. Someone
in his position could be expected to have his fling and do it in a
lavish way, but for that very reason, one would expect him
eventually to return to the life to which he had been born. And
how would Butterfly fit into that life, I asked? Would he take her
home with him? Surely he wasn't going to spend the rest of his
life in Japan? I could see that he wasn't comfortable with the

question and didn't press for an answer. In fact, I felt a little sorry for him, because he's going to have people pressing him—hard, too—once he gets home. I don't imagine his family will sit by and let him bring home a Japanese bride; but who knows? The rich are a race apart. A Pinkerton can permit himself things the rest of us wouldn't dream of.

May 16th.   Dinner with P. and "Mrs. Pinkerton," as she likes to be called. Japanese wives don't have the custom of entertaining, but Butterfly was eager to adapt herself to American habits— so P. explained. In any case it was necessary for me to meet her. Charlotte had reservations about going—"a scarlet woman," she sniffed—but finally went, I think as much out of curiosity as to avoid offending Pinkerton. The woman is charming, that I have to admit. We had all made the assumpton she was an unscrupulous schemer. Well, scheme she might, but it's all well tucked-in. Certainly doesn't give the impression of excessive unscrupulousness. Or am I taken in by her impeccable manners and appearance? C. is more reserved in her judgment, though admitting to being favorably impressed. One thing's sure: she has the knack to make him happy.

May 19th.   Pinkerton sailed. I went to the boat to see him off. His having entrusted Butterfly to my care seems to have created a bond of friendship between us that is quite new. I felt a real warmth when we parted, and I think he did, too. Which surprised me, because though we've always gotten along well enough, we could not have been considered friends in any but a casual way.

May 23rd.   Visit to Butterfly. She did the honors of the tea ceremony, and I had to get down that awful frothy green stuff. Ugh, to think of it! The ritual does have its beauty—I'm realizing

· *Butterfly* ·

that more every time I sit through one—and B. did it so gracefully that it was almost worth downing the bitter broth to watch her. Afterward she entertained me with stories of tea masters. The bowl I drank out of had once belonged to a famous master (Riko? Riku?). Her English is remarkably good. It puts me to shame, when I think of how rudimentary my Japanese is after two years of study. When Charlotte and I were there for dinner, she had let P. do most of the talking, but this afternoon she spoke quite freely. I had dropped in to see if she needed anything and ended up staying an hour and a half.

June 1st.   Delivered money to B. She insisted I go in. What a relief to get cool barley tea! She asked after the boys; I ended up talking at some length about their school and about life in America.

June 2nd.   B. kept slipping into my thoughts today. I hadn't realized how much I had enjoyed the hour I spent with her yesterday. Nothing noteworthy was done or said, yet there is a kind of pleasant aftertaste that seems to linger on and I have the funny feeling I haven't enjoyed myself so much since I don't know when. Could it be that I have more of a weakness for feminine charms than I believed? It was all very innocent, however, and neither my memory nor my thoughts of B. are in the least tainted. I guess it's just very pleasant to talk to someone who has such a genuine interest in things and really listens to what is said. Charlotte doesn't listen in that way, nor do most other women I know. I'm not complaining—I've certainly never missed anything in C., or even realized there might be anything to miss. But there's no denying that it is nice to come across someone who listens well. B. somehow manages to make me feel lighter by ten years.

June 15th. Attempt to persuade Charlotte that she should invite B. for a luncheon or an outing, or just for tea. But nothing doing! She wouldn't hear of it. Almost led to an altercation. Too bad. I think it would have been good for both of them—Butterfly is certainly eager to learn all she can about our ways, and it would have been a rare opportunity for C. to get to know Japanese life.

June 16th. Invitation from B. for tea! Had she anticipated my thoughts?

June 18th. Tea at B.'s. I went alone, without informing Charlotte of the invitation: I had no wish to re-open our discussion of the other evening, which still upsets me. A prejudice that refuses to give way before evidence of its injustice is a stain on a person's integrity and not worthy of an American representing America in a distant land—not to mention my wife. I am surprised and hurt that C., usually fair-minded, should be so perversely stubborn where Butterfly is concerned. She in return reproaches me for failing to understand her, yet she cannot point to what there is to understand. It is not as though associating with B. could in any conceivable way reflect poorly upon herself, morally or socially. It would be one thing if she disliked B., but she doesn't. Nevertheless, her obstinacy weighed upon my mind and kept me from fully enjoying B.'s company. But B. was in fine spirits and her gaiety almost made up for my distraction. She had written a letter to P. and was anxious to have me send it off with the next ship out. Our conversation this time turned around P. It eradicated the last traces of doubt from my mind: P. is loved as much and as well as any man could wish— and better than most ever are. Seeing that girl so ingenuously overflowing with tender feelings, I felt ashamed for having ascribed base motives to her, and doubly ashamed for having wished P. to extricate himself from her supposed wiles. Now I can only hope that he does as well by her as he has promised.

· *Butterfly* ·

June 28th. Note from P., who arrived safely in Frisco, together with thick envelope for B., which I took to her. Her excitement made me aware of how young she was. The attempts to hide her emotion were touching and full of charm. I let her pour me a cup of tea, but left after ten minutes so that she could read her letter in peace, which she was impatient to do, even though she was so happy, and so grateful to me for bringing it, that I almost think she would have put up with me if I had stayed longer. Not that I wasn't tempted! She was as flushed and radiant as a child that had just gotten a birthday present. Seeing her so was enough to dispel any suspicion of underhanded wiles. Happy man, Pinkerton!

July 5th. **(The entry is mainly about the Fourth of July party given by the American Consulate.)** . . . I did however miss B., even though I was not really expecting her to come. I had asked her on the spur of the moment and she had not refused (just as I suspected, she had not looked at the formal invitation that had been sent to Mr. and Mrs. Pinkerton). I knew she would not come unescorted, yet I was hoping, quite irrationally, to be surprised.

July 19th. Senator Pinkerton's obituary in the papers. His death should make things easier for P. in some ways. For B.'s sake, I certainly hope so.

July 27th. Letter from P. Had B.'s letter delivered to her, as I didn't have time to go by her house.

August 1st. B. seemed genuinely glad to see me and disappointed that I was there to bring her her money. She still had plenty left, she protested. In reality, she was disappointed I had not brought her another letter. In spite of the formidable

· *117* ·

heat, we spent a memorable afternoon together. I am a little surprised at the intimacy that has grown between us in such a short time. I should never have thought she could become so trusting and open toward me. I probably represent a benevolent uncle of sorts. As an older friend of P.'s, I am the closest thing to her foreign in-laws that she has seen. Would that they be like me!

I asked about her family and after a moment's hesitation she told me about the tragic circumstances that made her an orphan. Her father had come from a long line of warriors in the service of the *shōgun*. When the *shogunate* fell, he, though only a young man, adamantly refused to change his profession or his loyalties. The result was a life of constant frustration and hardship. Eventually, his intransigence lost him even the sympathy of his family. Her mother was a woman of great resource and courage, however, and she kept the family going, managing even to give B. an excellent education. But worn out by years of bitterness and want, she died when B. was still a child. Her death was a fatal blow to her husband, who took increasingly to drink. Eventually, over some offense to his honor, he committed the ritual suicide so admired by the warrior class. B.'s two brothers were taken away and later joined the army, while she, who was twelve at the time, was put in the custody of an aunt. This did not improve her lot, for her budding good looks and talents aroused the jealousy of her aunt and cousins, and she soon became the family whipping girl. An abortive attempt to run away only made things worse. In the end she was sold to a brothel in Nagasaki. There she spent a year as a servant-apprentice. Then by a stroke of luck, a famous geisha noticed and took a fancy to her—something utterly improbable because geisha and *tayū* seldom if ever set foot in the same house. If I understand correctly, *geisha*, like our ancient hetaera, by and large entertain through song, dance, and conversation, while the *tayū* use their bodies. That geisha brought her out and took her in as a servant, but upon discovering her talents, proceeded to make a geisha out of her. She was so assiduous and

· *Butterfly* ·

well-seconded that by eighteen she was on her way to becoming a well-known geisha herself. Spellbound by her story, which she told in a manner worthy of an accomplished entertainer, I was eager to hear more, but at that point she got up and opened the shutters to let in the last rays of the late-afternoon sun, perhaps purposely to dispel the melancholy of her story. When she turned to face me, she smiled broadly as if to say: And here I am today, in spite of all that.

August 8th. Charming note on beautiful paper from B., accompanying a letter she asks to be sent to P.

September 1st. Visit to B., who chided me for not having come around to see her for so long. "Is it only to bring money that you come?" In fact I had thought several times of going to see her, but something held me back. I feel uneasy going to visit someone with whom Charlotte refuses to socialize. I can't explain why. There isn't anything I should feel uneasy about by any standard, and yet . . . Is it simply the fact of enjoying? Is it guilt over enjoying something in which C. does not partake? But when was the last time we enjoyed anything together?

B. close to the lying-in period. Her condition has become quite visible, but until recently it was hardly apparent. She hopes P. will be there for the birth of the child. Seems unlikely, since P. would have to be setting sail just about now to arrive in time, and he did not mention it even as a possibility.

We talked about P.'s situation now that his father is gone. I of course knew next to nothing. It is only in B.'s eyes that I am P.'s intimate. In reality she knew more than I, since P. writes to her in greater detail.

September 20th. Thought again of having Charlotte visit Butterfly, but in the end resisted the temptation. I'll go check on her myself.

September 21st.   B. in great good spirits. Everything in order, all arrangements made. She is expecting the baby very soon. Her elation was infectious. I left feeling both reassured and cheered. Her maid, Sachiko, though young, seems to be a very capable person and quite devoted; I spoke with her for a few minutes on the way out, partly to practice my Japanese. She promised to send word immediately if anything unexpected should arise.

September 27, evening.   Note from Sachiko. B. has given birth to a girl.

September 28th.   B. surprised to see me—she didn't expect me so soon. She was going to write to P. that very afternoon so that he would get the news as quickly as possible. I told her to have it brought over by a runner.

The girl is named Etsuko—"happy girl"—because her mother was so happy in bearing her.

C. agreed to look in on her and take a present for the child. I was relieved that there was no discussion. It is Pinkerton's child, after all. But something in her manner gave me to understand that this visit was not going to set a precedent.

September 30th.   I was pleased that C. has gone to see B., but afterwards was irked to hear her lament the child's fate. When I objected, she retorted, "You don't imagine he's going to come back here and live with them, do you?" Although I am not a hundred-percent sure he will, I argued that there was no reason to doubt his word. Charlotte poo-pooed it. The rich can do whatever they want, she said, and never pay the consequences; once back in the States, a man like him will easily find himself a suitable wife when he wants one. Which is surely true, but I could not resist opining that it wouldn't be so easy to find one to

· *Butterfly* ·

match Butterfly. This incensed C., who showered scorn upon me. "She's really got you bewitched, hasn't she," she jibed with a virulence unfamiliar to me. "You men, you're all the same," et cetera. Pinkerton, however, wasn't as much of a fool as that, she concluded; he wasn't one to let himself be caught forever in her wiles. "Don't imagine him to be like you," et cetera. Her remarks were most disagreeable, indeed abusive. I was distressed and angered to hear her talk like that, but didn't see any point in quarreling.

October 1st. Could C. be jealous? It would be too absurd, yet I cannot think of another explanation for her attitude. When I first got to know B. better, I did express my admiration for her rather freely. It never occurred to me that C. would read anything into it.

I had B.'s money delivered rather than go myself. The reason I gave was that I was too busy this afternoon, but was I really?

October 9th. Finally went to see B. after days of procrastination. She was on my mind a great deal, and I did want to see her, yet something always made me draw back from it.

She, at least, was in fine shape, up and around for the past several days and chipper as a lark. And delighted with her pretty infant. Pity P. isn't here to see them. Perhaps she'll miss him less, though, now that she's got her baby to keep her company.

October 25th. Letter from P. informing me that he's sailing on the 8th of November. Took B.'s letter to her myself so that we could celebrate the news. We did, with some fine *sake*.

November 1st. Visit to B., accompanied by Charlotte. B. quieter than usual. I had the feeling something was troubling her—was it only C.'s presence?

November 24th. No word from Pinkerton for the past several weeks. I suppose he is in the middle of the Pacific. I went to see B., who was bearing up courageously. She has stopped writing since learning that he was sailing, and she misses it; writing, at least, brought her a certain relief. It is strange that he should be so silent over the birth of his daughter. Since he knew when she was expecting, I should think he'd at least have written, even if her letter had gotten lost or delayed. I sensed B. was worried, but she would not let on.

December 1st. Still nothing from P.; I guess we'll just have to wait for him to show up in person—his ship should be coming in soon. Even though I was quite busy, I went myself to give B. her money. This time she could not refrain from expressing her concern. Is he sick? Could something have happened? I tried to comfort her by saying that he had no doubt been swamped during the weeks before his departure; the explanation was perfectly reasonable, yet somehow I felt uneasy about his silence myself.

December 5th. Pinkerton's letter—I am amazed and do not know what to think or say.

46

(Pinkerton's letter to Sharpless, dated November 4, 1897)

My dear Sharpless,

I am at a loss to formulate what I am about to ask of you. After all that has happened, you are sure to find my behavior strange, the more so as I cannot explain in detail. Circumstances unforeseen have forced me to acknowledge

· *Butterfly* ·

what I have so long refused to see, namely that my union with Butterfly is without future. I have thus resolved to sever my relationship with her without delay, for any prolongation of it can in the end only create more pain both for her and for myself. If you would with your inimitable tact convey this to Butterfly, I should be forever in your debt—as indeed I am already. In view of the circumstances, I prefer to abstain from direct correspondence with her; it would be pointless to open a discussion that cannot but be futile.

I am sending a draft of ten thousand dollars for Butterfly, plus five hundred for expenses. Please do all that propriety and decency call for and if possible a little more. I leave everything to your discretion and put my trust entirely in your good judgment.

Yours in friendship and gratitude,
HENRY PINKERTON

47

(The Nagasaki ms.)

I cannot find words to describe the four months covered by the fateful contract. During the entire period I lived as in a trance. My strange role fitted me with surprising ease, as if the part had been learnt long ago and needed only a little prompting to be revived. Wide-eyed and impassive in the manner of a dreamer who wonders at all and nothing, I followed my mistress in her vagaries, and though they took us far, the landscape never seemed altogether alien. Indeed I was like a somnabulist obeying some unknown call from the soul's abyss.

Stretched between ravages of the flesh and ravishments of the soul, my life insensibly drifted away from everyday reason and became so insensate, so truly insane, that in clearer moments I felt I would, by closing my eyes and giving myself a good shake, awaken from what seemed a rapturous nightmare. And in retrospect, the events, for all their vivid detail, tend to merge in a dreamlike tangle that resists contemplation. For what I lived from day to day was beyond the mind's imagining—not beyond what imagination can produce, but what imagination can square with reality, with reality soberly distilled and reconstituted to the familiar formula. It is fine to contemplate Jerome Bosch's grotesque creatures on a canvas, but will our imagination consent to jostle one in the street? Are such imaginary beings imaginable in the flesh?

The peculiar quality of this period eludes my pen. What I have set down makes its extravagance seem caricatural and dissuades me from extensive description of what I suffered—the indignities of Marika, who "trained" me; the derision of the two women; the violence they did to my body, mind and soul. Perhaps it is as well to pass over them quickly, for seen from this distance, the details, though lurid, tend monotonously to merge.

But there is one thing that I cannot gloss over, and though remembrance is painful, I must speak of it, as it was the moral pivot around which my life would turn.

My titular mistress's first command was to sever all ties with Butterfly. Communication was to terminate forthwith. At Kate's behest, I wrote to the vice-consul whom I had charged to look after Butterfly, asking him to convey to her my decision to break off relations. The absence of explanation—none was permitted—made me a cad twice over, but in any case I should have been hard put to explain.

Nor was this all. Not content to banish Butterfly from my life, Kate set about with diabolical cunning and thoroughness to demolish the Butterfly in my heart. Every relic I possessed was confiscated and defiled in the most scurrilous fashion, then destroyed. Worse, in session after session of "confession," my memories were ransacked, the most treasured wrenched from me and so insidiously besmirched that henceforth I could only try to avoid them in my shame.

Why did I permit it? Why did I acquiesce in sullying the woman I had loved, and loved still? What inner demon drove me to witness and even participate in acts that made me sicken with self-loathing and the desire for death? By comparison, the other torments Kate inflicted were as balsam, for the most egregious yielded their measure of perverse pleasure; whereas Butterfly's desecrated love festered like the wound of a poisoned arrow, next to which all else were but flamboyant whiplashes upon the skin.

48

He had told her all there was to tell but still the inquisition pressed on. It was as if he had swallowed a piece of poison apple and were now racked by spasms which, though the stomach had rendered all, continued to pump stinging bitterness into his throat and mouth.

". . . so she cry 'Forgive me' when she come. Interesting. Tell us what names she call you when . . ."

Marika often surprised him with her knowledge of profane English; where could she have gotten it, if not from Kate? This, and the obscene testimonies Kate exacted, pointed to a familiarity with vulgar idiom hardly conceivable in a lady of her quality. But there could be no doubt about the skill with which she induced him to convert intimate moments into brutal, lewd language that disfigured them and stained them in his memory.

Nothing he could produce satisfied Kate, however. The farther she went, the more frenziedly she pushed on; it was as if she were wrenching at something that persisted in eluding her. In his abject abandon, Pinkerton did his best to help. But what she was after, he too could not reach. Although he could feel it almost palpably—as could she, no doubt—he had no words to grasp it.

Perhaps in evading their words, that fugitive quantity so grimly pursued escaped their hell. For if Pinkerton's hell was more than words, words were the precipitants that caused it to emerge and take form. What words captured, hell retained; but what lay beyond words remained free.

One day, as if a dam had burst, a deep sadness swept over Pinkerton, so swiftly and poignantly that tears spurted from his eyes. Marika would have beaten him, but she was stopped.

While he wept and for some time afterward, Kate stared in ominous silence. Her face was livid. "Damn you," he thought he heard her mutter. After that she no longer asked about Butterfly.

49

(From Sharpless's journal)

December 6th. Hard to imagine what could have happened. Pressure from his family? A hitch from the political side? Perhaps now that he is settling into his father's shoes, life is presenting itself as less simple than he had imagined, with rules that even a Pinkerton cannot escape. Charlotte's feminine view is that he has fallen in love with another woman. She seems very sure, but I am not convinced.

What to say to B.? Tell her outright what is in P.'s letter? Invent something less brutal? "Use my inimitable tact"—damn him! What tact in the world could make his message acceptable?

· *Butterfly* ·

I hadn't bargained for acting the go-between in this kind of delicate business. To my mind, if a man decides to run out on a woman, he ought to have the courage to tell her himself. It is not clear to me just why Pinkerton shouldn't, though I can understand how he might *want* to fob it off.

December 9th. Finally wrote to P. telling him to inform B. directly of his decision. Charlotte derided my hesitation, asserting that I was blowing it up out of all proportion: if I consent to P.'s request, I should do it without such a fuss. According to her it's no big deal. I should not have expected such callousness, because she is not a callous soul. Does this intense prejudice stem from B.'s immoral past, or from the fact that she is Japanese? I can't imagine Charlotte taking such an attitude toward an American girl in similar circumstances. Yet how can it escape her that whatever B. may be, her feelings are no different from those of any other woman? C. does agree that I have no obligation to transmit such a message, for P. or anyone else.

December 10th. Visit to B. I had gone with half a mind to tell her everything (I had come around to thinking that P. was perhaps not entirely wrong—probably I would break it more gently to her than an unkind letter). But in her presence my courage flagged. She was like a flower of love in bloom, breathing her faith as naturally as clear spring air. To utter anything against it would have been like brutally plucking petals in full blossom. Girding myself to deliver the little speech I had prepared, I had to remind myself forcibly of what necessity dictated. But at that very moment we were interrupted by the cry of the baby awakening. B. picked her up in her arms and started talking to her, asking whether she saw that I was there, the man who was her father's friend and who would be bringing him back to them any day now. (Not sure what she said, but with my poor

Japanese, that's what I managed to glean.) After that my resolve weakened and all I was able to get out was that P. had written briefly to say he had not sailed as planned, and that unforeseen complications were delaying his return: B. was not to worry, he would write to her when things let up a little. I was absolutely miserable saying this, and possibly that gave me away, because B. turned ashen. The transformation in her face was frightening to behold. The life, confidence, and joy that had so abounded drained away before my eyes and for a moment left her face void of life. Alarmed, I tried to reassure her, but she stopped me by saying very quietly, "He has another woman." I was startled that she should instantaneously jump to the same conclusion as Charlotte, and I began to protest that this assumption was groundless. Her grave demeanor, however, cut short my expostu- lation. It had taken her but a second to gather herself; during that time she had apparently sized up the situation and taken her stance. I was reduced to silence by her quiet dignity and courage in the face of an adversity whose extent I knew more explicitly, if not better, than she herself. In my eyes she appeared transfigured. At that moment, I would have given anything in the world to alter Pinkerton's decision, had it but been in my power to do so.

To me she asked, "He says he will write to me?" At that point I had no choice but mendaciously to assent; but I resolved to see to it that P. does not make a liar out of me. I read in her eyes the questions "Why did he not write this to me directly?" and "Why hasn't he written all this time if he did not sail?" but she did not press the point. I wished I could somehow comfort her and took my leave with a heart aching with sorrow and impotence.

December 11th.   Wrote to P. telling him of my interview with Butterfly. With all due respect for the reasons he surely has for his decision, I urged him to reflect again, before taking any step that is irrevocable, upon the seriousness of some things in life and the effects one's action may have on others. If he must abandon Butterfly, there is nothing for me to say, but he should, I again insisted, show at least enough consideration to write to her, and write in such a way as to cause her the least pain.

Writing the letter, however, did nothing to calm my unrest. On the contrary, I despaired at its futility. Deep down I do not believe I can influence him a whit in this matter. A change of heart, while not impossible, is all too unlikely. By refusing to act as his envoy, I force him to write her a letter, but what good ultimately is that?

December 12th. B. has written a long letter to P., which she brought to my office in a thick envelope. It oppressed me, perhaps with a feeling of guilt, for if I had spoken as I had intended, she would not have gone to this futile effort, whose product will elicit no response and might not even be read for all one knows. While putting her letter as usual into an envelope for diplomatic mail, I noticed it had not been properly sealed; seized all at once by an impulse I cannot explain, I opened it and with beating heart perused the pages. Though written in often ungrammatical English, it is an eloquent, even beautiful composition, at once reassuring and playful; while evoking their past happiness, it affirms the present that binds them more strongly than ever in the form of little Etsuko—of whom she paints a lively and delightful picture. She chides him for his prolonged silence, but very gently, and goes on to talk with great understanding about him and his needs—his future, his career, the need for freedom that a young man has. He should, she emphasizes, feel free to do as he wishes; she has no desire to tie him down in any way, nor does she feel they must necessarily live together all year round. She would feel comfortable with the arrangement that best suits his needs, however unconventional or strange it might seem to others, because the love that holds them together is strong enough to permit what others cannot afford. She clearly hints, though she does not explicitly state it, that she would tolerate another woman in his life—that, when it comes down to it, he is free to practice bigamy. This shocked me considerably. My first reaction was that no self-respecting woman could stoop to such a shameless proposal. I felt ashamed for Butterfly, and angry, for I felt somehow betrayed, I who had been treating her as honest when her mentality remained that of a kept woman. In thinking about it more, however, my censoriousness abated. I began to see that she had formed her own idea of how things stood and was proceeding according to a conscious strategy. This filled me with admiration, and also a certain uneasiness.

Would her strategy work? Judging from what Pinkerton wrote to me, I doubt it, though we won't know until he replies to B.'s letters or mine. I worry about the many weeks this will take, since she will be constantly waiting for a letter I have stupidly misled her into expecting.

December 17th.   Yesterday I did a strange thing. I drafted a letter to Butterfly, a letter that I imagined P. to have written— more correctly, a letter I'd have wished P. to write. I did it idly, as if daydreaming. The phrases were already there in my head; after I read B.'s letter, they started forming on their own. All I had to do was jot them down, and it was done in a trice, before I had quite taken in what I was doing. When I read the result, I felt ashamed and at the same time wildly excited.

A wave of euphoria came over me; I felt like laughing and talking to myself aloud. Suddenly I thought, Why shouldn't she read it? It contained no falsehoods, fostered no delusions; in fact the content was quite harmless, a gentle plea to be patient, no more. There was nothing P. might not have written, nothing inconsistent with the facts: He was being kept very busy, and—this idea came to me in a flash—he had broken his right hand in a fall from a horse. Reluctant to let his secretary into the privacy of his correspondence with her, he had written instead to me. His hand, however, was taking too long to recover, and now he had recourse to his sister for typing more personal things. This, I thought, would not only account for his long silence but for any difference in style or tone from previous letters written in his own hand; even a sister would considerably inhibit expressions of affection, for instance.

I waited until the others had gone home, then produced my typed copy on the machine by picking out the keys one by one. The operation was slow and laborious and I made numerous mistakes, which I soon gave up trying to correct; it is in fact reasonable to assume that P.'s sister is no more expert than I at operating such a machine. The problem was the seal; in the end I affixed a seal that only resembled P.'s, banking on Butterfly's impatience to help her overlook this detail. I was in a feverish state by the time I held the finished handiwork in my hands.

I was too worked up last night to record what I had done, and I lay awake for a long time. There were moments when it seemed like a silly prank, and at other moments it seemed fraught with unnameable peril. I certainly felt uneasy, yet no matter how much I turned it over in my mind, I found no good practical reason for not going through with it. The letter would surely bring comfort to B. and make her easier for a time—that is, until P.'s real letter comes (and I still hope against hope that it will say something unexpected); and there is no way it can harm her, since it contains no promises of any sort.

Nonetheless I had some difficulty getting myself to deliver it this afternoon. I trembled as I approached her house and felt almost ill when I handed it to her, but my anguish was for naught. She was delighted to get it, and at my insistence read it on the spot. I watched her peruse the page, her delicate features contracted from the effort of deciphering the alien script. I felt as if I were looking into a mirror to my soul, and my anguish turned into gratification as an inner light brightened her face like the sun shining through dark clouds. Her entire being seemed to dimple with new life; she was like a flower breathing in the dew. For that sight alone, I would have committed crimes less venial than my small deception.

We chatted for a little. When I left, I felt lighter than I had in days.

50

(The Nagasaki ms.)

For a long time I clung to the belief that if I had only imagined how things would turn out, I could have resisted Kate. But I no longer know. My pain was genuine, as was my despair, and yet . . . Can I be sure of not having perversely savored the pain? Did my very despair not threaten to spill over into a berserk holocaustal joy? If in defiling Butterfly I was trampling underfoot the dearest and best of all I had known, did that not feed my devotion to Kate and bind us tighter together in our unholy convenant? Did Abraham grieve to sacrifice Isaac, or rejoice?

Yet I would not have let Butterfly put that blade into herself, of that I remain persuaded. Although I could not easily have crossed Kate, who had become my life, I would have given up life itself before seeing Butterfly come to such a pass. Only I never imagined she might. I knew the strength of her love and could guess her suffering, but I also knew that everything in her character spoke against suicide: she was too strong for that, too solid and canny. Exquisite as she was, she was no hothouse graft but more a wild flower whose beauty rises irrepressibly out of the earth, nurtured by the sun and rain. And not in the most despairing circumstances could I have imagined the woman I knew to abandon her child.

What I did not know, alas, was the depth of Kate's rancor, and how relentless would be her vengeance.

51

Butterfly's had been small and tight, rising from the backs of her thighs like little apples. Marika's, even though her muscles were as well-developed, were larger and softer. There was an air of sensuality about them that sometimes struck Pinkerton as obscene; at such times he saw in them the same wanton twist that often made Marika's features seem to drip with lust. Considering how little mobility these anatomical parts enjoyed, they were curiously expressive; indeed at moments they seemed to be just as expressive as her face. Or did that only come from concentrating so long on them?

"No!" Marika interrupted, possibly for the hundredth time; her exasperation carried a hint of amusement and perhaps of malice. "No, no, no! You will never serve her if you do not learn better." Marika seldom referred to Kate by any term other than the third personal pronoun. "Your tongue is more strong than before, but still not enough strong. It must be able to go in and out like a finger and, how you say—*se tordre comme un serpent*. Eh?—yes, writhe like snake." She twisted around, and an astonishing length of tongue flashed out all the way to the tip of her nose, which it tapped three times before making an incredible flourish worthy of circus billing. Her demonstrations amazed him each time and made him despair.

"Again, from the beginning! You do not put enough warmth in your lips. Love, love with the lips. Slowly. No! You do not love, I feel you do not love them. Think they are hers, believe it—I tell you, you must love them exactly as if they are hers. It is not enough to pretend. Look first. They must be beautiful to you, most beautiful in the world; they must make you want to die. Look at them, love with the eyes. Then you really see. Make your eyes drunk, your nose, lips . . . Adore . . . Now the hands, gently, yes. Feel it all with the hands—make them sensitive, very sensitive. *Oui, c'est ça* . . . a little more. Slow, yes . . . harder . . .Concentrate. A slave must learn to concentrate completely . . . so completely that nothing exist outside his mistress. Concentrate, make yourself part of your mistress; go inside her skin, go inside her bum, become one with it. That is what being slave means: you are nothing, you have no existence, you are just a part of the mistress, a part that is completely *insignifiant*, no more than a *composant* of the thing she wants served—her bum, her foot . . . maybe a finger, a hair. . . ."

One morning early in his apprenticeship, Pinkerton had been called to Kate's bedroom. Kate lay hidden among the bedclothes while Marika, straddling her legs, massaged her thighs and buttocks. From where he was ordered to kneel, he could see Marika's face and movements, but nothing of Kate. Pinkerton had been impressed by the way the girl put her entire body and mind into her movements, and even more by her look of intense concentration that bordered on rapture. With its heavily drooping eyelids and half-parted lips, her face wore the expression of a woman rocking astride a lover or transported by religious inspiration. Fascinated but also a little embarrassed, he had let his eyes sink, only to be sharply reprimanded: he was there to learn, and that meant giving his entire attention to each moment and gesture. Did he imagine that competence as a slave could be

· *Butterfly* ·

gained without effort? Pity the fool given to such delusion! Not having reflected upon the difficulty of performing what he was there to observe, Pinkerton had taken the rebuke as another instance of the arbitrary fault-finding and needling that were apparently part of his initiation. But the subsequent sessions with Marika changed his understanding.

In the beginning, when Butterfly was still much on his mind, he would compare. It dismayed him to discover how shallow was his knowledge of Butterfly—what did he know of her heart's inner chambers or the treasury of her soul, he wondered, if he was uncertain about these outward regions where his pleasure had so often grazed and explored? For Butterfly, untrammeled by notions of shame, had offered her posterior as freely as any other bodily part, and his own avid attentions had never been shy; but their caresses, free as birds that seldom alight for long on a single branch, never obsessively dwelled but progressed contrapuntally, as it were, in a symphonic paean of love. At least this was how it seemed in Pinkerton's memory.

Those distant images, wistful and frail, dissolved all too easily, however, before the more substantial object of his daily devotions. Day after day, hour upon hour, its implacable cheeks were thrust at him to be nursed, rubbed, spoken to, fawned upon, and caressed with all the caresses his mortal parts could bestow; breathed, tasted, kneaded, contemplated, worshipped, adored. It became his companion, his mirror; his pillow, garden, shrine; his mentor and ward, his tormentor and mistress; his prison cell and his patch of sky. All this so intensely and for so long that in the end he needed no fleshly reminder to sense its solid presence and conjure up every detail: grafted to his mind, it had taken on a special reality all its own.

Then one day he noticed a subtle transparency in its surfaces and textures, and he could see darkly past it toward another, larger than life, that was starting to form in his interior vision.

52

(The Nagasaki ms.)

The terms of the contract, as Kate saw fit to implement them, wrapped around my life like powerful tentacles that untiringly probed and gripped every aspect and detail. Never for a moment was I allowed to forget that I now belonged to her, that I existed only as her thing.

Little of my time was spent in her company, but she made her presence felt in other ways. Ten minutes out of each hour I had to spend kneeling before her portrait; installed in my room upon her orders, the photograph served as my private altarpiece, my personal icon. This ritual and others were devised to keep my thoughts at all moments on a short leash; a number of them involved objects and relics, certain unmentionable, that stirred the senses and kept my excitation at a painful level. Stoked without respite and denied release, my passion mounted from day to day and sweltered unbearably as in an airtight kiln.

53

The photograph showed Kate in full face, with piercing eyes that looked straight out of the frame; her expression was serious, even stern, but a shadow of mockery played around the lips. By some inspiration or fluke, the photographer had caught a force of character that Kate seldom permitted to show; it lurked behind the exquisite features, a streak of steel in the finest fur. Catching the eye and yet eluding it—like the flash of a sword sheathed before there has been time to look—this glint of cruelty gave her beauty an incisive edge that made it all the more thrilling.

54

(The Nagasaki ms.)

My daily visits, after the ritual *baise-pied*, began with a "confession." For this, I knelt before a screen set up together with a system of mirrors to give Kate a full view of me without exposing her to my eyes. Any infraction of her orders—wilful or unwitting, physical or mental—had to be reported. On some days this lasted only a few minutes, on others it turned into lengthy inquisitions during which I would be beaten or subjected to other humiliating practices. I never tried to hide anything; in fact, I often experienced a peculiar satisfaction in revealing my innermost thoughts and feelings, some of which I had never dared acknowledge to myself. My only reticence came from a sense of embarrassment, caused partly by Marika's presence, which at first bothered me so much that I protested—with what baleful results one can imagine. No doubt I was also jealous of her, who though a fellow "slave" lorded it over me and enjoyed an intimacy with Kate that I hardly dared dream of. But I soon grew accustomed to Marika's position in the house, as I did to everything else.

At the end of my confession, Kate would mete out the punishment and issue her instructions for the day. I then offered my ritual expression of gratitude and would be granted a minute or two—never more—to kiss and caress her feet. This was the moment so ardently anticipated, toward which all my tormented desire was directed and for which I lived; for even though the contract permitted free homage to her feet, I seldom had opportunity to exercise that right.

The rest of the visit was taken up by menial tasks which Marika assigned at her pleasure—even these were given a ritual cast—or by "training" of a more specific nature.

The hour and a half specified by the contract would be extended, occasionally and later regularly, by as much as fifteen hours. But I was never spared the long ride home, even when it meant riding back again almost immediately; the ride too was part of the ritual. My visits were all but pleasant or pleasurable in any ordinary sense, yet not once in my memory did I not secretly rejoice at being kept longer, even when I knew what torments awaited me or what degrading or tiring chores; and I seldom left the house without feeling braced and mysteriously exalted.

55

It was of black morocco, so slight and delicately wrought that it seemed more suited to a woman's finer frame. "Do you know what it is?" Kate asked.

He knew, and blushed scarlet because he had known instantly. Women in medieval times were said to have worn them, wives of crusaders, mistresses of kings; but he had never seen one, or even known for certain that they existed. The thought of wearing such a thing drew from him a soft involuntary moan of horror and something else. His cheeks aflame, he shook his head.

"Liar!" hissed Marika. "How dare you lie to the mistress!" She took a quick step forward and her hands flew out at him, one after the other, deliberately and hard. The blows stunned and nearly knocked him over, and tears came to his eyes, as much out of vexation as pain, for he was not yet used to Marika humiliating him in front of Kate. He had to confess that he had guessed, but no one was interested when he tried to explain what he had thought and felt. Marika, grasping his hair, pulled his head so far back that his body, arching backward, exposed more clearly his condition—he was naked as usual. "Let the mistress see how big it make you," she sneered. She held him in the uncomfortable position for a long moment, then violently shoved his head forward in the direction of Kate's feet. "Now thank the mistress!"

Attached to the soft slender strips was a small elongated cup of hard leather with an opening at the end. It seemed tiny next to what it was intended to contain; he could not begin to fit into it in his present state. Eventually, after a long wait, his exaltation subsided, only to rise unmanageably again the moment Marika approached with the receptacle. In the end they resorted to ether; when he awoke, it had been fastened and locked. The sight of the fine black strips clinging to his skin made him feel a little sick, whether from disquiet—was this to be a permanent part of his body?—or from emotion he could scarce have said.

The belt was cleverly designed so that after a little habituation, its presence was felt only in a state of arousal; then, however, it became quite uncomfortable, and any manipulation caused intense pain. A small lock was built into the buckle that held together the different straps.

"I shall keep the key," Kate told him. "Marika will ask me for it when you need cleaning."

Pinkerton, who at this point was still capable of spontaneous protest, was considerably distressed. "But what if you should . . ."

"Lose it? Or suddenly die?" Kate laughed wickedly. "I guess your little peashooter will stay in there until it rots." Leather, of course, could easily be cut, but the mere idea of being permanently imprisoned in such a contraption caused an inrush of blood in more than one place.

Marika's lips curled maliciously. "Look at how he make the grimace," she observed. "*En plus* it excite him—look!" The two women joined in laughter, but the transformation in his anatomy caused Pinkerton too much discomfort for him to care; the pain sobered him, however, and that in turn eased the pain.

As he was forbidden to touch himself, it fell to Marika to wash him. To his surprise, she always did this in a matter of fact way, like a nurse, without repugnance or irritation or salacious commentary. On these occasions some of the affection he had once felt for her would come back. Surprisingly, the undisguisable pleasure he took in being handled did not provoke her derision; it seemed even to inspire a certain tenderness. Her only complaint was that it always took so long to get him back into harness; yet she never threatened to stop or change the practice. Once, encouraged by her bonhomie, he begged her to relieve the frustration that brooded so cruelly; the request got him a whipping he did not soon forget.

But this changed nothing; when she washed him, her attitude remained cheerful and distantly maternal. She appeared to him then like a simple country girl, and he would wonder fleetingly whether it was not only in these moments that she was really herself. She cleaned him conscientiously and with dependable regularity, much as she might have cared after a farm animal or a dog.

56

(End of Kate's letter of May 6, 1910, to her goddaughter Cécile; see Chapter 19.)

. . . forever his goddess, which is what the word "domination" means, as you, a good Latinist, needn't be reminded.

To conclude, stick to the two cardinal rules: first, keep

· *Butterfly* ·

him in a state of permanent frustration. Never grant him relief—never! His chastity is your surest guarantee of continued submission. There are many ways of enforcing it, and an ingenious little person like yourself will certainly come up with some piquant ones; but since chastity is not a natural state, a belt in the long run is most serviceable.

The second rule is to keep his frustration tied to your person through constant stimulation. Again the possibilities are limitless, but nothing is more powerful than your own body. The art of it lies in always granting him just enough to madden him with desire, but never so much that he feels he has possessed a part of you. Do not think yourself so secure in your domination that you can deny him entirely; deprive him of his daily dose of pacification and you may have a Spartacus on your hands.

These two rules constitute the essentials. Other aspects, such as the ritualization I spoke of earlier, are useful and interesting but secondary. Master the essentials, and everything else will fall into place by itself.

I close on a final word of advice: push your slave mentally as far as ingenuity permits, but physically no more than necessary. Corporal punishment has its place, but a self-respecting mistress will not use it in place of the imagination. The slave should fear the worst, but his fear should not be turned into fact. Mistreatment in itself is of no interest, and a maimed or dead slave is little use and much trouble. I know that you are a sensible girl, Cécile, but you have a spot of cruelty which, though a delicious finishing touch to your beauty, could, if excessively indulged, become your undoing.

And now, having thrown in my grain of godmotherly admonition, I shall send you off on your conquests with my blessing and wait for an account, which I trust will be delivered soon by your own pretty lips.

57

December 19th. Butterfly came in the afternoon with a letter for P. It was pretty nippy out and her face was ruddy. Or maybe just flushed with happiness. In any case it became her. Certainly in a gay mood, she bustled in like an excited child. I wanted to hug her and bounce her on my knee. It was gratifying to see the transformation, but also worrying that a letter, especially one so poor in content, could have such an effect.

After she left, I sat for a long time with her letter in my hands. There was no question but that I would read it, yet despite this foregone conclusion, I hesitated and went through all the throes of a rebellious conscience. In fact, it was more difficult than the first time, because then she had been troubled and I was prying solely out of concern, whereas now . . . Of course I had to check her letter for telltale allusions to the counterfeit, but in opening it I still felt more like a petty thief than a Robin Hood.

Once more her letter touched me deeply. I wanted to lay my head on the desk and cry. How many of us have ever received such a letter in their lives? It was poetic yet utterly unpretentious, light and playful yet informed by the deepest, most tender sentiments. Although there was no direct reference to my letter, everything she wrote was clearly in response to it, so that I could not but feel that in some way her words were addressed to me. It was not without a pang of regret that I resealed it and put it into the outgoing mail. If only that Pinkerton would better deserve it! I'm still praying for a change of heart and doing my best not to think further on it.

·   *Butterfly*   ·

December 20th. Finally, something turned up for B.'s Christmas present: an ancient Italian looking-glass in a rich frame inlaid with precious stones, very beautiful. The captain let me have it for two hundred and twenty dollars, swearing up and down that it was worth three-fifty if not four. I had been prepared to spend all of the five hundred dollars P. had sent for "expenses," but it is hard to find something really nice. I had thought of jewelry as being the most likely thing for P. to send, but what I've seen has not appealed to me. It had to be something Occidental, of course, and something Pinkerton might by some stretch of the imagination have chosen. For our gift, I settled on a jade pendant from China (which cost a bit more than what I told Charlotte—I have the feeling she would as soon have left Butterfly off our Christmas list, though she did not say anything to that effect).

December 22nd. Brought B. her presents. She was terribly pleased, and touched, and I do believe genuinely surprised. She was familiar with the Christmas tradition, but I don't think she was expecting anything from P., who did not even send anything when little Etsuko was born. The excuse was that he was expecting to return in person, but the argument, if reasonable, somehow lacks conviction. This was probably why she did not send him a Christmas present either, though she had thought of it—so she intimated—when she learned he would not be back so soon. We talked about Christmas back home and how it was celebrated at my parents' and at Charlotte's. She showed me Pinkerton's gift from last year, a beautiful ancient *koto*, and played a couple of tunes on it at my request—very prettily and, so far as I can judge, expertly. I should have liked to invite her for Christmas dinner—with the children back in the States, it was not unthinkable—but refrained as I knew it would not please

Charlotte. There is the Christmas Eve party at the consulate, but she would never consider going to that—certainly not without Pinkerton.

December 23rd. Spent most of the day on a letter to B. Just as opening hers was more of a hurdle the second time round, so was writing mine. Everything seemed difficult; I labored over each sentence, each detail. Should I open with "My dear" as I had last time? That question alone took an hour to ponder. Fortunately, the visit yesterday enabled me to work in a discreet allusion to the *koto* and to last year's Christmas. I then recounted at some length a story of how he had been shown the mirror by an antiquarian friend and immediately saw a vision of her face in it. It lasted for several seconds and was of breathtaking beauty. After that, of course, he simply had to procure it for her, over the protests of his resisting friend. I got rather carried away and had to prune my drafts considerably before arriving at a version that appeased my better judgment.

December 24th. Delivered letter this morning. It was a second Christmas present, and I suspect one that gave her as much pleasure if not more. She did like the mirror very much though—which was gratifying; she showed it to me excitedly, had never seen anything like it. I chided her for unwrapping her presents before Christmas and she blushed like a little girl caught with her hand in the stocking. She was so pretty it was all I could do not to hug her.

She had prepared gifts that she was going to have sent to us later that day: a lovely kimono for C., and for me a stunning dwarf maple called *yatsubusa*, apparently over thirty years old. There was also a box of sweet Japanese delicacies.

· *Butterfly* ·

December 25th.   A number of Japanese friends from the Christian community were at the party last night, and I caught myself thinking more than once that Butterfly would not have been out of place there. In spite of myself, I felt irritated with Charlotte, because if she had been friendly, we could certainly have taken B. My irritation continued all day today, and I had to make a real effort to keep it from flaring up against C., who of course was entirely innocent. The two of us spent the day quietly. This is the first time the children are away, and though C. prepared Christmas dinner as usual, the festive spirit was missing. I kept thinking against my will how different it could have been if we had invited B. It would have been a novel way of celebrating Christmas, but it would have been warm and fun, whereas with just the two of us, it felt cold and rather gloomy. I kept thinking resentfully that C. might have extended an invitation after accepting B.'s lavish gift. Her stiff-upper-lippish attempts at being merry only made me feel more peevish. I had intended to show myself affectionate and grateful to her on this special day; with this in mind, I had even looked forward to our Christmas alone. But I simply did not have it in me. My arms felt dead when I put them around her, and my lips seemed so cold that I was embarrassed to touch them to her cheeks.

December 29th.   For the past three days I've been making up another letter for B. in my head. Perhaps just to have a reason to go and see her. But putting it on paper is another matter.

December 30th.   Sachiko brought a letter to be mailed. I kept her for a chat. She asked me when I thought P. would be coming back. When I said I did not know, she asked me point-blank if he was at all. She clearly had her doubts. Apparently, both she and her mistress believe that P. has found another woman, but they are divided on its consequences. B. thinks she could still persuade him to keep her as his wife, or at least as a second wife; Sachiko is more skeptical, thinks B. should make other plans so as not to waste her youth in futile waiting. What did she mean, I asked? Well, she could marry someone else; it appears that a marriage broker had come with a proposition, which in Sachiko's opinion B. rejected with undue haste, even vehemence. I energetically defended Butterfly, but after Sachiko left, I began to wonder what was right. I had to admit to myself that the chances of P. coming back were slight. What ought B. to do? I imagined a letter arriving, embarrassed and full of self-serving explanations, and shattering in a single moment all her hopes and illusions— illusions I was helping to foster. Extravagant ideas came into my head, such as going myself to fetch Pinkerton. But they were all impracticable and thinking about them only made me feel powerless and despondent.

58

One may wonder at Pinkerton's persistent docility in the face of outrageous treatment. Granted that passion can give rise to the strangest behavior, and that in certain moments all is possible: what about all the other moments of the day? Was there no limit to his endurance? Had he never an impulse to rebel?

Indeed he had. During the first weeks, hardly a day went by without a resolution to end his absurd bondage. In the privacy of his room, he suffered fits of indignation. Then he would revile Kate's barbarity and defy her with resounding speeches; once he even wrote a letter. On sober mornings he swore not to go back to Creighton, not that afternoon, not ever again. But his resolve invariably weakened after lunch; at two-fifteen his horse would be waiting, and at four he would be confessing his velleities.

What compelled his unswerving adherence to a contract that no one could enforce? In the first place fear. Although only a negligible amount of bodily harm was actually inflicted, the threat of torture was never absent, and it was Kate's art to make him feel that nothing was beyond her imagination and power. Even in sober moments, Pinkerton would shudder at the thought that, should he break away, he might be pursued and gruesomely punished (as was provided for by the contract). Rationally, he was sure Kate would not take such extreme measures, but that did not cancel his terror.

The deeper fear, however, was of being definitively banished. If ever he should stay away, Kate had warned, he must stay away for good. This, his mutinous outbursts notwithstanding, he was never ready to do. For at no time did he entirely renounce Kate's love. Lost, her love was like a magnificent wine that had been spilled and whose dregs he now treasured almost more than the wine itself while the bottle was full.

Sometimes Pinkerton's mind boggled at his situation, it seemed so preposterous; at such moments he was tempted to tear up the contract. But the sense of absurdity, of hollow unreality, always veered back to a renewed reverence for his mistress, indeed to a quasi-religious awe, and like a penancing mystic after a bout with temptation, he would want to push back still further the limits of his surrender; had it been possible, he would have etched their covenant into skin and flesh and engraved it on his heart.

59

(The Nagasaki ms.)

As the weeks wore on, I lost myself more and more in Kate. Toward the end of the trial period, I became occasionally aware of a heightened concentration, as if the divers elements of my existence, from thoughts and feelings down to everyday odds and ends, were all converging in the person of my mistress, or at some invisible point beyond. As discipline leached my passion, that beauty which daily drew me on—and which I was forbidden to contemplate in the flesh though my life was organized to worship it—receded past its dazzling surface toward a splendor subtler than that of mortal substance lusted after by the mortal eye. From the woman I loved, Kate became the avatar of something beyond fleshly ravagements and fleshly desire. My whole life was nothing but a prayer to it—an idolater's, but prayer nonetheless. And to the extent that it laid waste my manhood, I came to know a bliss as ethereal and pure as a mystic anchoret's when he approaches oneness with the divine.

60

(The Nagasaki ms.)

After many weeks of dressage, I was gradually admitted into Kate's proximity. By the time our contract drew imperceptibly to its term, I was performing the services of a chambermaid. This new and hard-earned intimacy made it seem inconceivable that our bond should be severed, and though Kate intimated that she would be as punctilious in observing the contract's termination as in implementing its clauses, neither she nor I evidently believed for a moment that I would reclaim or indeed accept my liberty. On several occasions, a second and permanent contract was mentioned. The terms would be terrible and utterly uncompromising, I was given to understand, and I should do well to consider before binding myself to them for life. Such warnings did little more than fan the flames that consumed me and whose heat my lips sought feverishly to convey to mistress's feet.

What was my surprise when, upon expiration of our contract, Kate not only refused to consider a new one but proscribed all slavelike behavior as well as references to slavery. I was warned in particular against calling her "mistress"; and "unseemly" deportment such as falling on my knees would banish me forever. All those habits so laboriously and painfully inculcated during the four previous months were thus abrogated at a single stroke.

Abrogated, but not eradicated. After the very first day of enfranchisement, I knew to my alarm that never again could I be free; three days of it convinced me that I should go mad if I had to continue seeing Kate on this false "equal footing." For where the "slave" had enjoyed a degree of intimacy normally denied even a husband or lover, the "gentleman" had to observe the distance required of a stranger. Sitting stiffly opposite her on the divan with a teacup in my hand, I was bitterly struck by the contrast. While a slave, I had begun to fall in with her rhythms and to sense her predilections in a thousand little things, but now all those links and feelers dropped into the gulf that had opened up between the divan and Kate's armchair, and I became awkward and tongue-tied in her presence. When I tried to speak of this, Kate silenced me with a gesture of impatience.

I did not break the habit of presenting myself every afternoon, but our interviews were stiff and formal and became drier and shorter from one visit to the next; imperceptibly I had slipped into the role of the unwanted suitor whose presence is a strain on polite tolerance. But since nothing better came to mind, I continued my visits in the hope that something would change.

On the sixth afternoon, I was informed at the door that Kate was out. I was mortified at what I took to be my dismissal, which I had not expected to come so soon. I must have turned very pale, because Marika asked whether I was ill and wished to sit down. Then Kate really was absent! This assuaged my fears and I straightaway felt better, but I was grateful for the chance to talk with Marika, who, taking her cue from her mistress, was treating me with a distant, amnesiac politeness; I had once again become *Monsieur Henri*.

"She is out all afternoon," Marika told me. "So you must not wait for her. But I make you tea if you like."

I accepted a cup and, when she brought it, asked her to sit with me. "As *Monsieur* wish," she said and placed herself primly on the edge of an armchair.

"We're alone here, I presume, so why don't we drop the '*Monsieur*'? I don't see any reason for this ridiculous game of pretending that nothing's happened. Marika, surely we can speak openly, you and I?" I was at the end of my tether and spoke with a heated urgency.

Marika folded her arms and let herself fall back in the armchair. "As you wish. You want to say something particular to me?"

I was suddenly at a loss for words. "Well, you know . . ." I began, and immediately felt myself redden with emotion. "You know how I feel about . . . her. I would do anything for her, you know that, but she is making things so complicated. Why, Marika? Can you tell me? Because I don't understand it at all."

Marika stared at me as if she could not imagine of what I spoke. "Oh, you know very well what I mean," I burst out in exasperation. "This little game of politeness—this farce! If it's to get rid of me—certainly there are easier ways! But I'm not even

· *Butterfly* ·

convinced that she wants to get rid of me. We were, well . . .
she seemed satisfied with me, toward the end—she was, wasn't
she? Pretty much? So why stop? Why insist on making everything
different again? Is it just to play with me? I simply cannot figure it
out. What is it that she wants? Do you know?"

Marika fixed me with her large catlike eyes. "What do *you*
want?"

Once again I felt myself redden. "I? Oh, I . . . I just want to
stay with her. That's all I want . . . to be near her." The last
words trickled out tonelessly.

"As her slave?"

Surprised to hear the banned word pronounced that I had been
careful to avoid, I momentarily floundered. Part of me wanted to
object, but at bottom I knew the truth, even if a reluctance to
avouch it still lingered. "Yes," I murmured at last with lowered
eyes. "As her slave."

Marika was silent for a few seconds. "Why do you not ask for
her hand?"

"Her hand?"

"Yes, in marriage."

The idea seemed so incongruous that I simultaneously felt a
twinge of irritation and an impulse to laugh. "Please don't make
fun of me, Marika," I remonstrated dryly. "For me it is very
serious."

"I am serious too," Marika protested, but her eyes were bright
with mockery. "You are hopeless, you American men, you
undertand nothing. You come and you sit planted there stiff and
silent like a tree, and you expect a woman to give you what you
want. You do not make yourself agreeable, you do not bring
gifts—not even flowers! You do not give the smallest sign of your
sincerity, and then you say, 'I want to be slave, that's all I want!'
As if it is *rien du tout!*"

I stared at her dumbfounded.

"You think it is nothing to take a slave? You think it is easy to be a mistress? A mistress take responsibility for her slave, and it is for all the life. Only a husband is for all the life, but a husband, one is not responsible for him. You think marriage is a big affair, but taking a slave is bigger, much bigger! So one do not take a slave until he show himself really sincere."

"If anyone has shown himself to be sincere, it would be me," I protested heatedly. "How could she possibly doubt my sincerity? That's really absurd!"

"Then marry her."

Again I stared at Marika. "You talk as if all I had to do was ask! What about her? What possible reason would she have to marry me, if she is reluctant even to keep me as her . . . slave?"

"You are very innocent." Marika smiled. "You are from an excellent family, you are rich, you are *sortable*, you are docile. What reason more can there be? You make a suitable husband—and a woman always need a husband."

I had not thought of it this way and could not immediately adjust to the new perspective. "Do you think she would have me for a husband after . . . what we've had?"

Marika looked at me with a mixture of wonder and disdain. "But you do not imagine you will sleep in her bed because you marry her! *Ah non!*" She seemed tickled by that preposterous eventuality. "To the world you will be her husband, but at night you will lie at her feet, or outside the door." Her lips curled derisively and she added, "Like a dog."

· *Butterfly* ·

61

"So you think I should propose marriage," mused Pinkerton.
Even though he had done it once before and with success, all
that had happened since made it hard to imagine how he should
go about it now. "And you think she'll listen to me."

"She will listen to you," Marika said, "if you show you are
sincere."

Pinkerton threw up his hands. "What more can I do? If she
still isn't persuaded of my sincerity, I really don't see how I can
change it!"

"A little imagination, *Monsieur Henri*."

But his imagination, when he drew upon it, produced nothing
that Marika approved.

"Well, what would you do in my place?" he queried peevishly
when for the third time she scoffed.

"Write a pleasing letter," Marika threw out breezily. From the
tone of her voice, Pinkerton could not be sure whether she was
serious. "Ask for her hand, and say that you send her already the
wedding present. Attach your letter to a dog collar, put the collar
around your neck, and tie it to the porch." He looked at her in
wonder, so that after a moment she felt the need to expatiate.
"Then you ring the bell and wait, on your knees—in the snow is
even better. When she come to look, *remuer* your *queue* and lick
her feet." She looked at him fixedly while she spoke, but her gaze
was alive with little ripples of mirth.

"And forget not to bark!"

Laughter bubbled in her terrific eyes, and he could hear it
pealing long afterward even though he was not sure of having
heard it at the time.

62

Our engagement was announced in the middle of March. My mother, though less than overjoyed, gave us her blessing; I had feared her opposition because my father's will stipulated that she be given control of the entire estate in the event I should marry Kate. Lisa, on the other hand, was not as effusive as one might have expected. Since November, she had largely abstained from asking me about my relations with Kate, and this restraint had been too welcome at the time for me to question it; nor had she been seeing much of her friend. Only once, at Christmas, had the three of us been together, and then the festivities had helped mask the unnaturalness I felt; Kate as usual had been in complete mastery of herself. Sometime later Lisa did express concern over my air of preoccupation and on that occasion enquired about my courtship, for it was no secret that I was seeing a great deal of Kate; but she did not insist when I answered evasively. The reaction of my other relations went from grudging resignation to vociferous relief: whatever their estimate of Kate—and many had been influenced by my father's violent prejudice—they were all gratified that I had come to my senses in regard to Butterfly.

Two contracts defined my future with Kate. The first, the marriage contract, was nothing short of a travesty in its one-sided attribution of rights and obligations. While assuring her of a large fortune in every eventuality as well as unlimited freedom, it divested me in advance of any rights I should customarily and legally have enjoyed as her husband. Submissive though I had become, I could not but inwardly revolt against this outrage; but like yet another stone flung, it sank to the bottom of my heart's abyss and soon caused no more stir.

· *Butterfly* ·

The other contract specified the conditions of my slavery. Drafted along the lines of the temporary one but tauter and without a single escape clause, the implacable document roused in me a certain malaise. So far I had been dauntless in pushing back the limits of my bondage because, deadly earnest though it was, it had remained a game that would have its end; but now I became troubled by a murky presentiment of grave and sinister consequences beyond prevision or recall. This on the other hand only excited me further in my temptation and, like a novice trembling before the tonsure, I both dreaded and longed to contract that awful finality.

The contract of slavery was to be signed only at our wedding, whose date was not yet fixed. Kate had consented to a public engagement on the condition that she be assured of my freedom before marrying me. It was not enough to renounce seeing Butterfly again, however: I had to repudiate her in person, definitively and before Kate's eyes. This demand seemed highly perverse to me, but my opposition counted for nothing and an early date was fixed to avoid the hot summer weather. The prospect oppressed me considerably, for my heart still contracted each time I remembered the woman whom I had already so deeply wronged, and the thought of hurting her again was all but unbearable. But I knew that Kate would not be dissuaded and so tried instead to steel myself to the coming ordeal.

After our engagement, Kate and I slipped back into our former intimacy, with the difference that we now appeared in society as an affianced couple and consequently led a double life. I found the constant switching of roles strenuous, but it evidently amused Kate; gradually the strain diminished, however, and in time I became adept at changing identities at an instant's notice.

I felt uncomfortable writing to the vice-consul at Nagasaki to warn him of our arrival, for not long before I had received a letter brimming with indignation: he had pressed me to write to Butterfly, and I had declined.

63

(Text of the definitive contract.)

The undersigned Henry Benjamin Franklin Pinkerton, being of sound mind and body, hereby declares himself for the remainder of his natural life slave to the undersigned Kathleen Hamilton, who consents to proprietorship on the following conditions:

1· Mr. Pinkerton will relinquish autonomy over all mental, moral, and physical faculties in favor of Miss Hamilton; he shall at all times and in all eventualities be subject to her will and solely to her will. In obeying her, he shall disregard all other consideration of whatever nature, be it social, legal, moral, religious, or personal.

2· Mr. Pinkerton will forswear all familial, conjugal, social, and spiritual allegiance.

3· The person and property of Mr. Pinkerton will be put entirely at the disposal of Miss Hamilton. Her rights over these will be unconditional; they will include the right to mutilate, alienate, and destroy Mr. Pinkerton's person and property, or any part thereof, in any and every manner or form.

4· Mr. Pinkerton's condition of slavery will be absolute, permanent, and irrevocable; it will not be subject to abrogation by the will of the undersigned, singly or jointly. Mr. Pinkerton will enjoy no rights or claims of any kind.

5· Miss Hamilton will privately acknowledge Mr. Pinkerton as her slave; beyond this she will have no obligation whatsoever toward or regarding Mr. Pinkerton.

· *Butterfly* ·

64

[Editor's note: The following is taken from an interview I had in October 1978 with Mrs. Milly Davenport, widow to David Sharpless, a grandson of the one-time vice-consul at Nagasaki. Her account comprises not only memories of conversations but portions of dialogues and commentary recorded in the elder Sharpless's diary, which she had practically memorized verbatim through repeated reading. The first of the two pertinent volumes of that diary contains the entries reproduced above; the second was destroyed in 1976, when Mrs. Davenport lent it to a friend whose Irish setter, attracted by the leather binding, chewed it beyond restoration. The contents, however, have largely survived thanks to Mrs. Davenport's excellent memory.]

M.D.: Oh, Dada was riled all right when he got that letter—it wasn't even a letter, just a note, with no reasons given, nothing. And he was troubled, too, because what was he going to do now? Here he'd been writing those letters to her waiting for the day that Pinkerton feller's letter gets there, just filling in the time, kind of, and now Pinkerton says he won't write. Pretty fix, isn't it? Well, the first thing Dada did was to sit himself down and write to Pinkerton to tear a strip off him.

P.L.: Pardon? Tear a what?

M.D.: Tear a strip off him—it means to tell someone off real good. *(Laughs.)* Sorry about that. It's because your English is so good I wasn't payin' attention. I'll try to talk more properly.

P.L.: Oh, don't worry about that, I'm always happy to learn new expressions. But please go on with your story.

M.D.: Where was I? Oh yes, Dada's letter. Well, writing took a load off his chest, but it didn't get him out of the jam. He used to tell me it was the worst fix he'd ever gotten into in his life. There he was writing love letters to a married woman under her own husband's name—'cause love letters are what they were, no matter what he thought they were when he wrote them—writing them to a foreigner and him with a wife and family. 'Did you ever think of runnin' away with her, Dada?' I'd tease him. I wasn't much more than a girl then, and I was something of a hell-raiser in my time. He'd just smile, and you knew that the thought had been in his head, only he wouldn't say. Oh, he'd never have gone through with it, of course; he was a fine man, a gentleman like they used to make them, and not the kind to run out on his family.

"Well, supposing you hadn't had a family," I'd say, you know, just to prod him.

And he'd sigh and reply in that deep steady voice of his: "I dare say I might've done just that, Milly."

"Then you'd be sitting on a verandah someplace in Japan this very moment," I'd say, "talking Japanese to a Japanese grand-daughter-in-law."

And he'd get this misty look in his eyes and after a while he'd say, "Yes, I guess I would."

We'd had this same conversation I don't know how many times, because I loved to hear him talk about Japan—that was his great adventure, you know—and in those days we were alone a lot, the two of us. Dave and I'd moved into the house when we got married because Grandma Charlotte had died the year before and it was pretty lonesome for Dada to have that whole house to himself—it was too big even for the two of them, him and Grandma Charlotte. And then when Dave—"

P.L.: Excuse me, what year was that when all this happened?

M.D.: Let's see, we got married in the spring of 'thirty-seven, so Grandma Charlotte must have died in 'thirty-six, in the fall.

· *Butterfly* ·

P.L.: How old was your husband's grandfather then, do you know?

M.D.: Well, Dada was eighty-seven when he died, and that was 1940, just before Pearl Harbor. I'm glad he didn't live to see that, because with the soft spot he had for Japan, it would've broken him up. But the Lord was merciful, though I didn't think so at the time. I thought he'd have lived to be a hundred—but then he'd have been there to see Dave get killed. Another grandson, Dave's cousin Billy, also died in the war, but Billy was a pilot and you kind of expected it, but a doctor like Dave . . . Dada was born in 1853, if I recall properly.

P.L.: I didn't mean to interrupt your story.

M.D.: Oh, that's all right. Go ahead and ask all the questions you like, while I'm still here to answer them. (*Laughs.*) Anyhow, getting back to what I was saying, Dada and I had ourselves some real good times talking. I liked to tease him, but I didn't push it too far, because it'd been a painful time for him and some of the pain was still there even after all those years. But one time—I remember we'd been drinking some cherry brandy he'd made, and maybe I was just a little high on it—I asked him straight out what he felt.

"'Bout what?" he says innocent as can be, but I could tell he was just stalling.

So I looked him right in the eye and said, "About Butterfly. And about Grandma Charlotte."

He didn't say anything for a long time. I remember the way he spoke though when he finally did, even if the words are maybe not the identical ones he used: "Strange," he said—he drew out the word so that you really felt he was still caught up in the mystery of it after all that time. "Strange how a man can live with a woman for years without ever doubting he loves her, without ever looking at anyone else, and then one day in the blinking of an eye, before he's even had time to notice, everything's changed and there's not a thing he can do about it any more." He shook his head and sighed lamentingly. "Poor Charlotte."

To keep him from breaking off I said, "So you stopped loving Grandma Charlotte?" I remember feeling self-conscious saying it.

But he didn't seem to mind me, and I wondered if he'd even heard. But after a while he said, "I felt old when I was with her, Milly, I felt like an old man. The thing was that I never noticed until . . ." He couldn't finish the sentence, I recall, but then he picked up and said how it was like dreaming you're somewhere and then waking up to find yourself at that exact same spot, except everything's different. Now, Grandma Charlotte hadn't changed, not since the day before or the one before that, but all of a sudden Dada saw the fifteen years she'd put on since he had himself his last good look—it wasn't just looks either, he explained, it was the way she talked, the way she moved, the way her head sat stiff as a candied apple on those shoulders she kept hunched-up all the time. Maybe she'd always been that way and he just never noticed. But once he did, he started noticing all the time, like he couldn't help it. It made him feel funny. Old and gray. Had he really gotten so old? he'd wonder. Told me he felt like Rip van Winkle—scared to look in a mirror for fear he'd find he'd grown a long white beard.

I can also recollect asking him about Butterfly. Took my breath away just doing that. I guess there was a romantic girl in me waiting for him to say how beautiful she was, or something deep or heartfelt that would send a thrill up my spine. But he didn't, never did, just as he never declared his love for her. I remember the way his eyes went kind of blank. "Ah, Butterfly," he said, soft as a sigh; and that was all. But the next day he handed me those two volumes of his diary.

· *Butterfly* ·

65

(The last of Sharpless's counterfeit letters to Butterfly and the only one to have survived)

January 15, 1898

Dear Butterfly,

It is with more regret that I can express that I inform you of a decision that will cause you great pain. Nothing, I know, can justify my behavior in your eyes, and I do not ask you to pardon what I myself could not; it would, however, be a great comfort to me if you can at least understand that my action is not born of disloyalty or caprice.

For a long time, I resisted the pressure put upon me by family and friends to take an American wife, but as I began to play a more active part in our society, I realized to my distress that their views were not unfounded. I still hold that they are wrong morally, but they are not wrong in their assessment of the realities of our society. I had sincerely believed that we could live together as man and wife, in America no less than in Japan, but the past months have convinced me that this will not be possible. To play the part I have been assigned by birth, it is necessary to be an integral member of our society, and that society at the present time is not ready to assimilate a foreign element in matters of alliance and lineage. The temptation was great to throw over everything and return to spend the rest of my life with you and Etsuko in Japan, and believe me, I was more than once on the point of yielding to it. But what would have become of my family? Our family has a long tradition of eminence that I feel it my duty to maintain. For myself, I should not hesitate to abandon all for your love, but I cannot abandon the family that has a prior claim to my allegiance and to which I am responsible against my will. As you know, I have no brother who could replace me in my given role. It is my destiny and I cannot cast it off, not even for what I hold dearest in life.

In taking my leave of you, Butterfly, I want to tell you once more that you are the best thing that I have known. Nothing and no one can replace you in my heart. In abandoning you, I am abandoning my own happiness; yet I shall continue to draw comfort from my memories of the happiness I have had, which was greater than I deserved or could have hoped for. The time I spent at your side will remain with me; in my heart you will always be my wife. You will continue to be a vision and an inspiration; your beauty and goodness will forever haunt me like the exquisite and melancholic strains from your *koto*.

What I wouldn't give to see you once more! But I dare not, for fear that I shall never be able to tear myself from your side again. And for you, too, it is perhaps better that our separation should be allowed gently to take its course.

I can understand what you feel in reading this, I can feel your pain, for I know how you love me. In spite of this I must urge you to take another husband, even as I shall, with equal reluctance, take an American wife. You are young and still have a lifetime ahead of you which you must not let go to waste. I know that I have no right to give such advice and, furthermore, that it will hurt you to hear it from me, but I do care deeply about you and what

· *Butterfly* ·

you do with your life. Please be reasonable, Butterfly, for my sake as well as for your own; remember that whatever direction you may take, I shall be accompanying you in my thoughts.

Yours always,
HENRY

66

(From the editor's interview with Mrs. Milly Davenport)

When you came right down to it, there was only one thing Dada could do: if Pinkerton wouldn't write his own letter, Dada would have to do it for him. And that was hard. It was especially hard because he'd have liked to keep on writing those letters, and knowing Dada, he could've kept it up forever. Don't think he wasn't tempted either—he admitted that there were moments when he was ready to say "To hell with it!" and simply go on playing Pinkerton for good. But his better self won out in the end. He hadn't any business hiding the truth from her. She needed to know about Pinkerton, that he wasn't going to come back, so she could start getting on with her life.

Now, just how she might do that was a problem. Was she going to go back to being what she was before? Or marry someone else? It kept Dada awake nights, but to his way of thinking, loving her didn't give him the right to butt into her life. He was trusting though that she'd be sensible and maybe accept that marriage offer she'd had.

Now, I couldn't understand that; romantic as I was back then, I was scandalized. "Marrying someone she didn't love, that your idea of what was best for her?" I asked Dada. "Is that what you really wanted for her?"

"No, Milly," I remember him answering real serious, and there was such a pain in his eyes that made me wish I'd kept my mouth shut. I'd have changed the subject, but he wouldn't let me. "What do we ever want for those we love?" he asked me back. "Do you know, Milly?" That pulled me up, and I don't know what I'd have replied if he hadn't gone on himself. "If you ask me today," he said, "I think I might have an idea or two, but back then, well, I just wanted Butterfly to have what she wanted—God knows she more than deserved it—but since she couldn't have *that* . . ." Dada's right, there, what could he want for her if there's nothing she wanted for herself anymore? About the best anybody could wish for her would be, like he says, a secure life with maybe the possibility of being happy with someone else. And that's why he'd have liked to see her take that marriage offer, or at least give it a closer look. He'd also been thinking of her little girl, who needed a father; she needed some considering too.

Well, that was the long and short of Dada's answer to my question, and I had to say amen to it.

Of course, Dada's real fear was that Butterfly might go back to an immoral life, even with that money Pinkerton'd left her. Well, he wasn't far wrong, because that was exactly what she intended to do. Can't say as I'd blame her; I can see myself doing the same thing in her shoes. Beats marrying some man you don't even know and probably old enough to be your father. Anyway she was quite a girl. I wish I could've met her, I'm sure we'd have taken to one another. Was your mother spirited like that too? Did she take after her mother?

Getting back to Dada, he went through the torments of hell

· *Butterfly* ·

over that letter. It's bad enough trying to write a letter like that to someone you're actually running out on, but writing it to someone you love, and having to do it in such a way that the other feller, who you'd really like to dunk in tar, comes out looking halfway decent, because that's about the one thing you can still do to ease her pain—now that's hard, really hard. Dada spent a whole week writing it. He told me there were times when he felt he couldn't do it if somebody'd put a pistol to his head. But he just had to, for her sake.

He got it delivered to her while he sat in his office like on a pile of hot coals waiting for the three hours to go by before dashing over there himself. By the time he got to her house, he'd worked himself up into such a state that he was close to needing her to comfort him rather than the other way round. He was expecting her to be all broken up, but she was calm as could be. It wasn't that she wasn't affected, she was, he could tell. But she was one of those people who get stronger when the going gets bad. Dada told me that he felt awed by her composure; she was so dignified, he said.

She gave him tea and they chitchatted for a few minutes like nothing'd happened. Then right out of the blue, she asked him if he knew. Dada got all hot in the head and nodded uncomfortably, trying his best not to blush and not knowing what to say. Seems like they just sat there without either of them saying anything. After a while, she started talking about the plum blossoms in the garden. He had a suspicion she was saying something profound and literary, the way the Japanese sometimes do, but he couldn't figure out what.

There was a purity about her that made her seem imposing in Dada's eyes, so that he felt embarrassed about mentioning the money Pinkerton had sent, though he couldn't very well not talk about it. But soon as he did, she declared right off that she had no need of it. This was news to Dada, and by and by it came out that she was fixing to move out of the house, which was too big for her anyways, and start working again as a geisha. Dada tried his best to argue her out of it. If she didn't want the money for herself, he told her, she ought to take it for her child's sake; and it wouldn't be charity, either, for the father to provide for his own daughter. With the ten thousand dollars—it was a tidy sum of money back then—she wouldn't need to work; they could live comfortably and she could spend her time with Etsuko, which would surely be better for the girl. Well, Butterfly sat there as polite and patient as you please, but she didn't hardly listen. Which Dada noticed, of course, though that just made him argue with twice as much passion. But he could've talked himself blue in the face and it wouldn't even have begun to make a dent. However, Dada could be mulish too when he put his mind to it, and he wouldn't stop till he'd had his say in every blessed way he could think up at least three times round. Well, when at last he stopped, she thanked him and said quietly without batting an eyelash, "Please tell him we do not need money."

That left even Dada flat, but he didn't want to let the discussion end on such a definite note. "For heaven's sake take the money," he pleaded in a last burst of exasperation. "Take it even if you don't need it or use it or want it. Think of Etsuko— she's going to need a dowry someday."

"Not Etsuko, Itako," Butterfly said, as if the name were the only thing her ears had heard. "I have changed her name," she told Dada. "She is now called Itako." She said this in a "thin tone of finality that sealed off further discussion," to use Dada's own words. She didn't get up, but she made a little movement that told Dada he was being asked to leave. She saw him to the door no differently than usual, but he somehow had a sneaking feeling he wasn't being asked to come back. And here he'd been hoping that her misfortune might bring the two of them closer together. Instead she's shutting him out along with her faithless beau, as if their friendship was just an extension of her relationship with Pinkerton and didn't count at all in its own right. This was real hard on Dada, feeling the way he did about Butterfly. He even stopped writing his diary for a spell.

You do know that Itako means "child of pain." Well of course, since your mother kept that name. . . .

67

(The Nagasaki ms.)

I was unaware of it then, but the weeks preceding our departure were among the happiest I would know. The source of my worst anxieties—uncertainties in my relationship to Kate and the underlying fear of being banished—had been removed. Everything seemed to have been settled or disposed in a manner I believed to be enduring—as if things of this world could endure! But such is the vision of the newly betrothed, who see years and decades unfurled before them like long leisurely avenues in an open park.

Our engagement had been sealed by a macabre ritual as far removed from the usual exchange of rings as Kate and I were from the ordinary couple. Heated white-hot, a miniature branding iron wrought in the form of Kate's initial was applied to my thigh. It was a token of my full surrender, and I had been only too willing to espouse an idea that Kate had no more than breathed, though my alacrity would have been considerably tempered by a knowledge of how inhumanly painful would be its execution. But when the pain subsided, a deep sense of peace came over me and I had no regret. I felt that I at last belonged to the woman I loved, that I had been accepted as hers, entirely and permanently. And in the certainty of this unbreakable covenant, my servitude became a pure expression of the unconditional and limitless love I bore her; to which her tyranny was but the obverse, sharing its substance if inverting its form. To a heart that could imagine itself above contingency and beyond doubt, even violence and humiliation were as caresses and balsam.

68

The pain was so bad that Pinkerton, though determined to be stoic, screamed like a pig. Every cell in his body revolted against the glowing iron's inconceivable violation; he thought he would be sick. Quite possibly he lost consciousness for a few seconds.

One moment he was so hot that his entrails seemed ready to squeeze out through his pores; then it was ice cold inside him and he felt too frozen to ask for help. For the few seconds of eternity during which the branding iron tore, so it seemed, into his very marrow—afterward it perplexed him that pain inflicted on the skin could so deeply penetrate the rest of the body—he would have sent Kate to hell. He felt only hatred for her, for himself, for the thongs restraining his wrists and ankles, for the diabolical instrument of his torture: such a hatred that he could have annihilated all with his bare hands and fists. He lay drenched in sweat, and tears and mucus came out in irrepressible gushes. He was aware that the iron had been removed, yet the pain maddeningly persisted in the body's berserk alarm. It felt as if it would continue forever, and he gasped aloud for despair.

But the pain eventually became less intense, and his mind returned, and so did his senses, and his love for the woman who had laid this pain upon him; but he was still unable to move, though he could now picture his body as it lay, a crucified carcass frozen in pain. He sensed Kate's presence, and when with an effort he looked, he saw her petrified eyes fixed upon him with a strange and unholy passion, a chaos of hatred and triumph, love and lust. Instinctively Pinkerton feared for his life.

His fear lasted but a brief instant. He was convinced of her readiness to kill him for pleasure, but the thought, as it dawned in his mind, brought a profound relief, an indescribable joy. Though he had no wish to die, he realized that he did not care whether or not he lived, so long as his life or death was claimed by her whom he loved.

He was now hers, nothing, not even death, could cancel the mark that proclaimed it. A great peace came over him, and he let his eyes close. The pain, still present, no longer tormented him; he felt as if his whole body were breaking into a smile.

69

(The Nagasaki ms.)

Only the voyage to Japan, like rumbling storm clouds that spoil a sunlit afternoon, perturbed those weeks of grace. The prospect was troubling, but even more, it exasperated me. For what could Kate hope to gain that she did not already hold in the palm of her hand? What sign of devotion could she further want from one who already bore it indelibly in his flesh? To me her insistence was senseless and morbid; a wilful, gratuitious tempting of fate.

As our ship drew on toward its destination, my irritation turned into foreboding, and foreboding into dread—dread of confronting Butterfly, yes, but more, of something undefined and preternaturally ominous that, I felt, loomed beyond the horizon. I cannot name the hour, but it was at sea that the memory of that phantasmagoric butterfly came back to me; came with such startling vividness, and remained so obsessively present, that I hardly dared raise my eyes to the sky for fear of meeting it anew.

How had this stupendous vision slipped away for so long from my mind? Once back home, I had thought little more of it, though until then it had preoccupied me intensely; and it was the one thing I never mentioned in "confessing" to Kate the minutiae of my Japanese romance. But now it was back with a vengeance. With amazing clarity, I recalled that occult event in all its glory and strangeness. But if then it had seemed a wonder of heaven, I now descried in it something daemonic and menacing. I did not wish to remember, but it stuck with me obsessively, dogging me all day in corridors and up and down stairs; and at night I dreamt obscure dreams that left me wasted and anguished. Persuaded of an imminent reapparition, I lived in mounting terror as the days and hours crawled nervously on toward Nagasaki. All of Kate's efforts to suppress or soothe my rebel nerves were to no avail, nor did peace come at the sight of the port, or even of the dock. Only when my feet stepped from the gangplank onto solid earth did I accept, with as much incredulity as relief, that I was safe.

· *Butterfly* ·

70

Then came that letter saying they were coming, he and his new lady—all the way from Boston, and no reason given. No explanation, just a request to reserve the best suite of rooms in town. Dada was flabbergasted—I mean, of all places for them to go for a honeymoon! It was outrageous, positively indecent. Dada wasn't ever much good at figuring out what went on in that Pinkerton's head, but this time he was completely stymied. Couldn't for the life of him think of a reason, good or bad. All he knew was, he didn't like it, and he'd just as soon see them on the North Pole. Nothing he could do about it, of course. He got them their accommodations and had a man meet them at the wharf—damned if he was going to go himself!

But that was just a gesture, a protest of his outraged heart. The fellow could go to hell, he writes in his diary—he'd taken to calling him "fellow" or "that fellow," as if Pinkerton no longer deserved a name or even an initial. He might've liked to, I mean send Pinkerton to hell, but he couldn't, he had too much courtesy in his soul, and it wasn't as if Pinkerton had done anything against him personally. So the next day he called at the hotel. He couldn't have kept away anyhow, he was too curious—about why they'd shown up, about how Pinkerton felt about Butterfly. He was curious about the lady, too, the way men always are, though you won't admit it. Dada, well, he did when I put it to him, but that was years later and by then he'd reached the age when people become honest—some people anyway; but he didn't at the time, not in his diary.

Anyhow he got himself an eyeful. He was fascinated by that woman—though I did feel more embarrassed than fascinated reading what he wrote in his first flush of enthusiasm, embarrassed for Dada, that is. But it would've interested you more, I'm sure. It's a shame you can't read it—and that's one page I'm afraid I'm not much good at retelling.

So Dada got there and first there was Pinkerton all alone to receive him. Well, he didn't lose any time getting to the point, but as soon as he mentioned Butterfly—maybe even before—Pinkerton started looking sick. I reckon he could've stuck to his guns and grilled him right then and there, but Pinkerton looked so harried, he had such a hangdog air about him, that Dada didn't have the heart. Something had happened to Pinkerton, Dada had seen that first off; he wasn't the same man who'd left the year before. In fact, Dada was shocked. Because Pinkerton used to cut a fine figure—Dada said people felt he was somebody, whether you liked him or not. Seems they used to call him the "prince" in fun, and according to Dada, he had something the rest of them didn't, and it wasn't just money, either. Well, the looks were still there—it kind of made Dada's blood boil just seeing him so dapper—but leastways when they got talking, Dada got this queer sense that something inside him had dried up or run down or gotten broke. He somehow even seemed smaller than before. Now, Dada wasn't exactly bursting with kindly feelings for the man, but pretty soon he got to feeling sorry for him, for no reason besides him being so, well, diminished. Which was even more surprising considering the fact that Pinkerton's daddy had died and he being the only son and heir to all that wealth and prestige, and those aren't things known for cutting people down to size.

Dada was still puzzling over it when the lady entered, the future lady, I should maybe say; the intended. Then he understood. Not right away, and not all at once, but as he wrote, the spark of intuition came long before the flash of insight.

She was a beauty, if Dada'd got an eye in his head, and it'd

· *Butterfly* ·

seem she got everything else matching as well. 'Least Dada thought so. Not having laid eyes on her myself, I can't tell if she really was all he made her out to be, or just half, which'd be quite as much as a body would want. Maybe . . . well, I reckon women just don't take too kindly to hearing about one of their own being made out to be so high above their common lot, and they'd be dead right not to take a man's word for it—not even Dada's. But anyhow, this being his story, I'd better try to tell it the way things appeared to him.

So as I was saying, he was all bowled over by her, leastways in the beginning. It wasn't till after he'd left that he got to feeling something wasn't right about them. Of course, by then he couldn't be sure if he wasn't imagining things; but the more he mulled it over in his head, the more it struck him that there'd been something theatrical about the way the two of them behaved, as if they had rehearsed everything like a stage play. And that got him wondering. "What is the script?" he asks in his diary. The more he puzzled, the more mysterious it got to be.

Well, whatever the script might be, there sure wasn't a doubt about who'd written it. This was what Dada got to realizing by-and-by. It took a couple of days for it all to get itself in focus, and then came the "flash": that she was the one running the show. Pinkerton wasn't anything more than a pawn she could push around with her little finger, even against his own judgment and will; and that's the change in him. When did it happen, Dada asked himself, when did he come under her spell? Thinking back, he decided it must've happened in the fall, at the time of Pinkerton's change of heart. Well, Grandma Charlotte and Butterfly had hit the nail on the head, it had been another woman all right, but what a woman! Because it wasn't just a matter of falling for her, you understand, it was more like falling completely under her power, "ensorcelled"—I love some of these words Dada uses—like one of Ulysses's men who got turned into pigs. That was what had struck him in the eye first off, though he hadn't been able to put a finger on it. Realizing this made Dada feel cold to the core, because he knew how it could be with that woman, himself having felt the magic of her breath down his own neck, you might say. But what really made him shake in his boots wasn't that, it was thinking about what she might be after in Nagasaki. He went all hot and cold at the idea it might be Butterfly. But what in blue blazes would she want from Butterfly? He hadn't an inkling; fact is, it made so little sense that he told himself he was imagining things. But a little voice kept nagging at him and he couldn't keep it down. And then, what could it be if it wasn't Butterfly?

So there he was getting all wound up and not knowing where to turn. Desperate as he was feeling, he even thought of Grandma Charlotte, but what could she do to help, even supposing she'd see things his way? She sure as sure wasn't a match, not for that lady! He might go see Butterfly and warn her, but what against? And supposing he was wrong and they weren't meaning to go near her at all—then he'd just be stirring things up something awful, all for nothing. Worse than nothing, because she was better off not knowing they'd come—that was sure.

In the end it was the lady he went to see—or maybe he just took himself down to the hotel without anything in particular in mind and it just happened that Pinkerton wasn't there. Anyhow it suited Dada fine, because his being there would've made things more awkward. She was just as charming as ever, but this time Dada being on his guard, all that charm and good looks only made him feel more sharply the danger in her. She noticed, of course, and gave him his opening. I can still recall most of their pourparler as Dada set it down in his diary.

"You seem to have something on your mind today," the lady says in that crisp accent of hers that's got a hint of England in it. "Is there anything I can do to unburden it?"

Dada hadn't been expecting her to come out like this, but now that she was calling the hand, he was game to lay it out. "Yes, as a matter of fact," he replies. He's unsure about what to say, but again the feeling of danger pulls him up; looking her straight in the eye, he asks, "Why are you here?"

"Why," she answers, "the charm of visiting an exotic and fascinating country, which you'll admit this is. And if that's not reason enough, isn't it only natural for me to want to see the place where my future husband spent a year of his life?" And she looks at him with half a smile, as if to say, "Your move," because all this time he's giving her a look that says let's-not-kid-one-another.

But now Dada's steam is up and he isn't about to be stopped. "You know about the circumstances of his life here, I presume," he says meaningfully. He considered this pretty bold, but she didn't bat an eyelash.

"Are you referring to his charming Japanese companion?" she asks cool as if she were talking about her little boy playing with the neighbor's three-year-old. Dada just kind of nodded his head and tried to figure out what to say next. She let him sweat a little before going on herself, "Yes, Henry's told me all about her. A lovely . . . butterfly, isn't it? I'd like to meet her. I hope I shall, while I'm here. After all, she is among the best elements of the scenery, isn't she, at least for Henry?"

Dada said he couldn't tell whether his heart was rising into his throat or sinking into his stomach. "So it's true," he thought, "she did come for Butterfly!" It was all he could do to keep himself looking calm. "I wouldn't do that," he told her. "You would just be stirring up feelings that are perhaps settling down at last. She doesn't know you're here, and it'll be best not to let her know. She's been hurt enough as it is." Dada tried to make it sound like he was giving an objective opinion, but his voice came out all strangled and that gave him away. He found her looking at him with a queer little smile.

"What is your interest in her, Mr. Sharpless?" she asks suggestively.

Dada colored, I believe. He couldn't help it, he told me, it was that insinuating smile. "What are you trying to say?" he burst out after a moment of struggling to control his indignation. "I am a married man with grown children!"

"Oh, I'm not casting aspersion on your morals," the lady protested in a bantering tone Dada didn't much care for. "But she must mean something special to you for you to get so excited."

"It's nothing personal," Dada declared, and went back to talking about Butterfly's situation in such terms as he hoped might touch his countrywoman—he tried to think of her as that so as to defuse the hostility he felt mounting. He ended up appealing once again with a passion he never intended: "All I'm asking you, as an American and a Christian, is to do the decent thing, which is just to leave her alone.'

His hand is all laid out on the table now. After a little pause, the lady says, just as casual as you please: "I don't think I shall." Her smile had tightened, Dada notes, and the voice had something deadly and hard that made her playful tone sound sinister. "I was born in Europe, where we have a more complex notion of decency, and as for God, I have always numbered myself among the forsaken."

At least she was now in the open too. Dada wrote that his insides felt all—I'm quoting—"jumbled up in panic like a sentry's who's been uneasily watching foreign troops amassing and now sees them suddenly cross the frontier: he hasn't an inkling of the deep politics behind the move, but knows it won't be for the sake of a neighborly confabulation." In that instant, without thinking, Dada, like his sentry, "threw himself unheedingly in the path of the invader," knowing full well that one dead body isn't going to stop them, but by golly, they'll have to take the trouble of stepping over it to get to the one he loved. Before he knew it, he was crying out: "You can't see her! I won't let you!"

· *Butterfly* ·

71

A week went by while Kate played the tourist. Our purpose in coming seemed forgotten, and accustomed as I had become to serving Kate without question or comment, I dared not broach what she eschewed. My apprehension, however, grew from day to day as we explored in apparent leisure places I had known and things I had relished; these were invariably redolent of Butterfly and ushered her even more to the forefront of my thoughts.

Most often we were accompanied on our excursions by Goro, the same Japanese interpreter who had been instrumental in bringing me together with Butterfly. I had never cared for the man, and now he was more distasteful to me than ever; but he had been sent to meet us at the wharf, and Kate, taken with his natural servility or else recognizing his utility, had immediately requisitioned his services. His presence became even more intolerable as Kate took to treating me in a high-handed manner she usually forbore in front of acquaintances; Goro, of course, pretended not to notice.

But if the days were trying, they were well recompensed when, the day's tourist duty done, we retired to the privacy of our chambers. The long ocean voyage had brought us closer together, for Marika, who suffered on the sea, had been left at home, so that all her duties devolved on me. The bizarre and arduous training I had received now stood me in good stead, for not least among Marika's functions was to gratify her mistress's sensual longings. Kate had restrained herself on board ship, however, and it was only in Nagasaki that I came to know her appetites. Although every measure was taken to limit the pleasure I took in procuring hers—among others, the imposition of a

That took even her by surprise. The mask dropped, and, in Dada's words, "the darkness in her heart came flooding into her face." It didn't last but a second or two, but that was long enough. He saw it, and never forgot. "Milly," he said to me once, and I could feel the shudder going through him still, "it was a face from Hell. I didn't think so much hatred could go into a face. Hatred, bitterness, despair. Behind those flawless features, behind that supreme beauty. I could never look at her again. Ordinary mortals don't have the strength it takes to look upon such fatal mixtures."

While it was all happening, though, Dada hadn't got the time to think about that. In his agitation, he'd gotten up out of his seat in a spontaneous gesture of shielding Butterfly, as if he could by putting himself bodily between the lady and her prey. She'd risen too to meet him, and now they stood eye to eye in open enmity. "How do you propose to stop me?" she asks. He heard a challenge in the hint of laughter in her voice; there was no more pretense.

"I don't know," Dada conceded. He says, "I was hoping that by talking to you . . . ," but left off in the middle of his sentence as he realized he'd just confessed the hopelessness of his position more than he'd told of any hope he might've had, and to his own ears the words sounded foolishly ineffectual, like an "echo of his ineptitude." His body, which had been drawn tight as a bow, lost its tension; its combative posture went limp. He turned and aimlessly paced a few steps as if unable to stand his ground any longer. Crestfallen now, he was ready to bargain, or reason, or plead—anything, even beg on his knees, if that would help. Only it wouldn't. And he knew it; he had seen her face.

"I can't," he finally announces in an outright recognition of defeat. There wasn't a thing more to be said. All he's got left to do now was to clear the field, and he did that, in silence, without another look at his adversary. At the door, however, he turned back to her and added, "But I can pray for you."

contraption that not only effectively made me a eunuch but rendered painful the least stir of manhood—this equivocal intimacy with a flesh so extravagantly longed for and so rigorously denied, gratified me to a degree that words cannot describe.

72

Slowly, as inch by inch his hands pushed past the finely turned ankles, soft folds of silk and lace bunched and parted like a languorous, high-frothing wave over a slender reef, and in their wake emerged a lengthening expanse as dazzling as sunlit snow. His lips hovered in frozen homage, overawed, as if afraid to desecrate the tender surface of her breathing divinity, while his mesmerized vision fed upon the unveiled substance which, so persistently sequestered from his starving senses, had as steadily nourished his wayward dreams.

His dazed eyes followed the receding hemline, over the graceful calves and long thighs, and up the twin monticules at whose summit they came to rest, exultant and devout, like zealous pilgrims scarce able to conceive of attaining the sacred spot to which endless longing had given a quasi-mythical cast. The sleek double cheeks glowed softly, like blushing snow; a light fragrance swept over them, as cool and intoxicating as heaven's breath. To Pinkerton, whose manhood had passed under his mistress's heel, they had seemed no more accessible than a goddess's living countenance to the temple slave who dusts the sculptured image at her shrine. For like the latter, he had ministered to them in a slavish capacity, with ablutions and scents and fresh garments and pans to transport detritus from the crater they embosomed. But never were his eyes permitted to tarry in the sacred precincts; and his enslaved heart in all its ardor did not dare think of violating their mysteries. Nor, but for her explicit commands, would he even now.

As his face dipped to the enchanted valley, his eyes clouded with tears and he felt his love-racked soul ascend as to an inner heaven and explode in a spray of infinite stars.

73

(The Nagasaki ms.)

Sparse moments of eccentric intimacy thus emblazoned my unrelenting travail, like jewels on black velvet that capture all one's attention. Exorbitantly sensual and yet withheld from the senses, the singular gratification tormented rather than appeased; and constricted by that demonic contrivance to martyr desire, I sizzled like a toasting keg of explosives girt with steel bands and hourly doused to prevent its blowing up. It was a wonder that I was able to go through the motions of daily life with an appearance of sanity.

This aberrant state no doubt prevented me from being more attentive to the problem of Butterfly. In any event, it was not for lack of reminders: for one, the officious vice-consul whom I had once charged with certain practical matters concerning Butterfly and who had taken it upon himself not only to preach propriety but to compensate for my want of it. Having met Kate and scented, I know not how, the nature of our relationship, he invited me to his office for a tête-à-tête. Although I knew he was sensitive to Butterfly's plight, I was astounded to learn how far his sympathy extended: he had been writing letters to her in my name, so as to mitigate my unexplained desertion. He would not have confessed this but for his concern to safeguard her peace. In his attempt to dissuade me from invading it, he was insistent, even intrusive. Not knowing how powerless I was to comply, he quite succeeded in stirring up a turmoil of guilt and regret. My wretchedness was compounded by the realization, only now dawning, that Kate wanted and no doubt intended to hurt Butterfly. Did she imagine that in doing so she would reduce me further? Only later was I to understand.

74

(From the interview with Mrs. Milly Davenport)

Well, he'd lost the battle, and defeat was in sight on all fronts, but he wasn't beaten, not yet. He still had some fight left in him, and he felt better soon's he got out of that hotel. His parting shot had came out all on its own, you might say, and it had braced him. It'd had an effect on the lady, too. Because he'd seen the way she stood in the middle of that room, stock still, with her lips atremble—not a whole lot but enough for him to see. Dada had gallantly waited—or maybe it was more cunning than gallant— anyhow he'd stood a moment longer so she could have her say. But she never said anything, just stood there like her feet had grown roots. When he shut the door, he knew he'd scored a hit without ever intending to. Well, he *would* pray for her, he said to himself—or maybe against her, he didn't know. Maybe in God's eyes there isn't any for or against.

The next step was to see Pinkerton, but just how he'd do that wasn't real clear, because if he was sizing up the situation right, it wasn't going to be easy. What Dada finally did was to write a note asking Pinkerton to come by the consulate. Then he bribed a bellhop to hand it over personally and privately, which the boy did because Pinkerton showed up the next day. Now, Dada'd been trying to figure out how he'd go about saying what he had to say, but he needn't have bothered because this time Pinkerton didn't hem and haw but started in right away like a child who's done something bad, with excuses and apologies and all. "I suppose you want to know this and that, well, it's like so and so . . ." Well, Dada wasn't much interested anymore, he had other things on his mind.

"Fine," he said when Pinkerton had run out of steam. "What I want to know is what you want with Butterfly now, after coming all this way. You do intend to see her, don't you?"

The question clearly didn't make Pinkerton any too comfortable. He started talking confusedly about wishing to explain his behavior to Butterfly so as to make everything clear between them. This phoney talk got Dada's dander up.

"Explain!" he exclaims. "What's there left to explain? Isn't it clear enough? She doesn't need explanations now. Just leave her be!"

Pinkerton turned a little pale, but went on mumbling about putting things in the clear.

"Listen," Dada tells him, and I think I can remember most of the words he used. "Listen," he says, "it's too late for that. It's done, the explaining. You wouldn't do it, so I did it for you. In your name. Yes, I wrote her letters in your name, the letters it was your obligation, your moral duty, to write, the letters that you should have written out of common decency. But since you didn't, I did—I forged them, that's right! I forged letters in your name, so that the wound you inflicted might heal. Now it's all done, and there's nothing more you can do for her, not any more. Except to leave her alone."

Pinkerton didn't speak. Dada said he looked as limp as a puppet with its strings cut. Eventually he spluttered, "I see, I see."

"Then promise me you'll leave her alone," Dada demanded.

· *Butterfly* ·

Pinkerton withered and turned even paler. "I can't," he finally says in a strangled voice.

That took Dada a little aback. He felt like cussing but held himself in. So they just sat there both looking away and each one alone in his thoughts.

"She won't let you, eh?" Dada says after a spell.

Pinkerton turned red at that and he glared at Dada, though not for long. Straightaway his eyes were down again, but he nodded.

"Tell me," Dada asks, "what is it exactly that she wants from Butterfly?"

Pinkerton's eyes seemed to be going right through the floor; his lips quivered some but he didn't speak. In the end he made a little gesture of helplessness.

"You mean you don't know?" Dada asks in amazement. "You've come all that way and you don't know? Just what kind of relations do you have with her?"

Dada's questions hadn't been making Pinkerton none too comfortable, but this one really cut him to the raw and you could just about hear him stiffening and bristling. "Ask me anything," he said in his best starched manner. "But not that."

She really has got him under her thumb, Dada registered with a degree of surprise, even though he'd had that exact same thought before—oftentimes it comes as a surprise to see our own thoughts turn out so true. It was clear as day there wasn't a powerful lot of help to be gotten out of Pinkerton, but that wasn't going to keep Dada from speaking his mind.

"Okay, I won't ask," he tells Pinkerton. "It's none of my business. I'm concerned only about Butterfly. Look, it's simple: she loved you, and you abandoned her, even though she had every claim on your devotion. She loves you still, but she's accepted your jilting her; in her own way she's come to terms with it—though no thanks to you—and for better or for worse she's getting on with her life. Now, what more can you do for her, except stay away?" And he followed it up with an afterthought: "Unless of course you want to go back to her." But even while he was saying it, Dada was already thinking bitterly how superfluous it was.

Pinkerton's face went all to pieces and something between a wail and a whimper came out of his throat like it was being torn from his soul. "I can't!" Dada wasn't clear which he meant, staying away from Butterfly or going back to her; maybe both. "I can't," he repeated in a pathetic whisper with his eyes clamped tight as if wanting to shut out something too awful to stand looking. "I can't."

"All right," Dada says, speaking with what he defined as "that exacerbated indulgence with which one approaches idiots and drunks." "All right, I won't ask. Do what you have to; I won't even ask you to keep away. Just don't do anything vile to her. You can promise me that much, can't you?"

Pinkerton just sat real quiet and stared at the inkstand on Dada's desk. Looking at him, Dada got a feeling of pity and disgust and something close to hate; then suddenly something cut loose inside and he got just as mad as the blazing dickens. "I wanted to get right up and thrash him," he told me. "I wanted to grab him and throw him out the window. And by gosh, Milly, I think I just might have—honest to God! You know what most probably kept me back from doing it? It was a thought that came into my head all out of the blue, that it was going to feel like picking up a sack of potatoes. And somehow that quirky reflection let out all my fury. I just sat there and thought to myself: I guess I'll have to pray for him too."

· *Butterfly* ·

75

The interview, if it failed the vice-consul's intent, was not without its effect on me. The word "vile" in particular struck me with force—"Don't be vile," he at one point admonished. It had never occurred to me that I could be vile; but had I not been? And was I not? Had I not become vile in my condition, my conscience, my very flesh? I thought of the stigma I bore, of the degrading things done at my mistress's pleasure, and worse, of I know not what ignominious acts she even now had but to command. Yes, I was vile—worse than vile! At that moment I saw myself as the man sitting across the desk might have seen me if his eyes had been more penetrating, and a sickness came upon me, a loathing unto death.

My head felt heavy, too heavy to hold up; I had a sudden whimsical wish to lay it on a prie-dieu. But I could not have, even if one had been available. For I realized that I could no longer pray. There was no God for me anymore. Perhaps there never had been and I had not noticed. My head wanted to fall, to collapse; I would have laid it upon the vice-consul's desk, in humility, in fatigue, and it would have comforted me. But I could not, not even there. Only on Kate's feet could my forehead now rest; in the whole of the universe, there was not another place for it. So I thought, and despair poured over me thicker than honey.

From that moment thoughts of death came to me frequently. I no longer wanted to live. Will, hope, pleasure, desire, all had submerged in the sweet filth that engulfed me and dragged down my living spirit. Yet I could not die, for even my hand was no longer my own to command.

76

Inches above hung the flower of her femininity, its petals deeply flushed and peering as if eager yet shy to open. His eyes clung to them as he breathed deeply in preparation; he would have liked to touch them with his lips. Never had he looked at them for so long. Their loveliness made him ache.

Time slowed, almost halted. It was as if in the imminence of their obscene communion they had reached a timeless juncture of heaven and hell, where the divine merged with the abominable, the monstrous with the sublime. He had never felt the one so present or the other so near: in her hovering downpour, in his unquenchable fire. Never before had he felt so nakedly exposed to forces beyond his ken, never before so self-abandoned and so voluptuously possessed.

All at once, a small tremor broke out in the suspended patch of paradise, and a golden sluice descended, steamy and urgent, burning his throat and tongue and his very bowels with the stark, pungent taste of shame.

77

(From the interview with Mrs. Milly Davenport)

After that, there was just one thing left for Dada to do, and that was to go see Butterfly. He wanted to go that same afternoon but had to wait till the next day because he hadn't gotten her new address. She had moved a couple of months back to a more modest house and, there having been no invitation to visit, he hadn't seen her since. But even before that, she'd about faded out

· *Butterfly* ·

of his life—though in no way or manner out of his thoughts. She was, as Dada put it, "being absorbed back into the Japanese world from which Pinkerton had plucked her—like an enchanted figure from a painted screen come out to keep company with a favored guest and now receding back into it." Yet, Dada remembered wistfully, she had been ready to follow that guest into his alien world, to affront a new and foreign civilization, even to the extent of leaving forever the country whose subtle hues alone could match her own exquisite lines. Well, how's that for talking like a book! (*Laughs.*) There are parts of that diary I've read so many times that I can rattle off whole sentences pretty near word for word. Providing my memory holds out, praise the Lord—can't ever know at my age.

It was affecting for Dada to see Butterfly again. He thought she'd lost something of her youthful radiance, but otherwise she was fine and if anything even more beautiful than before. Sorrow or adversity had given her face a reflective quality, a maturity, which in Dada's eyes only heightened her charm. He'd have liked to be treated more intimately, though; she was charming as always, but seemed even more distant than the last time he saw her. I don't mean cold; she just seemed to have moved away some more from what Dada calls "the magical crossroads of East and West," and he got the feeling she'd gotten even more deeply immersed in a world he couldn't enter. She had even lost some of her ease in talking English.

Dada was inclined to tell her about Pinkerton and his lady right away, but she didn't give him half a chance. He had to wait till he'd been served tea and whatever else polite people do over there. The longer the words sat burning on his tongue, though, the harder it got to speak. Finally he took advantage of a moment's pause to announce he had something to tell her. She put on a serious expression and said "yes" like someone waiting to be given instructions.

"Henry is here, in Nagasaki," he told her, and hurriedly added so as she wouldn't misunderstand, "with someone, an American lady he's going to marry."

Dada could just barely detect a reaction in her eyes. She uttered a guarded little "oh" and he didn't give her time for more—not that more was likely to come, for her face was quite stoical.

"I think they want to see you," Dada went on in a cautious manner. "Or rather, she wants to see you, or wants him to see you."

He'd been expecting more of a reaction before, when he first broke the news to her, but now he was surprised to see her start the way she did. Her body gave a little jerk as if she were in the grip of some terrible emotion. But she got a hold of herself and kept her formal sitting position on the *tatami*—that's what they call those straw mats they have in place of hard floors, but you'd know that better than me. Anyhow, Dada's even more surprised a moment later when he notices her crying: tears are streaming down her cheeks, though there's not a sound. He would've liked to say something comforting, but he couldn't for the life of him think of a single appropriate phrase. So they just sat there in a silence.

"Now, I don't think you ought to see them," Dada ventures after a long while. "I know how you feel about Henry, but still I think it'd be better if you didn't see even him. And certainly not her. You don't have to, you know."

Butterfly looked puzzled. "Don't have to?" she asks in a tiny voice.

"Certainly not," Dada assures her. "If they come, have Sachiko tell them you're indisposed. But more likely they'll send word, and in that case you send word back either with an excuse—say that you're going away, or . . . anything would do—or simply that you don't wish to see them."

· *Butterfly* ·

Butterfly, who wasn't looking any too convinced, hung her head like she was deep in thought. "I think that will not stop them," she said by-and-by in a sad little voice.

"Oh, I don't expect they'd break in by force," Dada tells her half-jokingly. "They're up to no good, but I doubt they would do anything improper. You just have to be very firm in refusing to see them."

Butterfly didn't seem to understand. "Can't they send someone to take her?" she asks with obvious distress. "Police?"

Now it was Dada's turn to be puzzled. "Police?" he asks in wonder. "Take her? Take who? Where?"

Now both of them were confounded and looked across at one another in mutual incomprehension. With just a hint of exasperation, she stared unsmilingly into his face for a few seconds before bursting out, "Itako—who else do they want?"

That got Dada more confused than ever, because he'd forgotten that Etsuko's name had been changed to Itako. It took him a moment to remember, and a moment more to figure out what Butterfly was talking about. Then he understood: she thought they wanted her child. It seems that in Japan a child is considered to be the father's sole property. The problem simply hadn't ever occurred to Dada. Could it be they really wanted to take the child, he asked himself? He couldn't imagine what they'd want with her. It seemed too unlikely, and besides, Pinkerton hadn't mentioned it and probably hadn't ever considered it either. Certainly Dada wouldn't put it past the lady—he'd believe her capable of anything; but no, it wasn't the child she was after, he felt quite sure. So a moment later Dada was able to reassure Butterfly with conviction in his voice that it wasn't Itako they wanted at all. She took some convincing, but in the end she believed him. But then she couldn't understand what they wanted to see her for, or why they'd come to Japan. Dada didn't know any more than she did, but he did tell about his fears, especially concerning the lady, and he warned her once again not to see her.

Butterfly had regained her composure by then, in fact she looked even more serene than before—her face looked clearer and brighter, Dada writes, like the sky after a cloudburst. The French say "beautiful as the day"—well, that was how she appeared to him. She took counsel with herself for a second or two and then announced firmly, "I will see them."

Dada tried arguing with her, but after a while he could see he wasn't cutting ice. But having taken so much trouble already, he wasn't going to give up now. That lady, he tried to drive it home to her, spelled danger; she was up to something, he didn't know what, but sure and certain it was she didn't mean well by Butterfly. As for Pinkerton—Dada wasn't mincing words anymore—he was too doggone weak to oppose the lady, who chances are was cooking up something wicked. "Give him up," he pleaded. "You can't do anything for him now, no more than he can do anything for you. Stay out of his way, and above all, stay out of hers!"

But Butterfly's look was somewhere so far away that Dada wondered whether she had heard him at all. "I am not afraid of her," she quietly declared.

Dada could see that. He wrote—let's see if I can recite it: "I saw it in her gaze that was as clear as the deepest blue of heaven, in the sovereign erectness of her fine head, that indomitable woman's strength in her, and in my mind's eye I saw her rising in the hour of adversity like an angel of light that no darkness could overcome. I pictured their confrontation: Butterfly steadfast and sublime in her tensile, luminous grace, the other superb and dazzling with darkly amazonian splendor, two types of beauty, two kinds of strength."

Now, man that he was, Dada was powerfully taken with the image of two dueling women blown up by the male imagination

· *Butterfly* ·

to the size of pagan goddesses. Well, if that was the way he saw it, it was all out of his hands, wasn't it? There was nothing more to do than to watch and wait.

But his fear for her was gone.

78

(The Nagasaki ms.)

One evening Kate summoned me to her as I was making preparations for the night. "I want to talk to you," she said in a tone that announced a formal allocution. When I approached, she indicated that I was to kneel at a small distance from where she sat; usually I placed myself directly at her feet.

"Listen closely to what I have to say; I shan't need your comment.

"I have given instructions to Goro to bring Butterfly here tomorrow afternoon. Don't look so surprised—you've been waiting impatiently to see her, haven't you? Hush! Not a word from you. Just listen.

"When she comes, I want you first to see her alone. And as a free man, not as a slave. Mark that, as a free agent at liberty to do what he will, to determine the course of his own life. More explicitly, I want you to spend an hour with her at the very least—longer if you wish—and then decide whether you will remain her husband and free, or whether you want in earnest to become my slave.

"I know what's on your tongue: that your choice has long been made, that there is no question in your mind. But you've been reasoning as a slave; tomorrow I want you to think as a free man. It may be the last time, but do it—I wish it. It's for this that I put off signing our contract." She produced a copy of that document and reached over to hand it to me. "Here, read it again carefully and consider well the consequences. Tomorrow you can walk out under a free sky; after tomorrow, never again! For all you know, you may not even be alive, because the moment you sign that contract, I can order you to end your existence—and who can ever know what a mistress's whims will be? I myself don't know. Keep that well in mind. And remember what I've told you before and repeat now for the last time: only a fool among fools will put himself under such a contract.

"You'll receive her in the parlor; I'll be in here. Once you've made your decision, knock on the door. I want to see her before she leaves, and you too, of course, if you decide to accompany her. Take your time; stay with her as long as you like, but give yourself at least an hour. You can do and speak as you please. Touch her, embrace her. Don't let my being in the next room intimidate you. Get it into your head now that you'll be free, even if you should choose not to remain so—in which case it would be your last hour of freedom, so reason the more to grasp it by the lock. In fact, it would please me to have you feel once again what it is to be a man. Who knows, that might bring you to your senses, if nothing else does. You won't be wearing your belt, obviously; here is the key. I suggest, however, that you keep it on until noon tomorrow. Tonight you'll sleep in your room. I give you permission to use the bed.

"Is everything clear? Good! Now give me my massage; then go. I'll want nothing more tonight."

With that she held out her foot for the ritual kiss that terminated our audiences.

· *Butterfly* ·

79

He was wrong, however. Fatally wrong, you might almost say. It hounded him for a long, long time, and he did his almighty best to find out what'd happened. Not that it would've made any difference anymore, but he was eaten up by remorse and wanted at least to know where he'd been off in the way he'd had things figured. Because he'd been so sure, you know. He was sure she couldn't take her own life, even after she'd gone and done it. It must've been an accident, he'd think, or maybe they murdered her. He just couldn't square her killing herself with what he believed he knew about her. "I can still see her today," he told me. "The proud grace of her neck, the way she held up her head—so dignified, so self-possessed, so vital. I tell you, Milly, a woman who holds her head like that couldn't kill herself. It's a physiological impossibility."

I didn't know anything about physiology, but from all Dada had told me, it seemed mighty unlikely to me, too. "Maybe they wanted to take her child after all," I remember suggesting without being half convinced of it.

"Even so," he shook his head, "even so. Anyway it wasn't that. Pinkerton assured me it wasn't and I believe him on this point. But even if she'd have lost her child, which I guess is about the greatest blow a woman can suffer, it still wouldn't have done it. She'd have sorrowed, maybe rebelled, but she wouldn't have killed herself."

"How about to get back at them?" I speculated.

Dada had thought of that too. But no; it wasn't in her character. There was no spite in her, he was positive on that score.

I had it on the tip of my tongue to tease him about making her out to be such a saint, but something in his face made me hold back. "Well, they do have that gruesome custom of cutting themselves open," I said instead. "What do they do it for when they do?"

"Pride," Dada replied. "Honor. They do it to preserve their honor, it somehow redeems the honor they would otherwise have lost."

"Well, hadn't she been shamefully jilted?" I asked.

He allowed that it was the least impossible explanation, but still not one that satisfied him. "Because what happened had already happened," he argued as he must have hundreds of times in his head. "I mean it had been weeks since she was jilted. If it was a stain on her honor—and God knows what those people consider stains, that's something I'm afraid the likes of us will never understand—it was a pretty old one." At the time she'd never considered suicide, he'd swear to that and stake his life on it. No, if her honor was stained, it had to be something they did to her. "But doggone it, Milly," he said grimacing with frustration. "I can't figure out what it could be. All these years I've been trying, and I'm no closer to anything that halfway makes sense."

He'd gone to the hotel that night, Dada had, and just about dragged Pinkerton out by main force downstairs into the lounge, because he didn't want the lady to bust in on them. Pinkerton was in a state of shock, but Dada wasn't in any mood to let him off on account of that "What did you do to her?" he demanded. "I want to know what you did to her . . ." He used a couple of none too complimentary words that I won't repeat.

"I killed her," Pinkerton was muttering, over and over. "I killed her, I killed her."

"I know that, goddammit! But how?" Dada shouted; he was

· *Butterfly* ·

beside himself. "Now you tell me what happened, and you tell it right now."

Well, Pinkerton told it, but from what Dada records him as saying, there wasn't a heap of a lot to tell. They, he and his lady, had invited Butterfly to the hotel and she had gone. Pinkerton saw her alone. They talked for about half an hour. Pinkerton told her about his betrothal and how sorry he was about the way things turned out—just what he'd intended to say, nothing more. Butterfly seemed very composed, even relaxed, but understandably neither of them felt much like chitchat, and Pinkerton didn't feel he ought to ask personal questions—after all, what she did with her life wasn't any of his business anymore. She was getting up to leave when the lady came out. The two women met, but they didn't exchange more than a few phrases, in spite of them both being curious about each other. No, he affirmed, nothing'd been said that might be construed as an offense.

"Did anybody say anything about wanting her child?" Dada asked when Pinkerton'd finished telling about the meeting, and he was assured there hadn't been any question of that, that it hadn't ever been mentioned at all, in or out of Butterfly's presence.

"You must have said *something* to upset her," Dada insisted. To which Pinkerton mumbled that everything he said probably did.

"I don't mean that!" Dada cut in irascibly. "I mean something in particular. A new element, something significant. Something that changed the way she looked at things."

"But what?" Pinkerton asked.

"You tell me," Dada shot back in exasperation. Pinkerton seemed to turn paler, but he denied there was anything of the sort. Dada couldn't swallow that, but try as he might, he wasn't able to get a thing more out of Pinkerton. In the end he left the hotel feeling sick and frustrated and no wiser than before.

80

The first dreaded moments were mercifully taken up by Goro's bustle. He had no doubt expected to find Kate and made no move to go until I sent him away. His disappointment showed just enough for me to take note; I felt an unexpected pang of jealousy at the absurd thought that he could be providing services of a different nature.

Left alone, Butterfly greeted me with a formal bow and an elegant string of Japanese phrases. Unversed in Japanese politesse, and without a comparable repertory of my own to draw upon, I fumbled awkwardly for words. My embarrassment made her smile good-naturedly. "You have forgotten Japanese?" she teased in the familiar tone we had often used with one another and which contrasted with her formality a moment before. "Lucky I still remember English, is it not?" The little laugh we shared cracked the ice, though it did not melt. I ushered her to the divan and seated myself in an armchair a little distance away.

"So," she remarked as her glance swept the room. "This is how Western house looks inside?" I nodded, noticing for the first time how ugly the room was with its pretentious hybrid décor and pompous Second Empire furniture. It was clear, and all to her credit, that Butterfly neither approved nor felt comfortable in it. Nor did she appear there to her advantage, for the contrast was too stark, too strident; the grace of her delicate movements were crushed and her sophisticated hues swallowed up by that oversized, overbearing parody of European elegance. Seated unnaturally on the alien furniture, she seemed awkward and slight, and even a little pathetic.

Haltingly at first, like a swimmer braving gelid waters, then

· *Butterfly* ·

with great sputtering and thrashing about, I launched into my explanations—those ignominious falsehoods and half-truths I had lain awake nights to concoct. Butterfly sat on the edge of the divan at apparent attention, her eyes fixed on my face, but I could not be sure whether she was listening. Suddenly she broke in.

"Are you happy?"

Happy? I felt myself flush, and though I thought to reply in the affirmative, the words stultified my tongue and came out an incoherent mumble.

"Does she make you happy?" Butterly insisted. When still I did not answer, she looked down and said in a low voice, "Forgive me."

That broke the dam. "Forgive you!" I cried. "*I*, forgive *you*. Oh, Butterfly, Butterfly!" I was choked for words. Then, on a sudden inspiration, "Why, it is to ask your forgiveness that I've made you come! But I don't know by what right I could ask that, after all that I've done. If you only knew . . . how vile I am, how unspeakably vile. . . ."

Overcome with emotion, I closed my eyes. It could not have been for more than a few seconds, but when I opened them again, Butterfly had risen and was coming toward me with the quick, diminutive gait of Japanese women. A patch of afternoon sun caught her; she seemed a luminous spirit gliding to a mortal's aid. Then she was hovering over me, and her hands, those beautiful hands, gently touched my cheeks. Holding my head between them, she looked down into my uplifted face with a compassion that seemed not of this world. Her touch galvanized me, unknotting the tangled emotions in my breast, and I felt a sudden release. I would have fallen on my knees before her, in gratitude, in penitence, but even my knees were too sullied for that office.

"Forgive me," I whispered.

She smiled the faintest of smiles. "I have forgiven you a long time."

"No!" I cried. "You couldn't have—you do not know . . . there is so much you don't know!" I shut my eyes again as if my very regard could soil her. "If you knew," I groaned in anguish, "if you knew how I've been, how low I've sunk . . . I can't even tell you, I wish I could. . . ."

The pressure of her hands became firmer. "It is no matter," she said. "I forgive you, for all."

The words were clear and she spoke very distinctly, but a long moment passed before their import settled like heavenly dew upon my tormented heart. All! She forgave me all! I felt a twitch of joy, but my elation did not last.

"You cannot," I demurred. "There are things I've done that if you only knew would—"

She clapped a hand to my lips. "All!" she said softly but with a conviction that seemed to resonate through her entire being. There was no passion, only a certainty so strong, so absolute, that argument and doubt could only fall harmlessly away. The turmoil within me quieted, died; letting my eyelids drop, I slowly submersed in the peace of absolution. She has given me, I thought in wonder, what every man wants from a woman and never gets; and for that we build churches, say prayers, take communion, confess.

When I again lifted my eyes to Butterfly, her loveliness flooded my face like early morning sunshine. I saw her once more as in bygone days when I had basked in it so freely. It was as if her pardon had washed away all that separated me from her, all that encrusted and held me prisoner against the truest wishes of heart and mind. Our moment of deepest love suddenly came to me, with a vividness that transported me back in time. A current of sexuality, pure and potent, passed through our linked bodies, and my masculine core rose and surged toward her with an irresistible élan that the restraining garments could scarce contain.

· *Butterfly* ·

Butterfly's eyes never left my face, but swept along by the reflux of desire, the woman in her had awakened. I felt its response in an all but palpable emanation that enfolded me in its electrifying flow. My arms circled around her hips to pull her to me, but her willing body instantly drew away. "Not here," she gasped. She pryed loose my hold and, taking a step back, stood with my hands in hers. For a moment neither of us could speak.

She cast down her eyes and looked at my hands. "Your hand has healed?"

"My hand?"

"From fall."

"Fall? What fall?"

"Your fall from horse!"

"Where do you get the idea that I've fallen from a horse?"

She became flustered. "You . . . you say yourself, in letter."

I suddenly understood. Rash in my exaltation, I blurted out without reflecting, "I didn't write any letters! Oh, Butterfly . . . that was part of my . . . vileness."

"But I got letters. . . ." She flushed slightly.

I already regretted what I had said, but it was too late to retract. "Sharpless wrote them," I told her despondently. "He wrote in my name."

"So . . ." A shadow had crossed her brow.

I wanted to weep. "I am sorry," I said with an effort. "Can you forgive me?"

She could; she already did. Hadn't she said so? She smiled; her eyes had regained their clarity. I bent forward to kiss her hands. Clasping mine a little tighter, she drew me from my seat. The sexual call, for a moment suspended, once more sounded its claim.

"We go?"

The hint of passion in her voice made me thrill. "Butterfly!" I whispered. Awkward in my desire, I stumbled alongside her toward the door.

81

Pinkerton remembered perfectly. It had been one of the first really cold days. They lay pleasantly crushed under layers and layers of covers. He had slipped into her almost without intending, their bodies had become so perfectly attuned. It was difficult to move under the heavy mass, but hardly any movement was needed.

"I feel you," she had breathed. "So deep."

Possessed by love, their very flesh and blood seemed animated from within by its high purpose. Something stirred at the innermost center of his being, surged with a momentum unguided by his will. As his desire strove toward its destiny, he could feel the vortex of her response powerfully drawing him on.

"Now, enter now!" he had heard her moan or so he imagined, for the voice was muffled and the words in a language not his own.

And his life, deliquescing, flowed to her as if siphoned off in a stream, on and on. He could neither control nor stop it; it was marvelous, and a little frightening. The sensation was unlike any he had known. He felt transfixed as by an exquisite silver needle that pierced through his loins to hers, pinning them together for all eternity.

He did not cry out as he often did. Nor did she. Hushed as before an epiphany, they lay together in a suspension of time. It was as if God had breathed through their bodies.

"Now we will have child," she said. He nodded into her neck; he knew.

82

No sooner had Butterfly gotten the door open—I had turned the key in the lock to forestall any undesired intrusion—than a voice rang out from behind us.

"Are you leaving so soon?"

The voice brought me up like a leash whose existence I had momentarily forgotten. Through the connecting door to the bedroom, Kate had emerged and was coming toward us. "Henry!" she chided. "You knew that I wanted to meet your charming guest. I should have thought you'd be more considerate."

Discomfited, I introduced the two women. Kate was all smiles and amenities, while Butterfly contented herself with a bow and curt formal phrases. Underneath their polished behavior, however, I could sense on the part of one and the other a certain wary excitement, for each knew that she was facing a formidable opponent.

Kate was the first to attack. "Henry has told me so much about you, such interesting things, too, that I almost feel I know you." She looked down at Butterfly—in her high-heeled shoes, she towered a good six inches over her—with overbearing admiration. "Except that you are twice as lovely in person."

"He has been telling me about you too," Butterfly said meaningfully, though her face remained impassive. Her self-possession and delicate beauty, exquisitely wrapped in the splendid kimono, made Kate seem florid and vampiric for all her peerless natural beauty and studied simplicity of toilette.

"Oh? And you're still willing to take him back!" Kate, speaking with mock astonishment, turned to me. "Henry, she is an angel."

"Kate . . ." I began, half entreating and half threatening, for at that moment I felt a sudden antipathy for her and would willingly have wrung her neck to stop the pernicious needling. Butterfly, however, was a step ahead with her rejoinder.

"There is much more to tell, I am sure, and I am interested to hear, because curious," she said imperturbably. "But it is not important."

Kate's eyes narrowed. "I wonder if Henry would agree." Turning again to me, she smiled with cherubic malice. "The mark, for instance—how did you explain that to her? Or haven't you yet?"

The allusion was like a jerk of the leash to remind the dog of its condition. I colored.

"But that is none of my business now. It is clear that your decision is taken. A wise decision, too." She cast a significant glance in Butterfly's direction. "I congratulate you."

"Kate, you mistake my intentions," I said with a serious mien.

"Oh, no, I mistake nothing." Her laugh had an edge of bitterness. "And I approve the step you're taking, be assured. Especially now that I've seen her. I wish you both a long happiness.

"I am not leaving," I declared unsmilingly. "I'll explain everything later."

"There is nothing to explain. I'll be sailing shortly, the arrangements have already been made, so you needn't trouble about it or bother to send me off; in fact, I'd rather you didn't. I can manage perfectly well with Goro's help."

"I'm not leaving you, Kate" I repeated.

"Then I'll be leaving you," she said in a tone of playful melancholy. Our eyes met, and I found in hers—I had not looked into them since she made me her slave—a look that surprised me. I recognized it from the earliest days of our courtship; euphoric and dazzled as I was then, it had spoken to

· *Butterfly* ·

me of life's profound mysteries and the miracle of love. Now, though I did not overlook an unexpected amorousness, what I saw in those deep, dark eyes was above all sorrow. It was a sorrow without bounds, an oceanic sadness in whose murky depths seemed to lie buried every human woe. For the first time perhaps, I saw beyond her impervious beauty, beyond its public call for adulation to a mute appeal for something nameless and darkly private. It was this unspoken appeal, not to the slave but to the lover, that clinched my fate. For all the passion that I had ever felt for her rose anew like a geyser in my breast.

"Kate, I will never leave you!"

The expression in her eyes suddenly altered; I could almost see the shutters slamming, and yet they did not completely close. A ray or two still penetrated from their depths, a mere glimmer which yet kept my heart on the line like a hook the fish cannot disgorge. An old tenderness, revived and already overflowing, made me ache.

But the accents in which she spoke were those, terrifyingly and reassuringly familiar, of the despotic mistress; and her face had resumed the implacable beauty that unfailingly forced my heart to its knees.

"No, go! I don't want to see you anymore!"

She turned abruptly and strode toward the bedroom. Caught between hot and cold, overwhelmed by the unforeseen turn of events, my judgment faltered. Aching with revived tenderness and unable to imagine separating from her whom I adored, I did what I had done once before with such fateful consequences: I rushed after Kate and threw myself at her feet.

With a violent fling of the arm, she freed herself from my grip and took a step back—prevented by furniture from overtaking her, I had grasped one of her hands and tugged it so that she was forced to turn around. Her face was ablaze as I had never seen it: with cold triumph, with explosive wrath.

"Henry," she said in a voice like death. "Get up."

Astonished by her anger, I could only look up stupidly at her.

"Get up!" she hissed, this time louder and with a note of despair. "Damn you, get up!"

"Please, Kate . . . Mistress . . ."

She stared at me as if bewildered. Her breast heaved; a cry, terrible, unearthly, came as if torn from her entrails.

"All right then, be a slave!"

She fell upon me, her hands flailing out with hysterical violence as if wanting to knock me from the face of the earth, dealing blow upon blow until her arms could no longer for exhaustion, and still her desperate fury was not spent. Panting, her features contorted, she stood cursing me under her breath.

Butterfly had slipped away, I did not know when.

83

Kneeling at her feet, Pinkerton saw in a sudden flash the face that he had not been allowed to look upon for many months—the face not as it was now, ravaged no doubt like the wasting body, but as it had been one summer day fifteen years before. In his youthful ardor, he had been convinced that its beauty was immune to time, and for him it in fact had not changed.

The skin was so fine and clear and pellucid that he had felt as if he were dipping his face into fresh snow. It was the first time he approached her lips, and the kiss was as soft as moonlight upon an evening tuberose and as chaste. Their lips touched for perhaps a second, not much more, but it was a second plucked from time by the hand of God. As aeons hung upon their lips, the world around them, awakening from its age-old torpor, sprang alive in pristine beauty; it was as if they had with that magical act created anew all past and future, and perfused it with harmony and light. Were they not like two halves of an arch vaulting high above the earth and reaching irresistibly toward one another? And was their kiss not the keystone that brought them to their common pinnacle? Indeed, to the enraptured youth, it had seemed the final keystone in all Creation, where past and future, spirit and flesh, life and death, joined together in aspiring glory.

Their lips drew back as from some sacred mystery and did not touch again. In the peaceful, vibrant transparency wrought by their alchemical union, they looked at one another in wonder. Colors had become uncommonly vivid and luminous; the air brisker, more crystalline. His whole being tingled with a consciousness of awakened manhood, with a newborn sense of purpose. The universe was one with himself, and it was burgeoning into a plenitude of teeming young buds.

Tears had begun to drip from Pinkerton's eyes; they flowed uncontrollably, though he contained his sobs. Sensing his sorrow, she did not scold but reached out her hands and put his head against her knees. Then he could not keep down the pain and wept with racking sobs. When at last his convulsions quieted, she solaced him with the only kindness that remained to them; raising the hem of her gown, she eased herself forward toward the edge of the armchair and drew his head deep between her thighs, there letting his tears mingle with the secretions in which his dreams had drowned.

84

It was awfully hard for Dada after that. You know, when someone you love dies—'specially someone who's too young for it—everything else dies too. It's like the spark of life has gone out. The whole world starts feeling like cold gray matter, an empty desert forsaken by God. But if God's not there, where did He go? It always comes back to that, doesn't it? Where your God is, that's the question, not whether God exists—everybody knows God exists, even the atheists, deep down. But they don't know where to find Him, because God has a way of disappearing behind clouds, like the sun, but the light is still there, only you've got to know that the light comes from the sun. Dada kept on asking: Where was God when Butterfly died? Was He dead too, like that German philosopher claims? And if that's the case, what is the point of living at all? "Those were days when I couldn't see a spot of light anywhere," he told me. "Not in heaven, not on earth. I searched my soul, I turned it inside out, and all I found was darkness, and more darkness. I was appalled to look, and I was appalled that I hadn't ever looked before."

"And you didn't find your spot of light?" I asked.

"Yes, Milly, I did," he replied in his deep, quiet voice. "It was there all the time, only I didn't see it, not till later."

It was pretty late by the time Dada got home that night after seeing Pinkerton, because he walked around for a bit to get a grip on himself, but Grandma Charlotte was waiting up for him. Now, feeling low the way he did, about the last thing he felt like was having to contend with Grandma Charlotte and her hostility toward Butterfly. Of course Grandma Charlotte saw straightaway something was wrong and asked about it. Dada fobbed her off by

· *Butterfly* ·

claiming the Japanese dinner he'd had wasn't much agreeing with him, but he couldn't keep himself from blushing on account of her eyes being fixed on him so sharp and hard. She didn't say anything either, just kept on looking while he stood there uncomfortably wishing she'd leave him be. Then she shrugged like she was about to give up and go away, but at the last instant she changed her mind and spoke in a soft husky voice that he hadn't heard for a long, long time.

"Come on, George, tell me," she said in a jaunty, playful manner—you know the ways girls talk when they're trying to wheedle something out of a body. Dada told me she used to talk like that sometimes back in the days when they were first married, but that was a good many years before.

Well, Dada hadn't wanted to say anything about it, but hearing her ask like that, he just wasn't able to keep it in any longer. "Butterfly is dead," he blurted, and stopped because he was too choked up to get any more out.

For a second or two, Grandma Charlotte just kept on looking at him without moving while he did his best to stick his hands through the bottom of his pants pockets. "My poor George," she started saying under her breath, and next thing Dada knew she'd burst into tears and was sniffing and grieving her heart out. Dada was too flabbergasted to do anything. "I was standing there watching her come toward me with tears streaming from her eyes," he said to me. "And first thing I knew, she'd taken my head in her hands and I was crying too. I couldn't be, I thought to myself; why, I haven't cried since I was five years old. And for some reason, thinking that got me crying even harder, that and Charlotte's tears. I cried so hard my legs wouldn't hold me up any more. Charlotte got me shuffled over to the sofa and with her holding me, I bawled like a little tot, making up for the lulls by taking off again twice as hard. The funny thing was that in between I felt detached and amazed at myself: a grown man like me, hollering and carrying on because Butterfly was dead, and Charlotte of all people crying with me over Butterfly! I couldn't believe it was really happening." Dada looked so bewildered for a second that I thought he was going to start crying all over again right then and there, in front of my eyes. But he only looked into them with a mild expression and said, "That was my spot of light, Milly. Though it took me a while to realize."

The two of them didn't talk about it afterwards, and they didn't mention Butterfly any too often either, although Dada did end up telling Grandma Charlotte most everything that'd happened— everything he knew anyhow. But crying over Butterfly had brought them closer together. Before that, their marriage had somehow gotten twisted up into a hard knot, and this had dissolved it. They started talking to one another again, talking and touching. Dada said it was a little like getting married all over again; and this time it didn't get tied up. They stayed close right to the end, when Grandma Charlotte died. Dave and I used to be tickled when we saw them holding hands. The old folks, they were to us then. I guess they were pretty old, too. Anyhow, it was affecting.

85

(The Nagasaki ms.)

The door slammed shut, leaving me alone and in a daze. My first thought was that I had lost them both. Yet there was no impulse to follow either one in an attempt to retrieve. I felt oddly detached, like a spectator before an empty stage from which the actors had retired.

My bewilderment presently dispersed. For the first time in months, my head felt clear. It was as if Kate's blows had knocked

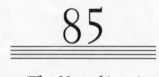

· Butterfly ·

me back into a saner, better world; I suddenly saw the divers elements in my life fit into place where before they had been violently juxtaposed. All the tortured ups and downs receded like a fading nightmare; what remained, what mattered, appeared simple and clear: I was back in Japan, I had been pardoned, Butterfly and my daughter were waiting. As for Kate, I felt that our destiny had run its course; I had loved her, betrayed her, and done my penance, and she had been right to impose freedom upon me. Tasting now of that freedom which before had been an empty word, I felt a surge of immense gratitude to Kate for having insisted.

I sat for I know not how long in the large empty room that a new and wondrous light seemed to transfigure. There was no need now for hurry or resolve; all my remaining years lay before me in seemingly endless leisure like an expanse of meadow in the afternoon sun.

I got up to announce my plans to Kate, but not hearing her stir, I decided first to pack my things and make certain practical arrangements. Thus it was late afternoon when I knocked at her door.

I found her in bed looking wan; I could see that she had been crying. "Oh, Henry," she said in a subdued voice and motioned me wearily to an armchair near her bed. Ordinarily such an invitation would have astounded me, but it confirmed me in my new identity and I felt it to be appropriate. "It's all right—you're still free for the rest of today. But first help me with the pillows. I want to sit up."

I had it on my tongue to announce there and then that I had come to say good-bye, but by the time I had made her comfortable and taken my seat, she was already speaking again.

"We've arrived at a crucial moment in our relations, Henry, a watershed. You seem bent on slavery, and apparently I can do nothing about that, but there are a few things I'd like you to know before we go on. I don't suppose they'll change your mind, but I do want you to know who it is you're marrying and making your mistress for life. It would incommode me for you to stumble blindly into this serious matter.

"To begin with, much of what you think you know about me isn't true. My father wasn't an English baron as I had given out; he was an adventurer who pretended to be one—he wasn't even English but Hungarian, though he grew up in England. Mainly he was a cardsharp and confidence man. My mother was a Viennese cabaret dancer. She did not want to keep the child, but my father, who was in love with her at the time, insisted. Afterward her attitude was that if God had let the child come into the world, God would also take care of it. Fortunately for me, my mother had an older sister who was a music teacher and one of the finest people I've known. She lived by herself, and I spent a lot of time with her, often weeks at a time. She gave me books to read, talked to me, taught me piano, and generally was a second mother to me. But she died when I was fourteen. Without her, things became worse, much worse. My father was losing his good looks and skills through drink and had trouble taking in the kind of money he was used to spending. My mother, too, was drinking by then. There were debts; my parents fought. In tight moments, my father would look at me in a peculiar way; I knew what he was thinking, and I'm sure he spoke to my mother about it, because she was afraid for me. Which was one reason why she espoused so eagerly his idea of sending me to my uncle in America. The uncle was my father's brother and he had immigrated there many years before; he was, according to my father, a "stinking rich businessman." So he wrote, and I was soon off to New York. With few regrets, I have to say.

"At first things went well enough. My uncle and aunt, who had no children of their own, really did want to adopt me, and I was prettier and smarter than they ever could have expected. But

· *Butterfly* ·

my qualities became my undoing. I found my aunt boring, and though I made heroic efforts not to show it, I was unable to keep her from gradually feeling it. But far more serious were my good looks, which I couldn't hide. By the time I turned sixteen, I was no longer a ravishing child but a beautiful woman, and my uncle was more than conscious of it—his wife, too, for that matter. For a time, I resisted his advances, but I ended by giving in, in a manner of speaking—in reality it was more rape than seduction. I had hoped he would leave me alone once he had had his way with me—I was still innocent then—but on the contrary he became frightfully inflamed. He wanted to come to me at night, to have me for his concubine; when I proved unwilling, he even spoke of divorcing his wife and marrying me.

"The situation became more and more tense. Failing to persuade, he tried to coerce. He did his best to impress upon me how much I depended on him: my parents had given me up, I could as well forget them; he was my legal guardian, I was entirely in his power; he would have ways of bringing me about, et cetera. But his threats only hardened my resistance; I ended by not letting him touch me at all. After that his passion turned into hate; the household erupted into open warfare. It was not hard for my uncle to turn his wife against me; already resentful, she was all too ready to swallow whatever tales he chose to tell. Soon she became even nastier than he.

"I was well aware that it was time for me to quit their house, and I began to look for ways. In the meantime I was determined that they wouldn't get the better of me. As I said, it was war and I expected underhanded tactics—I was not above them myself— but what happened was beyond anything I had imagined could happen.

"One day I was seized in the street by two men and put into a coach. They blindfolded me and took me to a house where I was quite literally kept a prisoner. It was a brothel, and I was to be one of the inmates. I resisted, of course, and for that I was beaten, tortured, starved, raped, and subjected to every conceivable pressure. I fought them in whatever way I could. I told them my uncle would find me; they laughed and said my uncle was the one who had sold me, and to convince me, they made him come and admit it. I told them I would escape; they laughed and said I couldn't, and even if I did, they'd find me and bring me back, only I should have it twice as bad then. I retorted that I would go to the police; they laughed and said nothing, but the next day a police captain came, and from that day on I have never thought of turning to the police for aid.

"Ultimately, I capitulated. More than anything else, I was afraid they would make me pregnant. But I was so sullen and cutting that clients were put off—except for certain ones. The worse I treated those, the more eagerly they came back. It was then that the madam put me in 'specialities.' With my temperament and my looks, she said, I was perfect; and once I became good at it, I wouldn't even have to let the man touch me anymore. She brought in an expert from the outside to instruct me, and I took to it immediately. I had developed such a loathing for men by then that I took a tremendous pleasure in mistreating them. This pleasure didn't last, but in the beginning it was quite real and helped make me an instant success, which improved my situation considerably. I remained a prisoner of sorts and continued to be shamelessly exploited, but I enjoyed a prestige that allowed me to do as I pleased in the house; in time I became almost comfortable there and was no longer watched. I was not happy, but I had sunk into a hebetude, not unpleasant, that drowned all initiative and will. Who knows how long I'd have stayed if I had been left to my own devices? But such was not my destiny.

"One day I had a distinguished visitor—he was not the only one, by any means, but he was special. It was the French ambassador, an elderly and elegant gentleman, highbred, cultivated, intelligent. An avowed voluptuary, too, but romantic. He was not one of the common ilk; he had heard about me, he explained, and was curious to see for himself what it was like. Well, he came back, though it was not for another 'special session' but to spend the evening with me—talking, because I no longer allowed clients, even the most distinguished, to touch me. And I charged him an outrageous sum for the favor. Far from being discouraged, he was back again the following day: he liked me, he said, he liked me so well that he wanted to take me to Washington with him. Was I willing? I was dumbfounded and at first did not take him seriously. But he convinced me that he meant it, and that it was entirely feasible. He was used to acting with vigor and proposed to take me with him that very evening. I said no. He gave me a deep, quizzical look, kissed my hand, and left. 'I always respect a lady's wishes,' he said as he was leaving, and then added with a roguish smile, 'But sometimes I know her wishes better than she.'

"I brushed him off as a romantic Frenchman who had let himself get carried away by a momentary infatuation, and was surprised when a letter arrived a month later. It was a beautiful letter—beautiful in every way. I spent two weeks framing a reply; fortunately, French was a language I could write correctly, thanks to my aunt's intransigence—in fact, I wrote it better than English or even German. He later confided that my command of the French language had impressed him as much as my beauty.

"That was the beginning of a fervent correspondence. Our letters were very fine—his especially; they ought to be published someday. Through them I came to know him, respect him, and almost love him. He had apparently thought about everything under the sun. And that included everything about me. I was impressed and touched to discover how attentive he was to everything I told him; I never touched upon a question that he did not pick up and elaborate on, and small details I hardly remembered mentioning would suddenly be alluded to. For five months, the correspondence was my entire life. Then he came and took me away.

"I spent three wonderful years in Washington. Much of the time I was alone—I could not appear in society as the ambassador's mistress, and he had a wife in addition to all his other activities. But I did not mind. I had a small but lovely house, a piano, books that came by the armful, and the best mentor in the world. I read, I practiced, I reflected; I was happy.

"Only love was missing. For I did not love my ambassador, though I had the deepest affection for him in addition to boundless esteem and gratitude. I endured our intimacies with the best of grace, but that was about the extent of it.

"Then he was recalled back to Paris. He offered to take me, but I chose to stay. I explained to him quite honestly that three years of that secluded life was enough, and that I had a plan: I wanted to go to college, as much to create a new identity for myself as to complete my education. As a student, I would quite naturally make friends with well-connected young women and through them gain an entry into society. My ambassador did not want to part with me, but he loved me enough to comply with my wishes, and to help. He left me the house in Washington, along with a modest but by no means negligible sum of money. To the last, his generosity toward me was exemplary.

"The rest you know. I sold the house to go to Vassar. All went as I had envisioned. I impressed everyone, faculty and students alike. A great many girls vied for my friendship, and I could have my choice. Soon I was being courted by a number of highly eligible young men—brothers, family friends—as well as some older but more interesting professors. Among my admirers were a few that were quite attractive, but I bode my time. Only with you did I finally let myself fall in love.

· *Butterfly* ·

"Our meeting was no accident. I knew about you before accepting Lisa's invitation, and I knew about your family of course. So you see, I was every bit the adventuress your father thought me. Yet in a deeper sense, he was wrong, fatally wrong. He saw only the hands reaching for his fortune; he didn't see the heart that directed them. He didn't consider my love for you, and what my love would mean to someone like you, somebody who apparently had everything—everything, that is, but character. And that was precisely what I could have given you. You needed me. *Me*, and not just another woman, because she wouldn't have seen it, your potential, and your weakness. At first sight you were just another rich young man, richer than most and rather more attractive, but that was all. I realized only after a time that you had something else, a sensibility that made your horizons elastic, a passionate core that could soar if it found its direction. That was what, taken together with your other advantages, made for such exciting potential. Perceiving that potential, I began to love you. And that love brought out the best in me. Part of me that had been forced under by circumstances now reemerged. I had ideals, talent, beauty, and I wanted to do things, great things, wonderful things; and I could do them with you. Oh, the things we could have done together! For me it was an awakening into a dream, a dream of life that was just beginning to dawn.

"And you destroyed it—you and your father.

"The worst was that he liked me. He would even have loved me, I think, if he had been able to love anybody. But he was suspicious on principle. He questioned me, as I knew he would, and my story was good. He believed it, but he sent detectives to check it nonetheless. Of course they found out everything.

"It was quite a shock for him, I believe. He was very shaken when he confronted me. But he realized that I truly loved you and used that to bargain. If I left you alone, he promised, you would know nothing. He would even play the villain who separated us. You'd be sent for a year to someplace faraway, during which time we would be forbidden to correspond; by the time you returned, I would have disappeared, faithlessly and without a trace.

"I had no recourse but to accept. I thought of making a clean breast of it to you, but I loved you too much to bear the thought of your scorn. And even if you had continued to love me, I could never again have felt at ease with you. Besides, your father would not have let me through the door. He would have destroyed me; and you, too, had you stuck by me.

"So I knew that you were lost to me when we said good-bye, and that most likely I would never see you again. Certainly, I had to keep to the bargain. I had no choice. Yet I still hoped that you would write in secret, at least once. I waited, week after week, but nothing came. One day, oppressed beyond endurance, I sailed for Europe.

"I traveled. I visited my aunt's grave, but I did not go to see my parents. They would have clung to me and pumped me—they who had abandoned me—and I had no desire to see how much further they had sunk. I should have settled in one of the larger cities and gone about establishing myself, but I couldn't. I was too heartsick. I wandered from place to place, as if hoping each time to leave behind a piece of the love I was trying so hard to kill. Eventually I returned to New York. It was just about when you were due back. Somewhere in my heart was still a hope I dared not avow, but the most I permitted myself was a card to Lisa giving my address.

"The reply came quickly. I could hardly believe my eyes: your father had died. I almost went mad for excitement. We could be together again, nothing could separate us now! Or had he imparted my secret to someone else—your mother, for instance? I put that terrible thought out of my mind for the time being and read on. Imagine what I felt when on the next page I learned that

· *Butterfly* ·

you had married in Japan. I could not move from the spot, and I wished a thunderbolt would really strike me there and then. All this time, my only solace had been that you loved me, and my greatest concern had been the effect my loss would have on you. And here I had been abandoned like some silly moonstruck girl! I could not believe it, even though there was no possibility of a mistake. But my disbelief faded as I read on. Lisa—together with your mother, she made it clear—wanted me to seduce you away from your wife! Her proposal astounded me, and I broke out in bitter laughter. As if I could take you back after you had so ignominiously betrayed me. Nor had you the shadow of an excuse. Remember that the bargain had been that you'd be free to marry me after a year of total separation, and for all you knew, I was still counting the days. But the proposal was a godsend, a gift from Nemesis, and a stroke of genius on the goddess's part. I would have a revenge worthy of my baffled love.

"I took the next train to Boston, where I had a meeting with your mother and sister. I consented to their plan, on two conditions: that I should have carte blanche to proceed exactly as I saw fit, with their full cooperation and no questions asked; and that I should be free to marry you if I succeeded. Your mother's manifest reluctance made me realize that she indeed knew my secret; but she had made her choice: better a whore for a daughter-in-law than a Japanese.

"My plan was already formed by the time my train arrived in Boston. If I knew your potential as no one else did, I also knew your weaknesses. I knew that what might enable you to rise higher than others could also be turned against you and make you sink lower. Given the right circumstances, any man can be dominated, but there are those who are particularly susceptible. Someone with my experience can spot them easily, and I had always known you were of that class. I was certain that you would prove as docile as one could wish; the only problem was how to draw you under my power. I could not very well make advances, and I judged from what I had been told that you were seriously attached to Butterfly. The obvious solution was to have Marika seduce you and deliver you up bound and trussed. The details we improvised as we went along. But make no mistake, everything that happened to you was part of a careful strategy; nothing was left to chance. You will remember, for instance, that on the day you were first whipped, Marika made you get up to shut the window—well, that was the signal for me to come and surprise you in bed.

"I watched with malicious pleasure as your will softened and disintegrated. I wanted to crush you completely, to reduce you step-by-step to the nullity I knew you could become, just as in different circumstances I would have gone about making you into somebody special. I also enjoyed triumphing over her, the woman who had taken what was mine. Pleasure I could have granted her, and you, but you had no right to love as you did— on top of that, you were stupid enough to tell everything, to spread before me all that the two of you had stolen. I rejoiced at your stupidity; I rejoiced in making you drag your love through the mire. But it wasn't enough. My rancor carried over to her; I wanted to see her suffer in the way I had suffered, but with even greater mortification. I wanted her to see with her own eyes what had become of your love, and what had become of her lover. It was for that that I made you come back to Nagasaki.

"But I failed. She was stronger than I had imagined. She came very close to getting you back; she would have if I hadn't intervened. I hadn't bargained for that. Her performance was admirable. In fact, it took away the hatred I had felt toward her, curiously enough.

"Oh, I saw it, I saw everything, heard every word."

In response to my puzzled expression, Kate indicated a large painting on the wall. "Go over and take it down. It's not very heavy."

I did as I was told and to my amazement found myself looking into the parlor, only a few feet from where Butterfly and I had sat. I remembered then that on the wall of the other room a large mirror hung at the corresponding spot.

"I had that two-way mirror put in. It wasn't easy, but Goro managed to find one and persuaded the management to install it, at a price of course. He's a resourceful little man. Haven't you ever seen one before? They are a standard fixture in bordels. You should know; if not, you've seen them only from the wrong side."

I was staggered by all that she had told me. Her words had shattered the world in which I existed. In a stupor, I put the picture back on the wall as she instructed and resumed my seat.

The lengthy account appeared to have tired Kate. For several minutes she sat gazing mistily at the picture, as if she were seeing the afternoon's scene replayed before her eyes.

"You broke my heart, Henry," she said at last in a pensive, melancholic tone. "When I saw you about to go through that door she had opened, it was as if she were taking you from me all over again, only this time I was there to witness it. It hurt me, and it made me feel vulnerable—I had thought I no longer was. Yet at the same time I rejoiced—or part of me did, the part that wanted to see you cast off your servitude and become a man again. The part of me that still loved you, and wanted you to be someone I could love—or even hate—not a doormat or a rag. Do you understand? Although my dreams had been destroyed, there still remained a piece or two, a mere tatter, but precious nonetheless. Somewhere inside me, I desperately wanted to preserve that last little piece, even as I worked to destroy you. I hated you, and because I hated you, I wanted to destroy you. But I also loved you, and my love wanted you to resist, to live out

· 219 ·

your betrayal of me like a man, so that I could at least hate you for it—because one can't hate a rag no matter how filthy.

"I suppose all along, at every juncture, some little part of me was hoping you'd rebel. But you never did. You never realized that each time you went down on your knees, you were crushing another piece of my dream. This afternoon it was the last, the very last." Her mouth had tensed and a terrible expression, more despairing than angry, came over her face. "I could have killed you! If I had had a whip in my hand, you wouldn't be alive now." She looked as if she were about to set upon me once more.

"Now you're no longer worth killing," she remarked venomously as she let herself sink back into the pillows. "You're nothing now, nothing, nothing, nothing . . ." Her voice trailed off to a whisper. A tear was making a glistening streak.

Her words had torn into my flesh like so many barbs, but that tear ate its way straight through to my heart, which gaped open to render its woe. I lurched forward and, kneeling by the bed, took her hands to press my face into them. "Kate," I pleaded, "couldn't we begin over? Couldn't we forget this nightmare and start again from scratch?"

Kate shook her head wearily. "Too late," she murmured. "Too late."

She continued to shake her head without pulling away her hands. "We had great stakes and a winning hand, Henry; we could have done some fine things. Now empty chips are all that's left. But we have to go on playing with them. We have to continue the game, together. That is the punishment we have brought upon ourselves."

· *Butterfly* ·

86

They had met in the garden, unexpectedly, for early morning strolls were not in the habits of either. The air was still misty; the first rays of the sun slanted through the haze.

As always, the touch of her arm thrilled him. They ambled aimlessly, talking of this and that. Once again Pinkerton wondered at the depth of her mind and her knowledge of life; at times he felt a mere adolescent at her side. Had it not been for her beauty and the grace of her every motion and phrase, he would no doubt have been a little put off.

A rose of a magnificent pink stopped them and they stooped over it in silent admiration. Wet with dew and resplendent in the early morning sunlight, it seemed the crown and quintessence of nature.

"It is like you," he said, somewhat to his own surprise. "So youthful in its vigor and yet so mature, so mature and yet so fresh. Its color unites the deepest red and the purest white and transcends both. Such passion and worldliness; such high purpose and refinement of mind. How proudly it opens, as if the whole sky belonged to it! And it has only just begun to spread its petals." He paused and added in a murmur, "I hardly dare look upon such beauty."

She made no reply, but when moments later he offered to cut the rose for her, she protested. "No, don't. It is more beautiful here in its natural state." Then, laughingly, "Besides, it'll prick you if you try."

Not knowing what to say, he bent over and kissed the glistening petals. The perfume intoxicated him; his lips lingered, as if they had touched something divine. The gesture was entirely spontaneous, but afterward he became self-conscious and dared not look at her.

That evening he found the rose at his bedside, freshly cut and exquisite in a crystal vase.

(The Nagasaki ms.)

I wept into her hands; I kissed their palms, their wrists, their fingers. They were gentle with me, but they did not hold out what I was reaching for in a flare of belated hope.

"I am hungry," Kate said after a time. "Have them bring some dinner—for you, too."

In her melancholy, Kate was softer and mellower than I had ever seen her. She continued to reminisce, but in a desultory fashion, sometimes engaging me in conversation, sometimes talking almost to herself. Her revelations had shaken me; mortified by what I had inadvertently wrought, I was at a loss to speak of all that pressed upon my heart. Besides, it had been a long time since our last civilized conversation and I was reluctant to break the mood or cut short her loquacity. I waited for an opportune moment, an appropriate opening or a lull, but none came.

After our brandy, I helped her prepare for bed and gave her her nightly massage. All was as usual, all but the mood—and the difference it made! My heart ached to think that it could always have been so, and that it would never be so again. All I could do now was to savor each poignant moment like manna that would melt before the dawn.

Had I hoped to render more intimate services that night? I do not know; certainly I was under her charm and would have been

· *Butterfly* ·

glad to see the evening prolonged or its intimacy advanced. No request came, however; she was tired, she would sleep. Tucked in under the covers, she looked up at me as I lingered still beside the bed. Her eyes in their melancholy were like the ocean in the dark of night, in which one can divine but not quite see the glimmering reflection of distant stars.

It would be the last time I looked into them. Too choked with emotion to speak, I bent and touched my lips to her brow.

(The following account is based upon the testimony of Itako, Butterfly's daughter; it consists essentially of what Sachiko told Itako in 1920.)

Sachiko pleaded with Butterfly not to see Pinkerton, but she would not listen. On her return from his hotel, she appeared absorbed and troubled, though no more so than might have been expected. The rest of the afternoon she spent alone with her child. When Sachiko served her dinner, she seemed self-possessed, even serene. After dinner, Sachiko saw her take out her writing implements. At one point she went to the kitchen and burned some papers. Later, perhaps around eleven, she summoned Sachiko, who was surprised because it was not her mistress's habit to call her in the evening, even when Pinkerton had lived in the house. She instructed Sachiko to have the bath prepared at dawn the following morning, and to fetch Pinkerton from his hotel; Sachiko should make sure that he came personally whatever happened and that he be there by eight o'clock. Sachiko's surprise grew when her mistress then presented her with two kimonos, a hairpin, and what seemed to Sachiko an enormous amount of money. Butterfly explained that she was going away soon and would not be able to take Sachiko with her. At first Sachiko was merely puzzled. Then, in a flash of intuition, she understood that her mistress was going to die. Horrified, she cried out in protest and ended up weeping in Butterfly's arms. "You must be brave and help me, not make it more difficult," Butterfly, herself moved to tears, admonished.

Sachiko asked what would become of Itako. Her father would take her, Butterfly explained; there was a letter for him which he would find together with her body and his child. Of course—that was why Pinkerton had to be made to come. Sachiko would have to help him with practical matters such as finding a wet nurse; once he arrived in America, he would see to it that Itako was properly cared for, but in Japan and aboard ship, it would not be so easy. Sachiko promised to care for Itako as if the child were her own. She understood that Butterfly was not to be deterred and now girded herself to play her own role the best she could.

The next morning Sachiko helped arrange everything and stayed with Butterfly until the last. A sense of excitement and responsibility permitted her to overcome her sorrow. When the time came, she asked to second Butterfly, and Butterfly consented, though neither of them knew what this should entail in their case. "I wish you were a samurai and could wield the long sword," Butterfly said. Clearly it was no easy matter to kill oneself with the short sword; the samurai most often had a second who would sever their head once they themselves had cut into the belly. There was a moment when Butterfly faltered, but she did not let herself weep, and once the ritual commenced, she performed it faultlessly. Her ancestors would have expected no less, but still they would have been proud of this descendant.

Sachiko was able to remain calm as long as her mistress drew breath. But seeing the beautiful body and the blood that was soaking through the white kimono onto the *tatami*, she broke down and wept. The idea of the faithless Pinkerton taking Itako suddenly struck her as unbearable—he who had so shamelessly abandoned the child and dishonored the mother. She, who was devoted to both, had been powerless to save the mother, but she would take care of the child. She knew at that instant what she had to do. Hastily, she wrapped the money Butterfly had given her in a kerchief together with a few necessities and the two letters Butterfly had left behind. With Itako attached to her back, she took one more look at Butterfly and hurried from the house.

At the hotel, Sachiko had some difficulty getting to Pinkerton, but eventually she made her way through to him. He was reluctant to comply with her request, but when she told him Butterfly was about to die, he turned pale and followed her. Downstairs, she had a ricksha waiting and made him get in—she herself would follow. The ricksha took him to Butterfly, but Sachiko herself fled to an aunt's house and from there eventually to Shizuoka.

Sachiko had expected to be pursued and in the beginning was very apprehensive. Days passed, however, without anything to indicate she was being sought. After a time her fear abated and she stopped living like a fugitive. For the first year or so, she worked as a servant to pay for Itako's wet nurse; after that she bought a small eating house with the money Butterfly had left. She did not marry until very late, when Itako had left to study in Tokyo. Itako never stopped feeling a little guilty, for she was convinced, no doubt with reason, that she had kept Sachiko from marrying and raising a family of her own.

Sachiko experienced a moment of great anxiety that fall when she found Sharpless waiting for her one evening. Her reaction was to run away as fast as her legs would run, which, burdened down as she was with Itako, wasn't very fast. Sharpless, understanding her fears, shouted after her that he was not there to take away the child. Heedless in her panic, Sachiko did not stop until her body gave out; but when, almost in tears, she turned to face her pursuer like a cornered cat, she saw from his face that he indeed meant no harm. When they had both recovered their breath, Sharpless explained to her that he had sought her out to arrange for Itako to have an annuity on the money Pinkerton had left her. Sachiko at first would hear nothing of it: she had enough for the two of them; she did not want Pinkerton's money. Besides, she did not trust Pinkerton; who knew what ties the money would bring? It took all of Sharpless's patience to persuade her that a trust fund could be set up in his—Sharpless's—name without any undesired ties of whatever nature. With his broken Japanese, it was a feat for him just to explain what a trust fund was. An arrangement was eventually made whereby Itako would receive an annuity until her marriage or her twenty-sixth birthday, whichever came first; at that time the full amount would be turned over to her; until she was eighteen, the income would be paid to Sachiko. In later years, Sachiko never tired of singing Sharpless's praises, but at the time her hatred of Pinkerton rubbed off sufficiently on him—"Pinkerton's friend," she continued to call him—for her to treat him with suspicion.

Although Sachiko spoke often to Itako about her mother and occasionally made depreciatory comments about her father, Itako did not learn the story of Butterfly and Pinkerton until she decided to marry and live in Germany. Before she left, Sachiko told her all she knew and also turned over to her the two letters that Butterfly had left. One, of course, was for Pinkerton; the other, as even Sachiko suspected, was for Sharpless. Sachiko would in fact have liked to give Sharpless his letter, but not knowing English, she had no way of deciding which one was for whom, and the letter to Pinkerton had to be kept secret. Itako, though curious about a document in her mother's hand, sent the letter unopened to Sharpless together with a note after obtaining his address through the American consulate.

Pinkerton's letter she opened, for she execrated him and had no scruples where he was concerned. To her surprise, it was written in Japanese. The contents chilled her; it was a letter that no doubt should have been put into her father's hands. Now it was too late, however, and she did not try to trace him through the address he had given when he went to Shizuoka to look for them six years earlier, in 1914. At that time Sachiko had prevented him from speaking to Itako: she told him how his daughter hated him, and he, sadly resigned, contented himself with a surreptitious glimpse of Itako when she returned from school. They were well provided for, Sachiko assured him, and wanted neither his aid nor his person. He left without protest but gave Sachiko an address in Nagasaki, where he intended to remain. He looked so pathetic that she almost felt sorry for him, but the memory of Butterfly lying in her blood roused her and she drove him away unceremoniously like a beggar.

89

(The Nagasaki ms.)

I spent the better part of the night writing a letter to Kate in which I set down all that I had on my mind. In closing, I excused myself for not saying good-bye: I could not, the evening had been so perfect. The letter would be taken to her with her breakfast; by then I planned to be gone.

I felt as if I had barely fallen asleep when a dreadful pounding aroused me. I was surprised to find Sachiko at the door. She was there to take me to Butterfly; I must go instantly. Sensing that something was wrong, I tried to question her. Sachiko would not listen; perhaps she did not understand my Japanese. "Hurry," she urged. "Hurry!" Seeing me hesitate—I was wondering what to do with my luggage—she burst out almost in a shriek, "She is dying!"

There could be no doubt about her veracity. I felt myself turn cold. Throwing on my clothes, I rushed out after her and at her behest jumped into a waiting ricksha that took me to a small house some distance from the center of the town. "Hurry," prompted the ricksha man when I hesitated before the unfamiliar gate. A feeling of doom gripped me; I charged into the tiny front garden. "Butterfly, Butterfly!" I cried, as if my voice, preceding me, could already succor her in her distress. There was no reply. The only sounds were the song of birds and the placid trickling of water in the small fountain.

I was too late. She lay on the floor. Beneath her, blood had soaked into the *tatami*, making a dark, sinister splotch. The body was already cold. Half crazed, I took her in my arms. "Butterfly, Butterfly!" I repeated, as if the name could rouse her. To awaken her again, if only for a minute, a second even . . . But her lids did not flutter, her lips would not stir. I remained with her for I know not how long. At last I noticed that the body had become stiff; it no longer seemed related in any way to the woman I loved. I got up as if in a dream and stumbled out of the house. It was a bright day. Birds, trees, flowers—all were in bloom, but the world seemed unreal to me. I cannot remember what thoughts went through my head; I only recall thinking with complete detachment, as if I had been a mere passerby whom it did not concern, that someone should notify the mortician or the police.

Apparently I wandered about the city. Sometime in the afternoon, I was taken to a police station. It seems that I had tried to jump into the Urakami River, or looked as if I would. I told the police about Butterfly. The consulate was notified; Sharpless and another American came. The latter took me back to the hotel and explained to Kate as best he could what had happened. Kate turned rather pale when she heard about Butterfly.

After the man left, neither of us spoke. Out of inertia, we resumed the seats we had occupied in his presence. I felt no sorrow, only emptiness, as if the blood had drained from my veins. "Kate," I said eventually. "Let me sign the contract."

· *Butterfly* ·

90

(From the interview with Mrs. Milly Davenport)

By the time Dada got himself over there, they'd already taken away the body. It being an unmistakable case of suicide and the circumstances being what they were, the police weren't exactly itching to start an inquiry. Dada did ask about a suicide note, but it seems there wasn't any. There wasn't any sign of Sachiko or little Itako either, but Dada was assuming Butterfly'd made arrangements for her child and thought it'd be better to refrain from asking. He recalled how upset she'd been over thinking that Pinkerton might take Itako and decided maybe it was just as well for Butterfly's wishes to be respected—he sure didn't much like the idea of the child falling into the hands of that lady.

Well, there doesn't appear to have been much danger of that, because plain and simply Pinkerton never even asked about the child. He and his lady sailed on the next ship for home. Dada didn't hardly get a chance to say good-bye. Now, he still had that ten thousand dollars Pinkerton'd sent, and seeing as Butterfly wouldn't take it, he couldn't think of what to do with it except giving it back; but when he tried, Pinkerton didn't want to hear about it. He wouldn't really listen, just told Dada to do with it what he thought best. "Donate it in her name," he maundered with that apathy that vexed Dada more than anything, "or give it to the child. Or whatever."

Dada did what he could to get ahold of Sachiko, but she'd vanished into thin air. At first he wasn't too concerned—he was too distrait himself to be bothering much about it—but after a few weeks when there still wasn't a sign of either her or Itako, he realized he'd better start doing some serious looking. Well, it wasn't easy, but after a time, maybe three or four months, the people he'd set on her track finally located her in some place far away, Shi-something or other, I can't remember. Shikota? Shikoza? Eh, how's that? Shizuoka, that's it—he went out to see them in Shizuoka.

She being out of the house, he went around again later in the afternoon and waited. It was dark by the time she finally came clattering around the corner in her wooden clogs; she had Itako strapped to her back and was carrying a bundle in her hands. Dada felt all excited, it was a little like seeing Butterfly again. He waited till Sachiko'd gotten pretty close before accosting her. But soon as she saw who it was, she turned and ran like she'd seen the devil in person. He called out, saying he wasn't intending to take Itako away if that's what was making her scared, but she wouldn't listen. So he ended up running after her, not too fast, you know, so as not to get her jittery, until finally she'd had to stop for breath. Even then he went up to her real careful. At first she looked as if she was going to scratch out his eyes, but then she must've seen he wasn't meaning to do them harm, because she calmed down some. He explained then that he'd come to arrange something with the money Pinkerton left. She wasn't in any hurry to hear it, but in the end she did take him home and fed him dinner, and in the evening they talked. She was pretty misdoubting of foreigners by then, and she bridled just to hear the name Pinkerton pronounced. But after a whole lot of persuading, he did manage to convince her that a trust fund could only be to the child's advantage. It was exhausting to have to do all that explaining in Japanese, but he was happy because he'd seen them at last and could finally go about setting up that trust fund. In the beginning Sachiko wouldn't let him touch the child, but as he was leaving, she made him go over to the cradle so he'd see how sweet she looked when she was sleeping. Dada said he almost broke down and cried for the second time in his adult life. He suddenly caught himself wishing—maybe not really wishing, just dreaming—that he were the father; he could

· *Butterfly* ·

see himself staying there with them, marrying Sachiko and bringing up Butterfly's child. Thinking about it made him feel awful foolish, but he wasn't near so surprised as he would've been a few months back. And he realized that he had learned a whole lot about himself since getting to know Butterfly, and maybe changed some as well.

That place, Shi-whatever it is, I've already forgotten again. (*Laughs.*) Shizuoka—thank you—was far and out of the way, so Dada never went out there again, even though he often thought about the child and even about making another trip. It wasn't until years later, twenty-two to be exact, that he got the letter, like that, out of the blue—by then he'd retired from the foreign service and was living back home. It was from Itako, who was happily married and living in Germany. Before leaving Japan, Sachiko had given her an envelope her mother'd left behind at the time of her death. When she'd realized who it was for, Itako had written to the U.S. Consulate and gotten Dada's address and now, at last, she was forwarding the letter with an apology for the long delay.

It was hard for Dada to believe that he was getting a letter from Butterfly after so many years. It was like getting mail from the other side. If you like, you can read the letter—the original is buried with him, but I made a copy. It's very short, but it said just what Dada needed to hear, and it was without any doubt his most treasured possession. I say "needed," but probably by this time he wasn't needing it anymore; he had aged so beautifully—I only got to know him ten years later, but I'm sure he was already as fine at sixty as he was at seventy or eighty. I often used to think how it was too bad that he couldn't have gotten that letter when she meant him to, because it would've given him so much comfort then, when he surely was needing it. But now I incline to think maybe there was a reason for it, like there is for everything here below. Anyhow, Dada turned out just as fine as anyone can wish, so it's all for the best. And this way, when he finally did get the letter, it was like a bonus, or a prize held in reserve and awarded when he'd shown how well he could do on his own. Which in a way is just as nice, isn't it?

91

Dear Mr. Sharpless,

I write to you first and, sadly, last time. To say good-bye.

You are good to me; I always knew, but not how much. Henry told me about letters. I am deeply moved, and I am happy that you wrote them. Yes, happy because I understand. Although I cannot return your kindness, I hope that we meet again in another life and be together what in this life many things permit not.

Please think of me but not be sad. I go because I wish, and because my destiny is. I feel not regret but happiness.

BUTTERFLY

92

(The Nagasaki ms.)

In the weeks and months that followed, I was haunted by memories of the cold, rigid body I had cradled in my arms, and of the woman who only the day before had held my hand and offered me life. How could that life-giving woman—Death himself would not have dared breathe upon her yesterday, I thought—have voluntarily yielded up her teeming, boundless vitality? Whence the mortal poison that overnight could make a

· *Butterfly* ·

corpse of one so rich in life? From me, I thought in despair, from me alone! Death was in me—on my fingers, in my heart—and it had killed Butterfly just as it had killed my dreams, my loves. But why, how, did I come to be its cursed carrier? And what fateful hand detained me yesterday when I could and would have gone to her? Had it been dire but meaningless coincidence, or was there a significence beyond my ken?

I did not know, and perhaps it was to learn the answer that I could not die. For I wanted to, fervidly. Having made myself Kate's creature, I prayed to Kate to make me die, but she would not. Once, even, the desire overrode my devotion to her. It was on the voyage back. Standing on deck, I had a sudden vision of the rocking sea as a vast cradle of death upon which tiny specks of life floated for a few paltry instants before sinking without a trace. How pathetic, how absurd our passions, our hopes, our quixotic fight against pervading death; how vain! Perhaps the vibrant Butterfly had understood this in a similar moment of black illumination; perhaps her self-inflicted death was the natural, inevitable expression of this understanding, and the ritual suicide of the Japanese but its institutionalized version, artfully preened and civilized. No wonder then that she'd left no note, no message; she had merely let herself slip into that sea of futility. Thinking this roused me to a savage joy; wild with dark exaltation, I climbed onto the ship's railing to leap.

All of a sudden I heard close to my ear, "No, no yet!" Low, almost a whisper, yet entirely distinct, the voice was Butterfly's. I recognized it less by its timbre than by the intonation I knew so well from intense moments when she spoke to restrain me. My resolve vanished; I suddenly felt dizzy and hastened to descend from the rail lest I be seen.

Although suicidal thoughts continued to prey, I never again was incited to act. My guilt and self-loathing, however, drove me to welcome and to revel in punishment, in bodily pain. Where before I had but thrilled at submitting to her whom I adored, I now began to take a brutal pleasure in the physical maltreatment, previously dreaded, that henceforth increasingly accompanied my subjugation. Indeed I provoked it. Even in moments when I cried out for sheer pain or, at the limit of endurance, begged for mercy, even then there would be an inarticulate wish somewhere deeper for my mistress to push the punishment to its ultimate end, to flog me veritably and inexorably to death.

So did I attempt, in the months and years that came and went, to snuff out my memory of life: in the asperity of my mistress's rod, in the sweetness betwixt her thighs.

93

(Butterfly's final letter to Pinkerton. This letter, meant to be found with her body, was removed by Sachiko and later given to Itako, upon whose death it came into the hands of the editor. Except for the opening sentence, it was written in Japanese.)

Dear Henry,

I shall write this letter in Japanese; please make translation to read.

When you read this, I shall have passed into another world. But I shall continue to watch over you—you and Itako.

As I sit here, many things come to me that I should like to say to you. But they are things of the world I am about to leave and there is no time to write of them. My decision is taken, and I must be quick in its execution, for I do not

· *Butterfly* ·

know what she will do. At this very moment, she may be pursuing your destruction.

I cannot understand her. To me she is a demon who wants to destroy you. Why? I do not know. Perhaps she bears a grudge against you from another life, or perhaps she is jealous, as demons are. Perhaps it is simply in the nature of demons to prey and to destroy. In any case, she is powerful.

I sensed your danger before I met her. Inwardly I knew that I had to take you away. If you are with me, I can protect you, but not otherwise.

Ultimately, however, it is not for me to protect you; you have to do it yourself. But as you are, you cannot, for you are too weak. Forgive me, I must say what I have to say. You are weak because you have no purpose in life. You bend with the breeze, because you yourself have no direction. You obey your desires and not your destiny. To possess a sense of true purpose, to harken to the call of destiny— that alone can give one strength to walk the high road. The demon is beautiful, but her beauty enthralls you because your eyes are unsteady.

For you do not see. Looking with your senses, you see things but not the life that shapes and transforms; you see the petals but not what makes them open and close. Thus you do not see yourself, you do not see your destiny.

While I live, though I would give you all, I cannot give you purpose; though I would look for you, I cannot make you see. But in dying, I shall leave you with both purpose and vision. When I am gone, our child will be yours. It will be up to you to care for her, to raise her. And you alone will be answerable—to the gods, to me, and the life you planted in me, which is more than either of us.

You must take Itako and go back to America; Sachiko will help you. If you accept the charge, as you must, the demon cannot touch you. Do not be careless, for she will still be powerful. But Itako will save you: whatever happens, hold on to her like a floating branch; then you cannot sink.

Do not grieve for me, because I am happy in my destiny. If I seem to sacrifice myself, it is not for you alone but for us—for the love that joined us and brought forth our child, for the love that you must continue to nurture from day to day. Do not grieve, but think of me. I shall always be at your side, because every day you will discover me anew in Itako. Find her a good mother, bring her up patiently and steadily, like a plant you watch with love and water with care. Watch her grow and you will learn to see. As the child grows into a woman, so will you grow into a father. What you make out of her, that you yourself will become.

Your wife in death as in life,
BUTTERFLY

Part Three

Keine Ferne macht dich schwierig,
Kommst geflogen und gebannt,
Und zuletzt, des Lichts begierig,
Bist du, Schmetterling, verbrannt.

Und solang du das nicht hast,
Dieses: Stirb und werde!
Bist du nur ein trüber Gast
Auf der dunklen Erde.

(No distance discourages you,
You come flying and enchanted,
And in the end, avid for light,
You, butterfly, are burnt.

And as long as you don't have it,
This 'Die and become!'
You will only be a gloomy stranger
On a dark earth.)

—GOETHE

Once Chuang Chou dreamt he was a butterfly, a
butterfly flitting and fluttering around, happy with
himself and doing as he pleased. He didn't know he
was Chuang Chou. Suddenly he woke up and there
he was, solid and unmistakable Chuang Chou. But
he didn't know it he was Chuang Chou who had
dreamt he was a butterfly, or a butterfly dreaming he
was Chuang Chou.

—Chuang Tzu

94

Kate and I were married that fall. At her
instigation, I began to dabble in politics. However,
despite some ambitious plans and initial success, our
interest flagged after a year or two, for neither of us really believed
in my career or cared. On her side, Kate made a triumphant
entry into society but soon tired of it, for it satisfied neither her
intellect nor her senses. Our life in Washington had plenty of
bustle but no memorable events. To the world at large, we were
the epitome of the bright young couple, fêted, admired, envied;
privately we lived by our contract, with minor innovations and
no revision. In our own way, we led quite a normal married life.

As Kate became bored with Washington, she began to consider
moving to New York or Europe. In the end she set her sights on
Paris and for a while had me angling for a diplomatic post, but
soon she became restless and decided to go in a private capacity;
the ambassadorship was not within immediate reach, and
anything less, she felt, was not worth the constraints imposed on
a government official. Although my personal ambition did not go
much beyond my mistress's pleasure, I felt uneasy about giving
up my political career. Being public figures molded the way we
lived; it determined our schedules and activities, defined images
that adhered to us most of the day, and even imposed a measure
of restraint and sanity upon our private relations.

In Paris everything changed. Immediately we were—or rather,
Kate was—drawn into a maelstrom of pleasure. All stops were
pulled. We were answerable to no one, and Paris was a city
without restraint. A few weeks sufficed to transform Kate; the
Washington socialite, poised on her respectable eminence, had

been left behind on the staid Maryland coast. Lovers, male and female, were soon drifting in and out of our flat on the boulevard Malesherbes. Kate flaunted them and, to them, my servitude. When I protested, she responded by humiliating me first in their presence, then with their participation, and finally to their fancy. On occasion I rebelled, not purposefully—for I was past genuine revolt—but like a blinded, crazed animal; whereupon I would be beaten, and the outrage redoubled. I endured it, because no torment could overcome the fear of being sent away. For however much Kate made me suffer, the feel of her foot upon my neck at least absolved me of responsibility for my suffering.

Yet at times my love for her would turn into hate; more than once I was close to murder. But Kate sensed with uncanny precision that receding threshold beyond which endurance runs amock, and with Circean art she would draw me back each time. Then there would be the sweet moment of reconciliation, when weeks of torment, jealousy and rage would pour into her lap in a torrent of tears. After which all would recommence.

95

The door opened and Marika emerged. Her eyes, formerly so impervious and crystalline, were puffy and red as lately they sometimes were. She stopped at the window and stood looking out with an abstracted air. As she turned away, she noticed Pinkerton with a start. Immediately she drew herself up, but the traces of tears could not be erased. Suppressing an impulse to hide them, she went over and, crouching, peered into his face. Although they saw each other every day, she had not looked at him for many months. "Poor Henry," she said, wincing slightly from pity or self-pity, and caressed him the way one would caress

· *Butterfly* ·

a dog lame with age. "We are getting old." In fact, tiny fishbones were now etched at the corner of her eyes. She had lost some of her bloom and feline naturalness, but possibly she had gained in allure. There was little of the soubrette about her now; she had become quite the young lady—and, he thought a little sadly, not so very young anymore either. At that moment he was free of resentment. Her insolence, her betrayals, her little cruelties that were as gratuitous as her kindness, all were forgotten; he saw only that she, too, was suffering now. How long ago it was that he had come upon her for the first time in Kate's arms and turned away in shocked reprobation; his heart fainting from jealousy, he had fled, but their laughter had pursued him without mercy. But that day now seemed faraway.

For a moment longer, they looked at one another as if tracing each in the other's face the lines of their own sorrow. Thinking to comfort her, Pinkerton reached out to take her in his arms. But at his touch, her eyes turned cold; pouting with disdain, she thrust him away and strutted from the room.

Later, as Marika lay with Kate, Pinkerton, sleepless outside his mistress's door, listened to their laughter shrilling deep into the night.

96

(The Nagasaki ms.)

Our life in Paris was a ten-year slide into depravity. Where I was concerned, it was an unending demonstration to my soul that its existence had been cancelled and that my body was no more than a hollow shell, animated for and to my mistress's pleasure. No more capable of sustaining life than a vase without earth, it had to be filled anew each day, each hour, with her commands and abuse, with her perversities and her effluvia. Oblivious of my soul, I worshipped her, worshipped in her the godlike part that is our universal birthright and the basis of all true freedom, and which I myself had wantonly abdicated.

Yet the mystic intensity I had once experienced was gone; I did not relive the transcendent emotions discovered in my early winged devotions. There was, on the contrary, something like a transcendence downward, as if a degenerate deity, incapable of assuming her own divinity or drawing up her devotee, were dragged down lower and lower until she too sank in mire.

Sated without being satisfied, Kate turned to alcohol, drugs, and debauchery. Imperceptibly, her senses dulled, her intellect clouded, her will eroded. In later years a despair sapped her even as it pushed her on in her frenzied excesses. So that I, who in the beginning had wondered about my sanity, feared in the end for hers.

97

Once someone mentioned *Madame Butterfly*—the play was having a great success in New York—and asked what Pinkerton thought of it, he who had lived in Japan. When he replied that he did not know the play, the woman gushingly pressed them to see it the next time they went up to New York, or even to make a special trip. Kate's enthusiasm had made him want to wring the woman's neck, but to his relief Kate had not pursued the suggestion. Later, however, she had made him read to her the story by John Luther Long from which Belasco's play derived. Long, in turn, had apparently taken the story from a newspaper article. And where did the journalist get it, Pinkerton wondered with the rage that rose every time he thought of those parasitic

· *Butterfly* ·

literary excrescences. Probably from someone in the Nagasaki consulate who knew of Butterfly's death and a few odd details but nothing more; the journalist's imagination had supplied the rest, which would explain why the story was so garbled.

Belasco's play was put on in 1900. Their life had been very different then—in retrospect a model of moderation and balance. In those days Kate was never cruel to him, not in the vicious way she had since become—at least it seemed that way to him now. But when Puccini's opera premiered at La Scala four years later, she had gleefully planned a trip to Milan to see it and had taunted him mercilessly when he squirmed. But in the end other pleasures retained her and they did not go.

Now it had come to the Opéra Comique and there was no way to get around it. He tried to steel himself but deep down knew it to be impossible. Ten years had passed since Butterfly's death, and she had gradually receded from where she had loomed in the forefront of his mind; but she was still the one thing that tormented him beyond all else.

The opera made him suffer even more than he had anticipated. Everything was so distorted as to be hardly recognizable; nonetheless he could not help seeing himself and Butterfly on the stage. The representation was a grotesque caricature, and it was obscene that he should attend it kneeling in Kate's box. But the worst part was the music; for images and words he could keep at a distance and shut out at will, whereas the singing voices floated up and enveloped him like a penetrant perfume, living phantoms of the timeless sorrow or joy contained in moments long buried.

The scenes in the opera resembled none that he could dredge up from his memory, and yet they belonged somehow to his past. Not the words, not the decor, but the emotion; and this emotion he was forced by the music to relive and to suffer afresh. For the voices bore on their song more than the words attributed by an ignorant librettist, they recreated the sinuous movements of the soul in ecstasy and in pain. Their love, their separation, the betrayal, Butterfly's lament and death—he was made to relive it all, as it were, from within.

Friends came to see Kate in her box and together they laughed at the sentimental slave who wept over an operatic *fait divers*.

98

(The Nagasaki ms.)

For me at least, life in Paris eventually settled into an almost monotonous routine. In the welter of new companions and distractions, Kate, though never relaxing her hold, left me more to myself. In the beginning I whiled away the leisure hours with desultory reading; in time, certain subjects caught my fancy and were pursued more intensively. Kate, always avid for knowledge, spurred my diligence; it did not escape me that I was treated best when her intellect was regaled with spicy, consistent fare.

I spent many afternoons at the Bibliothèque Nationale and, as I became more immersed in topics relating to art, in divers museums. These excursions, I might add, never led away from Kate's dominion, for the least stir of desire brought an excruciating reminder of my condition and of my mistress; thus restrained, I did my best not to notice the beguiling faces and figures that I passed, and my expeditions were always narrowly purposeful. Some of my research eventually found its way into certain obscure journals; few and insignificant as these are, they did much to render my life bearable.

By some fluke of destiny, Butterfly was dragged into the public eye. With deplorable distortion and increasing notoriety, her story was publicized in the news, then in a magazine, then on stage, and finally as opera. Much against my will, I had to

· *Butterfly* ·

accompany Kate to the Paris première of the last. It was a cruel experience, and it stirred up memories of Butterfly which until then I had largely succeeded in suppressing. To channel off my preoccupation, I took to studying things Japanese. The obsessive memories eventually abated, but not my interest, and once again I approached the language that I had begun to learn under Butterfly's tutelage. Kate, in whom the short sojourn in Nagasaki had kindled a lasting curiosity, was only too happy to broaden her knowledge and encouraged me in my struggles with that difficult tongue. The greatest impetus, however, came from my lost daughter, who began drifting frequently into my thoughts. I had no hope of ever meeting her, but that did not prevent me from daydreaming, and in those imaginary encounters we spoke in Japanese.

Would Kate have undertaken a second voyage? Perhaps; but if she contemplated another visit, she waited too long.

99

There were five or six of them, elegant, high-spirited, ferociously handsome women; at one time Pinkerton might have been titillated to find himself at their mercy, but now he abominated their willful immodesty and their vicious laughter. Above all else he hated to see Kate in their company.

". . . and how old is she?"

"Twelve, thirteen . . . What is it, Henry?"

"Thirteen—too delicious! The cherry is just ripe. You mustn't let it go to waste, darling."

"Do you want it? To pluck for your birthday?"

"Oh, I'd love it!"

"I'm sure you would, my dear Françoise, and so would I, but

don't you think it'll be more piquant to have Papa here do the plucking?"

"An excellent thought, Anne-Marie. Bravo!"

"I suppose we're all invited to the show?"

"I can hardly wait . . ."

"Just think, a family of slaves! Papa here can make her big and soon there'll be three generations."

"How amusing! If they breed well, you can sell the little ones. Baby slaves, guaranteed-pure incest, ha, ha—they'll sell like hot rolls. It's a gold mine, better than the Suez Canal. You'll make millions, Kate."

"Seriously, darling, why don't you get the girl over here. I'm sure that legally Henri has every right to claim her, with the mother dead."

"You know what, we ought to have our slaves inter-breed. . . ."

"Haven't you ever thought of having Marika or Chantal breed with Henri or . . ."

Pinkerton had long since learned to suppress all emotion in front of his mistress's friends, for any sign of dismay or protest was sure to bring out their worst, and some among them had less restraint than Kate, as he well knew. But this time he was unable entirely to conceal his fear. Would he stoop to that as well, or would he at last rebel? Already the confrontation loomed, and he almost felt he could rise to the occasion.

Luckily the ladies, intoxicated with hashish and champagne and their own dissipation, noticed nothing and perhaps for the same reason did not apparently retain what had so roused their enthusiasm: for months he lived in dread, but the matter was never taken up.

· *Butterfly* ·

100

I have often wondered what our life would have become if Kate had not taken ill—or would the illness, by an inner necessity, have ineluctably struck? At forty, though marked by time and debauchery, Kate was still stunning. But as the disease gnawed from within, that proud veneer of beauty began to fade. Not swiftly, not from one day to the next, yet for us who revolved around her like planets about the sun, the disintegration came with a speed that took away our breath. When bravado and denial fell away, there were no farewells, no explanations—there was not time; lovers, friends, servants, slaves, all were dismissed in a packet. Only Marika and I accompanied her to our property at the foot of the Pyrenees—near the beautiful cemetery at Valcabrère—purchased a year earlier as if in anticipation. There we lived secluded in a moldering old house without luxury or comfort, without servants, and with not a mirror on the wall.

The doctors had given her six months, possibly a year. But the following spring it appeared that she was, if not recovering, at least holding the assailant at bay. Her pain seemed less insistent, and she was able to listen to me read for long periods. She even took to riding on days when she felt particularly strong. Months went by and there was no relapse. We settled again into a semblance of normal life, and if death still sat in the ante-chamber, we no longer paid any heed. The routine of daily life had reasserted its claims.

101

Pinkerton was forbidden to look at her face, though he could not help catching glimpses now and then; in any case, he did not have to see it to follow the course of the disease. Her sleek body wasted away week after week like a worm-infested tree; she seemed to shrink before his eyes. Some days she was so weak that she could not move; in his arms she was like an antique doll with fragile limbs and peeling paint. Only her voice did not change, but she had not always the strength to talk.

And still the debauched mind refused to relinquish its pleasures; perhaps it was a desperate effort to stave off death. Each day she would have Marika hold her skin to skin against her own vigorous body; and the cold lips, barely moving, continued to demand the smiles and kisses of love. Pinkerton noted with relief and also a certain surprise that Marika never showed repugnance; he had always admired her apparent immunity and at the same time found it alienating. Far more surprising was the fact that his own desire for Kate did not subside but grew instead. An insane longing now possessed him, a longing impossible and wayward: to have her child before she died. Such was the new obsessive yearning that his strangled instincts began to torment him as they had not since the belt first imposed its tyranny. One day, on the verge of frenzy, he confessed it to his mistress; it was the first time in all their years together that he had dared speak of his own desire.

Unprepared for such an outlandish declaration, Kate let out a little laugh, half in embarrassment and half in anger. A tense silence followed. He, on his knees before the bed, did know what more to say.

"Look at me, Henry," she ordered unexpectedly in a hard voice. "Look at my face."

· *Butterfly* ·

She was half-reclining, with her head a little sunk into the large square pillow against which it lay propped. The long dark hair fell in a cascade of sensuality; in its midst lay a mask of death. But death transfigured, for the skin that stretched over the skull and its tenuous shreds of flesh was still fine and seemed to glow in its fragile translucence, while underneath the contours and features rose and fell in eloquent testimony of past glory. To Pinkerton, her face had been the most beautiful thing on earth, and she, knowing that, had guarded it jealously from his eyes, in former years to sharpen his passion and in past months out of pudency. Death now veiled that face, but when the initial shock wore off, he was able to discern the beauty, so ephemeral now and so frail, that clung piteously to the baring bone. Tears came to his eyes; he did not know whether he was moved more by the vision of enduring beauty or of fading life.

"Do you still want my child?" she asked with bitter mockery. Her emaciated lips twisted into a ghastly smile that once again conjured up the vision of a death's head come to life. He had to force himself not to avert his eyes. She was watching his every reaction; set deep in the pallor, her dark eyes looked unnaturally large and burned with he knew not what unquenchable passion or fever. Too seized to speak, he stood up in front of her, and taking her hand in a manner unwonted, brought it to where the answer could be touched.

Her smile slowly faded. She did not take her hand away, but after a while drew him toward her onto the bed. When his face was sufficiently close, she took it in her hands and gazed long into it as if searching for some remnant or reminder of better, bygone days. In her eyes he saw no defiance or derision, only a deep, quiet sorrow.

"It's too late, Henry," she said mournfully. "I shall never have a child now. Never." The terrible earnestness of the last word seemed to linger in the air; her despair made him want to weep.

"But I'll unlock you," she told him with unaccustomed

gentleness. "Not today—I'm feeling too weak." Drawing him closer still, she held his head so that his face pressed against her neck. "Some time when I feel better, I'll unlock you," she continued soothingly. "I shall. I promise."

102

(The Nagasaki ms.)

As the days became warmer, Kate went riding almost every morning. Swaying a little stiffly in the saddle with her exquisite skeletal head proudly thrown back—for she no longer hid her ravaged beauty—her long gaunt figure wrapped in its black riding cape could have been a Romantic artist's vision of Death. The peasants, understandably, did not like to meet her. She always rode alone, often for hours and returning too exhausted to dismount or call for help. Marika and I had to take turns watching.

One day she did not return. I went looking for her at noon, but it was a hopeless undertaking, since I had no idea what direction she had taken. Late in the day, gendarmes brought back her body; a peasant had found her. Her neck was broken.

We cleaned off the grime and laid her on the bed as we always did. Marika wept. Dry-eyed and dazed, I contemplated the face that had ruled my life. It seemed at peace and despite the extreme emaciation very beautiful. Her eyes were closed, her lips almost wore a smile; she could have been sleeping deeply. These fifteen years she had been my wife and yet we had not once lain together. All that time I had not even dared hope for what would have seemed a defilement; I, her slave, her dog—it had been right to contain my animal desires with that terrible lock. Yet she

· *Butterfly* ·

had let others defile her, I thought with rage, and remembering her recent promise to consummate our marriage, I was buffeted by waves of the bitterest despair.

103

"Marika," he turned and said suddenly. "Where is the key?" He was kneeling in his usual position at his mistress's bedside.

Her sobs had quieted, but her face was still blurred from weeping. "Why?" she asked with a trace of suspicion.

"I'd like to have it."

She glared at him. "Why?"

Her insistence made him flounder. "Marika, please . . ." Helplessly, he lowered his eyes.

Suddenly she understood, and her face flushed with anger and incredulity.

"You dare!"

"She promised . . ."

"Promised? Promised what?"

Reflected against her indignation, his shame burst; he felt it spread over him like a sticky corrosive varnish. Yet his heart flared, not with desire but in a frenzy of berserk frustration.

"She promised to unlock me!" he wailed, but softly, as if fearful of being overheard. "Just once, before she—"

"Lying dog!" Marika, rising, fairly screeched. "Get away from her. Get away! Filthy swine, I'll kill you before I'll let you dirty her." She rushed up to drive him away from the bed with kicks and blows, but then, changing her mind, went instead to the chest of drawers and rummaged there impatiently. When she turned around, she was holding up a small key between her thumb and forefinger.

"This is what you want, isn't it?" Her eyes glinted maliciously. "It is here," she said as she approached him step by step, the key still held clearly in view. "But I don't know if I can give it to you. It isn't mine, you know, and it certainly isn't yours." She stopped, contemplated the little piece of shining metal, and shook her head as if deliberating. "No, I really don't think I can. It's hers; it'll have to remain hers." So saying, she turned to the dormant figure on the bed. Gently, as if afraid to disturb her mistress in her rest, she pushed up the hem of the nightgown in which they had dressed the body. Using one hand to pry open the lips, she inserted the key and with two fingers slowly pushed the offering deep into the inert flesh. When she had at last satisfied herself that it was well ensconced, she turned to the consternated Pinkerton.

"Now you are hers for always," she said in malicious triumph. "You should feel happy."

Pinkerton stared at her disbelievingly. He had been too astonished to interfere and now it was too late; even if it were possible, he could not bring himself to fish the key out of his mistress's body, and in any case the rage had subsided. His only thought was how he would clean himself.

As if she had read his mind—perhaps she had guessed from his face—Marika said, "I cleaned you only yesterday, so it won't be necessary to do it again." She had become serious and spoke quietly in a matter-of-fact way. "In two or three days she will be buried. It will be pointless for you to go on living beyond that. I don't see how you could, even if you wanted to—but I know you don't.

"I think she has left me everything. That in principle would include you, but I don't think it was what she intended. We never discussed the point—for some reason we always put it off. She never gave any indication that she wanted me to have you, and I

· *Butterfly* ·

think we both assumed you would be hers to the end. You did too, no?"

Her nonchalance stung him. It was true he had no desire to outlive his mistress, but there was something shocking about the way Marika stated it. She looked at him a little in surprise and the mockery returned to her eyes.

"You don't want to accompany her? I'd have thought you'd be overjoyed. Or are you afraid of death? Look at her, look at your mistress. Look how beautiful she is now." Her voice became soft and dreamy; she seemed to be talking more to herself than to him. "Can you imagine death to be more beautiful? Can you still be afraid when you see her lying there?"

But her words did not calm him—quite the contrary. A terrible anguish, so intense that he felt his entrails sucked up as by a violent tourbillion, came over him. Possibly his consciousness grasped only at this moment the fact that his mistress was gone forever and that he was left alone with life and death and all that lay between the two.

Seeing his tears, Marika contemptuously curled her lips. "Do you prefer to be my slave, then?" She seemed to toy with the idea. "Is that what you want, eh?" She stepped closer and in a graceful movement brought a foot against his cheek.

"Kiss it," she ordered; but as he turned his mouth to obey, she stepped back with a dancer's agility and brought the foot to the floor in front of her with a little tap. "No! Down, all the way!"

These sharp commands brought him an indescribable relief. Obeying spontaneously, unreflectingly, with the involuntary eagerness of one who reaches for a saving hand without asking to whom it belongs, Pinkerton prostrated himself full length on the floor and pressed his lips to the waiting foot.

Shifting her weight, Marika lifted her other foot and slid it over his head and neck; she let it come to rest on the nape and slowly ground his head against the floor. A profound and familiar voluptuousness took hold of Pinkerton; a feeling of release not unlike happiness went through him almost in a pang. The temptation at that moment was overwhelming; yet he did not pronounce the word that already soughed lightly over his tongue. For at that instant he knew in his heart that he could not belong to another.

Above him he heard her ask, whether herself or her dead mistress he did not know, "Should I?" Her foot continued to bear down for a few seconds longer, as if she were venting her indecision.

"No, I can't take you," she said, releasing the pressure on his neck; her casual tone made the words seem trifling. "Sorry. You're hers; you'll have to be hers to the end."

104

(The Nagaski ms.)

At first I thought that Kate might have left written instructions for me; when nothing turned up, I felt a mixture of disappointment, relief and resentment. She could, and considering how seriously ill she had been, should have provided for such a contingency. Was it not her duty to do so? Was it not part of our contract, which bound us until death, hers and mine? No doubt there had been a tacit understanding that I would die with her, and I could not imagine she had intended otherwise; but why then had she not spoken? How could she, after fifteen years of total domination, leave me at the final juncture on my own? My death, like my life, had been hers, and she herself had once rebuked me for begging her to let me die: a slave had no right to wish for death. This was the meaning of the ritual thanksgiving: that the slave had not only to endure whatever pain the mistress inflicted, but

· *Butterfly* ·

to be thankful for it. Death—unless it be for her pleasure—was the ultimate escape from the mistress's power, and to want it was to reject the life granted by the mistress's will; as such it was the ultimate betrayal. But if I had no right to claim my own death, Kate for her part had no right to abandon me to it. That was the crux of our agreement. The contract quite explicitly placed the entire burden of my moral existence upon Kate's shoulders: in return for absolute obedience, I would be freed from moral imperatives and purged of moral poisons such as guilt, remorse, ambition, hatred, even sorrow. Yet there I was, alone and betrayed.

But if the business of dying seemed more than I could undertake on my own, that of living was far worse. In fifteen years of slavery I had not had to make a single decision or to take responsibility for a single act; now she who had animated me and determined every detail of my life was gone. I had to die, because I could not live.

Despite my lassitude, I did not want to leave my affairs in disorder and the following morning, after arranging for the funeral, I went to see the solicitor who took care of them. Formerly, Kate was to have inherited everything—that is, everything I had not already made over to her, for during the first two years of our marriage, the greater part of what I owned had been put into her name, and now she had left these extensive possessions to Marika. My holdings, though reduced to a fraction of what they had been, still represented considerable wealth; I now made a new will bequeathing them in equal portions to Lisa and to my long-abandoned daughter, Etsuko.

From neither had I had any news. I knew nothing of my daughter's fate, and my relations with Lisa had been severed for over a decade. During the early years of my marriage, when Kate and I were living in Washington, we had seen her regularly; it was something of a strain for me when she stayed with us, and she no doubt caught a disquieting glimpse now and then, but on the whole Kate succeeded admirably in keeping up appearances. Later, however, when Lisa visited us in Paris, Kate had made no effort to conceal the kind of life she led or the nature of her relations with me. In fact, she tried to corrupt Lisa. She failed of course, and the attempt was for me an alarming sign of her deteriorating judgment. Profoundly shocked, Lisa fled back to America; she never wrote after that, and I in my shame also kept silent.

I thought of writing a last letter to Lisa and to Etsuko, but when I tried, I found that there was nothing to say.

105

Her silent, bitter tears flowed as from a fountain of reproach, so filling him with despair that he would have hanged himself like Judas on the nearest tree.

Then the tears too were spent, and she only stared. He, unable to endure the horror in her eyes, spoke to her, coaxing her to speak. In an ultimate plea of his writhing heart, he cried out that he loved her, that he would always love her. The words fell absurdly short of what he felt, yet they were in their primitive way true and pure where a more circumstantial representation of his feelings would have veered into the false or grotesque.

Presently she turned her eyes upon him; they were dry now, dry and empty.

"Damn your love! Your love has killed me, can't you see? It sapped away my life, more than any hate could have. Look at me now. I'm . . . nothing. Like you, nothing." She continued to stare vacantly, her eyes seemed to look right through him. "Prime fruit, the best on this earth—we held it in our hands, we whiffed

· *Butterfly* ·

its aroma, and we let it rot. Let it rot and ate the putrid flesh. It poisoned us; we're going to die from it now." She looked down at her wasted body and suddenly began to laugh. Hysteria, erupting shrilly from some dark pocket of the soul, racked her poor body with spasms of mirthless, inhuman laughter. To Pinkerton, it was more terrifying than the shrieks of Hell.

106

(The Nagasaki ms.)

The undertakers, from a considerable distance away, were to come the morning of the funeral; at my request, they were to bring a second coffin for a spouse who, also ill, was not expected to survive. My plan was to keep a last vigil that would end with my joining her over whom I watched.

After an active day of practical dealings, however, I began to have doubts, for it seemed patently untrue that I was incapable of living; indeed, it seemed absurd to imagine that my faculties could have so atrophied. No, it was not that I was unfit to live, but that I had no wish to prolong a life whose sum total amounted to less than nothing. My life ended the night Butterfly died, or rather, the day I left her side. The phantasmagoric butterfly had been an annunciation, a call I should have done better to heed.

These fifteen years had produced nothing. No insight, no atonement; only degradation. While Kate lived, remnants of passion had drawn me on, and the inertia of habit. But now all of it seemed sordid, preposterous, empty—even Kate herself. A corpse, today still marked by pleasing features, tomorrow festering like any other and leaving behind nothing, no child, no grain of life, no legacy of spirit. Had she ever been more? Perhaps not;

but what was I then who had worshipped her? Yes, I had to die, because my life sickened me, sickened me to death.

Such thoughts, like a swarm of Furies, pursued me into the night. Although sunk in despondency, I adhered to my plan as a miscreant might yet cling to ritual. But there was no enthusiasm, no thrill or hint of exaltation. Mine would not be the love-death dear to the romantic imagination. Even the sight of Kate, beautiful as ever by lamplight, moved me but slightly. Less in arousal than to rouse myself, I touched my lips to her feet, but their unnatural coldness made me shrink back in distaste. Even that last illusory pleasure was denied.

I had intended to die at the crack of dawn, but exhausted by the day's activity and two sleepless nights, I fell asleep against my will. The morning sun woke me. Not knowing the time, I started; but it was still early. Nothing stirred; Marika was not up yet and the undertakers would not arrive for another hour or two. Still, there was no time for dawdling. It would be nice to wash and have a drink, but to what end? I dismissed the temptation with contempt. Better to get on and have done with it.

I rose only for one last look at Kate. Gazing down at her face, I recalled that fatal night in Nagasaki when I had kissed her good night for the last time. To think of all that could have been—but no, I refused to be host to idle regrets. Steeling myself, I kissed her quickly on the forehead and turned away.

Practiced as I was in administering Kate's daily dose of morphine, it took me no more than a minute to prepare the hypodermic syringe. The acute feelings that had assailed me a few hours before were gone. I felt nothing in particular, only my body's stiffness and an unclean dryness of the mouth. Already I was, like Kate, an empty shell, passing from void to void.

The very moment I inserted the needle, a fluttering sound caught my ear. Though faint and of short duration, it was quite distinct in the stillness. Looking up, I saw a large yellow butterfly

· *Butterfly* ·

at the window; it had been butting against the glass pane trying to get out.

Now it was perched on a lath; I was struck with the oddest impression that it was beckoning me to set it free. I stopped dead in the middle of my operation, and after a brief hesitation withdrew the syringe. But when I opened wide the double window, the butterfly did not stir; again I had the feeling it was watching me. Fascinated, I stood and observed it. It seemed unthinkable that such a bold expanse of color and design could be animated by a body so small and frail. Who could have thought to fashion such a perfect and unlikely creature? And that such creatures should inhabit the earth, and live and fly and propagate—it was a miracle beyond conceiving.

Presently I shut the butterfly's half of the window, leaving only the left side open for its exit. Still it did not move. To encourage it, I blew on it lightly and slowly put out a finger. The butterfly was not frightened; it almost seemed to await my hand. Very carefully, I clasped it and set it upon the window's outer sill. There it rested a long moment before finally taking flight; even then it did not immediately depart but hovered leisurely in front of my eyes and, before setting off, circled once as if for a last look.

I gazed after it in wonder. What thoughts if any went through my head I cannot say. The thoughts came later. I only remember feeling strangely that the butterfly was part of me, and that it had drawn out something in me that now accompanied it in its flight. It was as if life had for a moment touched me with its pure essence. Giddy with new awareness, I felt life washing up in great waves to the latticed window behind which I stood. In every insect, in every leaf, petal, blade of grass, I felt its vital force; and I saw how it pervaded the earth, the sky, the very air I inhaled, fusing all into a stupendous whole that comprised equally the winged butterfly and my heart's consuming fire.

107

"*Satori*, yes," the abbot replied. "You could say it was that. But it was not really *satori* in our sense.

"An illuminating experience you might have at any time, but unless you are properly prepared for it, it will soon fade. On the other hand, if you prepare yourself well, you can almost do without it. So the day-to-day preparation is the essential thing.

"Suppose a flash of lightning lights up a dark night. For a moment you see the entire lay of the land. But a second later, how much do you still see? And in an hour? In a day? If you know precisely where you are going, that flash might get you there; otherwise it won't take you far.

"This is not to say it is useless. It can orient you, and it gives you knowledge of things ordinarily invisible. But knowledge by itself is vain. If you let it guide you in your everyday life, you may get far. If you merely cling to it like a precious object you find on the road, its light is no better than the obscurity of its absence.

"In the end there is no difference between brightness and obscurity, between object and eye, between knowing and being. The true light is where there is no light, no darkness. But that you will not see in a flash, but only through long, patient work."

108

(The Nagasaki ms.)

What had happened, what had changed, that the world should have become so clear, so crystalline? I did not know, nor did I know how life in such a world would be. But my body felt light,

· *Butterfly* ·

my movements free and effortless. As to why, whence, whither—
I had no idea; I only knew that I was no longer a slave.

The first thing I did was to cut the belt that had been the
symbol and instrument of my servitude. I shuddered to look upon
it; the severed thongs seemed obscene and strangely unsubstan-
tial, like a spider dead and shriveled. The sight aroused in me an
emotion between horror and nostalgia; and curiosity. Who was I,
who had been contained in them all those years? And who was
Kate? Suddenly I saw her again as she had appeared to me the
first time, so bright and splendid in the richness of her person,
and from the darkness of my memory came forth beautiful
moments sparkling like jewels. Could such gems be corrupted or
cast away? It all seemed a dream from which I must awaken, a
dense forest from which I would yet emerge, intact and into the
sun.

Later that day, I dropped the belt into Kate's grave. As I
watched it fall, a violent longing overtook me unexpectedly and I
had a fleeting urge to hurl myself into the pit; but I steadied
myself and came away knowing I had buried the slave with the
mistress he so adored.

But my love was not buried. Only the stranglehold of perverted
passion was broken. Like a cancer, that delirious outgrowth of
guilt and thwarted desire had devoured the love it was both one
with and at odds; now it had consumed itself. As life returned to
me, my love for Kate also revived and with time recovered some
of its original purity. For love, like life itself, is irrepressible. In
the nature of miracles, its demands match its amplitude, and not
to meet them is wasteful, perilous, sometimes tragic.

By some extraordinary grace, the miracle had visited me twice,
and twice I failed it—a sin, redoubled, for which my slavery was
an unconscious expiation. The day I broke free, I began to
understand. At first there was only the quality of clarity, without
definition or detail: I knew what I had to do without being able to

anticipate or explain. Comprehension slowly followed and little by little insights took form.

The butterfly that had guided me back to life also led me back to its namesake. For years Butterfly had hovered at the periphery of my thoughts, not so much forgotten as neglected like furs in a warm climate. Now a plethora of memories rushed upon me, vivid, overwhelming, and I began belatedly to feel the full extent of my loss. Her image was constantly before me, while Kate's seemed to lurk behind my back, waiting to confront me each time I turned. Once again I was torn between them, but this time it was their ghosts that tugged over my soul. One day, without apparent reason, I wept and could not stop; for an entire week my tears flowed, for the one or the other I did not know. Then they dried. And imperceptibly, in a process that continues still, their images began to harmonize and at moments even to merge.

109

"What are you doing here?" Marika was surprised to find him in the kitchen, since she had known of his plans. Her keen eyes— the years had only made them sharper—took in the garden shears he had been about to replace; he had tried first to cut the thongs of the belt with a pair of scissors, but these had proved inadequate against the fine steel wires sewn into the soft leather. From the shears her crass attention darted to his trousers, bringing life to the newly liberated organ.

"Bugger!" she exclaimed under her breath. Her face darkened and for an instant he was afraid there would be a contest of force. But the frown lifted. "So much for the fidelity of slaves," she quipped and broke into a quizzical but good-natured smile. There was something in her movements as she approached that seemed to invite him to fold her in his arms; perhaps the shears in his hand restrained him. Casually, she palpated the excitement of his flesh, then let her hand wander up his body and to his face. "I see you're still in one piece. Nothing like a resistant slave." Then with a wicked trace of a smile, she hissed, "She should have cut it off. I would have, and I would have been right!" She looked into his eyes and asked in a more serious tone, "How did you find the courage?"

He did not know how to reply, but his regard was steady. Finally he said with a certain firmness, "I am not a slave anymore."

"I can see that." She was looking him over with a proprietary air; like a prospective buyer, he thought. "Do you want coffee? I was just about to make some. There's not much for breakfast, I'm afraid. I am leaving tomorrow."

He, having eaten little the night before, was grateful to find some dry bread and cheese and a bottle of the excellent claret purchased for Kate's palate. Marika sat over her café au lait and watched him eat; in the stretches of silence, their eyes met, and met again.

What would he do now that he was free? He could not say.

"Listen," she said. "I'm going to see the *notaire* at Saint-Gaudens after the funeral. I don't know when I'll be back—in any case, I don't want to sleep with you here in this house, you who ought to be keeping her company. But tomorrow I'm taking the train to Toulouse and then to Paris. If you like, we can go together. A coach is coming at seven." Their hands touched in a promise of passion; he remembered how he had been seduced by her younger charms, yet thought he had never desired her more.

But in the morning he was not there at the appointed hour, and if the coach waited, it was not for long.

110

I could not stay in France, and I had no wish to return to America. Eventually my way led back to Nagasaki. Why I had come was not clear, but when I arrived, I knew it was here that I would live out my days.

The two women I had loved and wronged were dead, and there was nothing I could do for them by way of amends. But I found a purpose in work I imagined they would approve. With what means I still possessed, I tried to provide for lost women and abandoned children. My efforts, at first lavish but awkward, in time became less prodigal and more efficacious. Memories of the two women kept me from succumbing to discouragement, though I could have done with Butterfly's counsel and Kate's inspiration. Kate's ambitions had surpassed anything I could accomplish, but I did the best I could and liked to think that she would not have been displeased.

There are times now when I think I have expiated my sins; the faces of Butterfly and Kate seem friendlier, and sometimes I imagine them to have made their peace with me and with one another. But just when I feel myself to be reconciled with the world, some too-lovely memory or imagined scorn would jolt me back into despair. In black moments I would pray to one or the other as to a heathen divinity, and as often as not I would be comforted.

Only Etsuko continues to weigh on my mind, even though I feel intuitively that she is well. Some time after my return to Japan, I was able to track her down to Shizuoka, but when I went there, Sachiko would not let me see her. To my daughter, Sachiko told me, I was not a father but the man who had betrayed and killed her mother, and if I wanted to do anything for her, it would be to stay away. Etsuko had everything she needed, and I could only upset her if I imposed myself. The abuse Sachiko threw at me pained me, but I understood her bitterness and saw that she was right. I left deeply saddened, but resigned myself to the separation as part of my penance. I made no further attempts to contact Etsuko; I did leave Sachiko my address and kept her informed of my whereabouts in case my daughter, in growing up, should want to get in touch. Twenty years have gone by, however, and there has been no news.

(The Nagasaki ms. ends here. Pinkerton himself was no doubt dissatisfied with the final pages, which show signs of carelessness, and it may well be that he abandoned the plans for publication because he was unable to write an adequate ending. From the scattered notes, it would appear that he had in mind a more extensive commentary on the moral significance of his experiences.)

111

(Editor's note: In the summer of 1979, I visited Nagasaki again in the hope of picking up information about Pinkerton I might have missed twenty-five years before. I was surprised at the number of people who still remembered Taizan, as he was called, but none could tell me anything I did not already know. An exception was the Zen priest Ikkyū. In 1952 I had already heard of Pinkerton's connection with the old abbot, Benku, of Jindai-ji temple, but Benku had died and neither the new abbot nor the inmates could tell me anything. This time, however, I had the leisure to talk to many more people and one of them directed me to Ikkyū. I called on him without high expectations, but I was struck by his remarkable personality and knew that the interview would not be without interest. The mobile, expressive face and the mischievous twinkle in his eyes were anything but what one would ordinarily associate with a Zen priest. "My old drinking partner!" he exclaimed joyously when I spoke the name Taizan. "I should say I knew him." When I explained my interest in Taizan, Ikkyū showed a rare openness. The following is a summary of what he told me.)

Ikkyū Roshi: I will start at the beginning. When I was twenty, I had a mystical experience that converted me to Zen, and I had every intention of becoming a monk. My teacher, Benku, however, wouldn't allow it. Each time I mentioned taking vows, he would tell me to go work in the family business and get married. I was a lively and tenacious youngster, and in spite of my great respect for my teacher, he couldn't convince me. I kept pestering him, and one day he told me to go talk to Taizan. I asked him why.

"You're so interested in stories," he replied. "He can tell you one." No, he didn't know the story himself, he wasn't interested, but since I was—I wrote stories and poems those days and fancied myself a man of letters—he was sure Taizan would be willing to tell it.

"I thought I was supposed to forget about stories," I objected.

"Get out!" was all the reply I got.

So I looked up Taizan and discovered that he had a taste for *sake*. Well, I had too, so we became pretty friendly. In fact, we were quite alike in having sybaritic tastes that we almost sincerely wished to be rid of. Together, we felt better about indulging them. I had come from an old merchant family and though I had just spent four years studying in Tokyo, knew the town inside and out; I was proud to show around a foreigner of comparable background and tastes.

· *Butterfly* ·

It turned out that Taizan wasn't particularly eager to tell his story, at least not to me, though after a while I got to hear most of it. He was more interested in talking about Buddhism and social conditions in Japan, and I was most interested in finding out more about the West, but often we ended up on geishas' dresses and other such exciting topics. At first I was rather patronizing— I was the man-about-town, I was the one who had had a sudden enlightenment and knew all the Zen stories, my family had been on familiar terms with Benku from before I was born. But by-and-by I realized that this foreigner knew more about Zen than I; in fact, he knew more about everything that counted. I finished by having to admit that he was simply more advanced on the path of life—a mortifying admission, he being only a foreigner and not one my teacher made much of either. Yet, just being what he was, he showed me up for a callow youth who imagined himself a sage. That was pretty depressing, but I got over it and even got so I could laugh at myself. Then one day I discovered almost to my surprise that I was going to do just what my teacher had suggested. When I told him, he smiled very sweetly; he knew I would be back.

The war came, I was taken into the army and sent to China. There I saw some terrible things. Then came the bomb. My parents, my wife, my children, our property—everyone, every-thing, was wiped out. Taizan, too. I went to Benku. "You're too poor now," he said, and refused to take me in.

I went to Tokyo and with what money I could raise bought land. The city was devastated and land was dirt cheap. I didn't have to wait long for the prices to skyrocket, though. And there were plenty of opportunities in those days for anyone who opened his eyes. In a few years I was richer than I had ever been; I was successful in everything I touched and I enjoyed my success. I had been holding off getting married again, but now I was able to make a very fine match.

Well, the morning of the wedding—it was a beautiful day late in March—I looked out at the blossoming garden and saw the whole world smiling at me. Transported, I stepped out onto the veranda and descended the steps. Perhaps too caught up in my elation, I stumbled; I just managed to keep myself from falling, but something jolted loose in me. At that moment I understood.

I tried to call off the wedding. The parents were mortified, but the daughter declared that if this happened that very morning, it was surely in our destiny and she was not going to go against the course of nature. Previously, I would probably have been astounded like her parents, but in my state of mind, her answer delighted me and suddenly it all seemed as right as could be. So we went through with the wedding. Shortly afterward we retired to Yamaguchi, where I devoted myself to Zen. Later, after I had received my dharma transmission, I moved back to Nagasaki.

You mustn't imagine that I had been immersed in a crassly materialistic life during the preceding years. I had lost my youthful taste for debauchery, and since the war I had assiduously practiced *zazen*. The war had made me quite disciplined, really. So it didn't happen out of the blue.

It may seem strange to you that I've talked so much about myself and so little about Taizan. But there is not much I can tell you directly about him that you do not already know.

P.L.: What is your personal view of Taizan and his rather unusual life? And has that view changed since you first became friends—in the 1930s, I suppose?

Ikkyū Roshi: That's right, I met him in 1934 and saw him regularly until 1937, when I entered the army. I understood his life to have been determined by deep bonds of karma between him and the two women. Which is not to say that it had to be what it was. Our lives are shaped as much by how we respond to our karma as by the karma itself.

· *Butterfly* ·

Back then, I used to think that Taizan was too good. That is, he wanted too much to do good, he was too eager. From the Zen point of view, such zeal showed attachment, and all attachment is an obstacle; so I sometimes chided him for it. I told him he should let go of his guilt feelings. We talked about it a lot, and in fact he himself saw things quite clearly, only that didn't change the way he was. I was young then, and impatient. Now I see that striving to be good, though it made knots in his life, was part of the process of untying a greater knot. I had disapproved of it as a method he had adopted of appeasing his guilt, but it was not a method but rather the other side of that guilt, something that he could no more jettison than the guilt itself.

P.L.: It is very interesting to me to learn that you talked about his guilt feelings. Could you tell me more about his attitude at the time, what he thought and felt?

Ikkyū Roshi: Like most Westerners, Taizan had a penchant for theorizing, and I was interested in Western thought, so our discussions tended to be speculative. At this distance it is hard to recall their contents, or who said what. I do remember, however, some of our talk about guilt; since you ask, I'll repeat some of it, for what it's worth.

Now, what is guilt? It is identifying with something different and separate from yourself and then judging yourself from its point of view. That other can be society, or God, or an abstraction like the law or humanity, or a person like the father or the mother. The greater the distance you put between the other and yourself, the greater the sense of guilt. In the most clear-cut instance, there is an act, a crime, that alienates the doer; but there doesn't have to be a crime, or a consciously identified other.

In the West you have the idea of original sin. It comes from the sense of being alienated from a transcendent God. An entire theology and way of life are built upon it. God is good, so man is bad; God is omniscient, so man is blind; God is everything, so man is nothing. This is fine so long as you believe in God. But where does it leave you when this God before whom you prostrate yourself begins to seem a dubious proposition? You turn to substitutes—"idols," they used to be called. The best is a woman, at least if you are a man. It is easy to channel sexual passion into free-floating guilt. Taizan was ready to worship his European wife even before he became guilty of betraying her; the betrayal was almost an excuse. A deep, unspecified guilt was already there waiting—the guilt of being a nothing, a born sinner, before a God whose reality was uncertain. There are other possible substitutes, but none with a woman's presence and immediacy. The undeniable reality of her body ensures an ironclad illusion; an infinite, unbridgeable gap is compressed into the distance between skin and skin; transcendence is brought within reach of a kiss or a kick.

For us, to whom all reality is immanent, the very notion of transcendence is an aberration, a source of perversion even. Divinity is not elsewhere in some greater, transcendent reality but in the very nature of things right here, all things at all times. Someone asked: What is Buddha? A shit-scraper, answered Ummon. A thing is itself, that's all, and its it-ness is the ultimate reality—or Buddha, divinity, God, call it what you like. When you experience it in one thing, you experience it in all. But if you seek it elsewhere, in some "higher" reality, you will end up perverting it.

P.L.: But the Japanese are certainly not immune to perversions.

Ikkyū Roshi *(laughs)*: It's our talent for imitation! And we're a competitive people on top of it. Anyway, God is not the only transcendent reality: there is the state, and the company, just to name two to which my countrymen are easily addicted. But since the distance between these and the individual is so much smaller

· *Butterfly* ·

than that between God and man, there is less alienation—both quantitative and qualitative—and guilt comes mostly in packets small enough to be confined to the fantasy chamber of a "love hotel."

P.L.: You said earlier that Taizan was more advanced in Zen than you at the time. You also spoke of the obstacles of guilt and "goodness." Do you think he was close to overcoming these? And do you think that he might have attained what one might call "enlightenment" before his death?

Ikkyū Roshi: He was more advanced in the sense that his experience of life was more genuine. He was not looking to be enlightened, he was even a little suspicious of it. He met my teacher, Benku, by accident, and many years went by before he approached Benku for instruction. Even then, it was with a certain reserve. But he had been working on his own in a spirit that was quite compatible with Zen. In coming to Japan, he had left behind a good deal of the excess baggage we are all burdened with. If he made errors—and who is to say what is error and what is not?—the errors were authentic.

It is hard to talk about enlightenment. When the war ended, I spoke with several people who had known Taizan. According to one, he had been active and fearless in helping people evacuate after the atomic blast—the area he was living in was quite far from where the bomb hit. But the accounts do not agree. The woman who took care of him told me he had been blinded and severely burned. Perhaps that was later, the result of exposure to fallout; I don't know. In any case she had been impressed by the fact that he seemed happy in spite of his obvious pain. He told her that he saw light. She thought he was touched in the head, but it was certainly something else.

112

(Reconstituted from the editor's notes on his interview with Midori, Taizan's housekeeper, on October 19, 1952. Midori died in 1957, at least partly because of exposure to radiation.)

I went to see Taizan two or three days after the blast. I had hoped that he might have stayed home that day, because he was living far enough away not to be affected. But unfortunately that was not the case. His condition was frightening. Large portions of his skin had peeled off and his body resembled one big wound. Furthermore he was blinded. How he managed to get home was a mystery; he himself did not seem to know. I did what I could for him, which wasn't much. It was clear to me that he was going to die, but despite his weakness and terrible suffering, he seemed somehow almost cheerful. I attributed it to damage to his head. He was very concerned about me and my family, however, and asked me to forgive the Americans. I told him I held nothing against him. The one request he had was to burn some papers; there were several stacks. I consented, but afterward something held me back and I kept them, I don't know what for.

I went there every afternoon after that. One day when I arrived, he was dead. The day before, he had seemed particularly excited and spoke to me about the light he was seeing. I saw that he was raving and knew the end was near. He also mentioned seeing people he had known. It was heart-wrenching to see him in such a state, but at the same time I was glad he could be so distracted from his frightful condition.

· *Butterfly* ·